H
U
S
H

**DYLAN
FARROW**

WEDNESDAY BOOKS
NEW YORK

First published in the United States by Wednesday Books, an imprint of St. Martin's Publishing Group

HUSH. Copyright © 2020 by Glasstown Entertainment and Malone Farrow. All rights reserved. Printed in the United States of America. For information, address St. Martin's Publishing Group, 120 Broadway, New York, NY 10271.

www.wednesdaybooks.com

Designed by Anna Gorovoy

Endpapers, map, and interior illustrations by Rhys Davies

The Library of Congress Cataloging-in-Publication Data is available upon request.

ISBN 978-1-250-23590-9 (hardcover)
ISBN 978-1-250-23591-6 (ebook)

Our books may be purchased in bulk for promotional, educational, or business use. Please contact your local bookseller or the Macmillan Corporate and Premium Sales Department at 1-800-221-7945, extension 5442, or by email at MacmillanSpecialMarkets@macmillan.com.

First Edition: 2020

10 9 8 7 6 5 4 3 2 1

For Evangeline

EXCERPT FROM THE HIGH HOUSE MANIFESTO

It always starts the same: a deepening blue in the veins about the wrists. This much is common knowledge. What follows is shallowness of breath, coughing, fever, and muscle pain. Once contracted, one or two days may pass before the darkened veins spread throughout the body, at which point the sclera of the eye will become tinged and mottled. The coloration reaches the extremities next, turning the fingers and toes a dark, thundercloud blue. In the final stages, the veins become increasingly sensitive, pulsing and ready to explode.

In the most severe cases, they burst beneath the skin.

Eventually, the pain becomes unbearable, accompanied by varying degrees of delirium and paranoia. As one Bard famously reported, "They are even more afraid than we are."

The current epoch has been irrevocably tainted by death and chaos; our streets, fields, and homes run thick with the foul, rotting stench of disease. A cloud of smoke rises above Montane from countless thousands of funeral pyres, from the homes we must burn to purge the affliction.

The means to end this tragedy lie in understanding its origins.

The disease, referred to as the "Indigo Death" or "Blot," was first reported in a rural manor in the southwest. As if contracted by mere word of mouth, no sooner had word reached a village than the outbreak would claim it. It spread so efficiently that, in only a few days, outbreaks had been reported in every corner of Montane. Anyone displaying the telltale symptoms was immediately quarantined, but isolating the afflicted did nothing to stem the tide of death. Riots ensued. Pandemonium reigned. We were a nation consumed by pain, fear, and chaos.

There are those alive today who still remember the grim processions of masked doctors through the countryside, leading caravans of blue corpses to their final fire.

It was only after careful dissemination that the Bards of High House discovered the nature of the enemy:

Ink.

We had welcomed it willingly—in our stories, letters, and news. We had invited it into our homes, passed it along with our hands, and distributed it in our very warnings.

But together we shall rise above the ashes of our fallen and usher in a new era of peace in Montane. The time is come to join High House in ensuring this tragedy is never repeated. The tyranny of the Indigo Death can be overthrown.

Our history shows that vigilance and caution are tantamount to survival. Burn the ink from the page. Turn away from forbidden words, toxic tales, and deadly symbols. Cleanse the country of this malignant blight.

Join us.

Shae sat beneath the old tree outside the house where her brother lay dying.

Only the loudest, most keening wails of mourning could reach her there, and they had lessened as he grew weaker. He was not gone yet, but he would be soon.

Before her sat a basket of rags. She ran her fingers through them, tearing the fabric into long strands, grief seizing in her throat. Once Kieran's death ribbons were hung from the tree, everyone would know the Blot had come for her family.

She thought about the blue veins crawling over her brother's skin and shuddered. Her elders kept her from going near him, but she had seen the telltale signs of the plague worsening through a cracked bedroom door. She heard the sounds he made, mostly screams of pain and violent coughing.

He was only a child, younger than her by three years. It wasn't fair.

A dark pull in the pit of her stomach swelled as she stood, preparing to ascend the tree, and another long, keening wail came from the house. The only sounds for miles were Kieran's haunted cries and Ma's soothing voice, carried away on the wind down the gray mountainside.

Shae shoved the ribbons she had darned in her pocket and began climbing. She found a spot to sit, and reached up, beginning to tie the dark blue ribbons to the branches. The bleached winter sun peeked out from the clouds, throwing the gnarled shadows of tree branches over her cottage.

Shae shuddered. The shadows looked like plague veins.

From her high perch, Shae saw three men riding horses in the distance, swiftly making their way up the path. She had never seen such beautiful horses, though she'd heard about such creatures, so different from those of her village. Everyone in Montane knew the story of the First Rider: long ago, centuries before the plague came, he tamed a wild horse, a beast, they say, who was born from the sun. On its back, he galloped through the empty darkness of the unborn world, bringing forth life with the words that flowed from his lips. Where he trod, the land sprang into being and color.

These horses' manes and tails flowed like they were underwater and seemed to glisten, even in the fading light. The beautiful animals could only come from one place: High House.

The Bards were coming to burn her home.

Though their faces were hooded, Shae swore she saw the Bards' lips moving steadily in the shadows. The wind blew harder as they approached, and the wails rose to match its fevered pitch. The tree branch lurched beneath her, and Shae lost her balance. She slid, the branch above slipping through her grasp.

All she could see as she fell was a frenzy of ribbons, furious and wild, snapping in the wind.

Snap. Snap-snap-snap. My eyes whip open, and I'm in my bed, its thin unpadded pallet stiff beneath my back. That same dream, as vivid as when it happened, five years ago.

A dark figure stands over me, snapping her fingers. "Rise and shine!"

"*Shh!*" I whisper. "Keep it down, or you'll wake Ma." *She needs her sleep worse than I do.*

Fiona huffs, stepping back from the bed and into the line of gray dawn cast from the window. She is less fearsome in the light. Tall, willowy, and blond, with the highest cheekbones in all of Montane, she is like the dappled sunlight beneath a tree—beautiful in a way she herself cannot see. My parents were both brown-haired, short, and stocky. I never stood a chance of growing up tall and fair like Fiona. Neither of them were tormented by thousands of freckles on their faces, however—that seems to be my unique misfortune.

My friend shrugs. "Somehow I doubt that, if she sleeps as heavily as you."

I glance at my mother. Tucked beneath her covers in the bed across the room, she is a frail form, her ribs gently rising and falling with every breath. Fiona might have a point. My mother sleeps like the dead.

"What are you doing here?" I pull the ragged quilt off my legs and begin massaging out the crick in my shoulder.

"It's the first quarter moon, remember?"

Fiona's father sells the wool from our sheep and repays us with food from his general store. They are one of the only families in town that will associate with mine since the Blot touched us. And so, every month at the first quarter moon, Fiona stops by and we exchange the meager goods that allow our families to survive.

"But why so *early*?" I stifle a yawn. My feet ache as they hit the cold floor, my legs trembling with exhaustion. I couldn't sleep last night, even after a long day in the fields—dark dreams hovered at the edge of my mind, full of faint whispers and shadows. I sat up for hours, squinting at my needlework under the pale light of the crescent moon through the window, stitching to distract myself.

Fiona follows me to the other side of the room where my clothes hang. A simple white shirt, faded green skirt I embroidered with thread spun from wool, torn and muddied at the hem, and a matching vest lined in soft rabbit fur—far from fine, the opposite really, but the only apparel I own. I prefer pants for working the overgrown pastures, but after years of growing out of them just as soon as I'd finished their hemming, it became easier to wear a skirt, tying it in knots above my knees when it's hot or the terrain is rough.

Fiona politely turns her back, rolling her eyes at my modesty as I change out of my nightgown. Once dressed, I usher her from the bedroom, closing the creaky door as quietly as possible behind me.

"Pa wants me back at the store before we open," Fiona says, watching my hands—callused and raw from spinning—as I place the prepared skeins of yarn in a basket for her. "The Bards arrive today."

The Bards. Suddenly I feel as though the house has been encased in ice. The town elders say there's power in words—that certain phrases can change the world around you. The same was said for the color of the disease. Indigo was avoided as if merely the sight or sound of it would cause a resurgence of the sickness. Now it is referred to—when absolutely necessary—as the "cursed color."

Only the Bards can harness words safely, through their Tellings. Everyone in Montane knows that any fool can speak disaster into existence by uttering something forbidden.

Some say my brother was one of those fools.

They say the Blot started with the written word. The havoc it wreaked has long since turned to terror at all words, written or spoken. Any careless utterance could be enough to revive the pandemic.

It was enough for Ma to stop talking completely after losing Kieran.

A familiar feeling of dread snakes through my gut.

The Bards arrive once or twice a year with barely a day's warning, a message delivered by a raven to the town's constable. He, in turn, summons the town in preparation for their arrival. They collect the town's tithe for High House and—if they are pleased—they may perform a Telling to grant blessings to the land and its people.

They are rarely pleased. Aster's offerings are meager: an armful of wool, a few bundles of pale wheat. The hide and antlers of a buck, if we are lucky.

A Telling in Aster has not occurred during my lifetime, but the oldest of the elders, Grandfather Quinn, often recounts one from his childhood. After the Bards left, his family's wheat farm produced a harvest that lasted six weeks.

The last time I saw the Bards was from a distance, the day Kieran died. After, Ma forbade me from seeing them—the final words she ever said aloud to me. But it's not as if I have time to peer in on their visitations. With the land scrubbed dry by a merciless sun, I often have to drive our flock miles away to be sure they're fed at all. Last month, we lost a three-week-old ewe lamb to starvation.

Now I understand why Fiona came so early. If the meager skeins of yarn from our sheep make the town's tithe look even a little bit better, perhaps the Bards will aid in ending the drought. The village of Aster has not seen rain in nearly nine months.

"Are you all right?" Fiona asks quietly.

I jerk my head up from the yarn and look at her. Lately, I've been haunted by strange things I can't explain. Dreams that seem more like terrible, nonsensical predictions. I awaken with the growing fear that something is deeply wrong with me.

"I'm fine." The words fall heavily out of my mouth.

Fiona narrows her large green eyes at me. "Liar," she says bluntly.

I take a deep breath as a desperate, foolish idea starts to make its way through my head. With a quick backward glance at the closed bedroom door, I grab the basket of yarn with one hand, Fiona's wrist with the other, and walk purposefully out of the house.

The sun has barely touched the sky as we step outside, and the air is still cold and dry. The mountains that surround us cut a dark, jagged line ahead and cast the valley in a veil of gauzy shadows while mist rises from the withered grass.

I lead Fiona around the side of the house in silence. Despite the chill in the air, my skin feels hot and prickly. My mind is spinning. I worry that if I turn to show Fiona my face, even for an instant, she will somehow know the truth.

I could be in serious danger, and by just being near me, so could she.

It started about a year ago, right after my sixteenth birthday. I was embroidering one of Ma's headscarves, black birds arcing across the fabric, when I lifted my face to see a flock of them forming an arrowhead through the sky. Not long after, I was stitching a hare with a white tail onto a pillowcase, when one of the neighbor's bird hounds came into the pasture with a bloodied white hare in its teeth.

A warm tingling began to fill my fingers whenever I sewed. Not unpleasant, but strange.

I spent countless nights lying awake, staring at the austere wooden beams of the ceiling, trying to figure out if I was mad or cursed—or both. There was only one thing I knew for certain: the shadows of sickness had fallen on us before. We have been touched by the Blot. We can't possibly know what other catastrophe might befall us from that contact. And ever since I discovered my embroidered fantasies echoed in the world around me, Ma's silence has felt more and more deafening. The house echoes with everything that is unsaid.

Loss. Exhaustion. Gnawing hunger, day after day.

The morning air sends a shiver through me, stirring the frigid fear in my gut. When we reach the side of the barn, I finally release Fiona, but can't help another wary glance over my shoulder. The little gray wooden house is still and silent in the morning mist, as we left it.

"What's gotten into you, Shae?" She quirks an eyebrow, suspicious, but intrigued.

"Fiona," I begin, biting my lip hard as I realize I'm not sure how to say it. "I need a favor." It's the first truthful thing that comes to mind.

Her eyes soften. "Of course, Shae. Anything."

Instantly, I want to choke back my words. I try to imagine what might happen if I simply explain the truth to her. *I might be cursed by the Blot, so I want to ask if the Bards can cure me.*

At best, I risk losing my friend out of fear that I've brought my curse upon her, and the whole town will know within the day. Her parents will cancel their deal with Ma, no one will buy our wool, and my family will starve.

Even saying such a thing aloud is forbidden; any word that conjures thoughts of malice must never be spoken. Such words are said to harbor curses of their own, upon the speaker as well as those who hear them. The words would likely summon such an occurrence into existence all on its own.

Worst case, I spread my curse to my dearest friend in the world.

I can't take that chance.

Staring at Fiona's sweet, eager face, I know I can't. I can't risk losing her too.

"Can I deliver the wool to your pa?" I ask instead. "I'll need you to bring the flock up to the north pasture while I'm gone. They shouldn't be too stubborn this morning, and I can give you all the instructions. You've seen me do it plenty of times."

Fiona's brow knits. "That's all? Yes, of course. But why?"

My heart starts pounding heavily in my chest. I take a deep breath, leaning against the rough siding of the barn to steady myself and clear the scattered thoughts in my head, frustrated by how terrible I am at this.

"Oh, I know what's going on." A sly smile tips the corner of Fiona's mouth and my heart suddenly goes quiet as it plummets into my feet. "You're going to see Mads, aren't you?"

"Yes!" I breathe a sigh of relief. "Exactly." No one would question why I would go to town and see Mads unprompted—or if they did, their suspicions would be far from the ones I'm worried about.

"Shae, you don't need to be embarrassed." Fiona laughs. "I completely understand."

I force a thin, hopefully convincing laugh, though it sounds more like breath getting caught at the back of my throat. "Thank you. I owe you."

"I'm sure I'll think of something." She leans in and hugs me. I'm tempted to pull away, as if even my touch could infect her. Instead, I let her scent of fresh dill and brambles and stream water wash over me, feeling, in this moment, not cursed, but *lucky*.

Fiona and I have always been an unconventional match as far as friends go. Where I'm short, she's tall. I'm dark and she's fair. Where I'm broad and husky, she's slender and soft. She has suitors, and I have sheep. Well, sheep and Mads. But it's all just as well. Fiona is loyal, thoughtful, and willing to put up with all of my moods. She's the kind of person who would happily assist me and expect nothing in return. She deserves better than my secrets.

"He adores you, don't you think?" Fiona asks, pulling away. The sly smile has become a full-fledged grin. "I never thought you'd be married before me."

I let out a real laugh. "Let's not go *that* far!"

If Fiona has a flaw, it's her love of gossip. And

young men tend to be her favorite topic. If as many of them paid attention to me as they did to her, it might be mine as well. Mads seems to be the singular exception in the entire town of Aster.

He kissed me once, last year after a disappointing harvest festival. The next day, the constable declared that the drought had returned, and Mads and his father left for three weeks on a hunting trip. We never spoke of the kiss. Even now, I'm not sure exactly how I feel about it. Maybe everyone's first kiss is underwhelming, and they just lie about it to make everyone else feel better.

But Mads is the least of my worries. I only hope that I can sustain this little act of subterfuge long enough to make it to town and back without Fiona or my mother knowing the real reason—and without any prying neighbors finding out. In Aster, anyone could be watching. Everyone usually is.

"You promise you'll tell me everything when you get back?" Fiona asks, driving the knife farther into my chest.

"I promise." I don't meet her gaze. "Here, let me show you what to do with the flock while I'm gone."

Fiona obediently follows me around the weathered old barn toward the gate. Like the house, the wood siding has grayed with age, along with the shabby, thatched roof. It's impressive that it's still standing, if barely, let alone that it manages to keep predators and thieves out.

The flock bleat and shuffle around happily as I

unlock and open the door. They waste no time trotting outside to the pasture. Mercifully, they seem to be cooperative today and stick together as they file out into the valley. Only Imogen is a little slow, but I forgive her for it. She's due to give birth within the week. Giving us another lamb is worth the extra time it takes to wait for her to catch up.

We lead the sheep to the hilltop east of the valley, which can't be seen from the house, before I turn and take Fiona's hands.

"What?" she asks with a confused look.

"I almost forgot. I have something for you." I reach into my pocket and produce my latest project, a handkerchief dyed red with a mix of beetroot and petals, stitched with dark flowers that look like eyes. Another one of my strange dreams, though this one can't possibly come true.

"It's beautiful," she whispers.

That's another thing about Fiona. She loves everything I sew, even the odd and disturbing images. Sometimes, I think maybe she sees the world the same way I do. Other times, I think she loves what I make precisely because she does not.

Because to her, the world appears simple. To her, the sun is merely light, not a scourge. To her, the night is a blanket of stars, not a swath of fear and silence. What I cannot say to her—what I cannot even understand myself—is that sometimes, I fear the dark will swallow me whole.

Most travelers have to navigate a treacherous pass to reach town, but from our house, it's only an hour's walk north along the shore of what used to be a pond. The walk is easy enough, if a little dreary. Without rain, the dusty countryside is all the same dull, washed-out brown. The pond dried up long ago and is simply a dark crater in the middle of the valley—a scar on the skin of the earth, reminding us of what once was there.

Nausea and dizziness roll in my gut the nearer I draw to the village, my vision spotting as if I am stricken by sun fever. The tall watchtowers loom ever closer, ominous and unmoving in the distance. Stepping toward their shadows only adds to my unease.

Even if I do speak with the Bards, what are the chances they won't simply execute me for my impertinence? What if they do find a trace of the Indigo Death in me and banish us? Burn our home for a second time? A cold chill rolls over me in waves as I recall tales of the Bards' past punishments. Fiona's mother once saw a Bard seal a woman's mouth shut by whispering in her ear.

To calm my racing heart, I try to remember the

sound of Ma's voice. If I concentrate, I can hear the warm tremor of it: deep and gentle, like the summer wind echoing in a well. Before she went silent, she used to spin bedtime stories for Kieran and me— stories of a place beyond the cloud-capped mountaintops, where we will all one day rest. Stories of Gondal, a land of magic and beauty, where flowers grow twice the height of man, where birds speak and spiders hum, where trees thick as houses burst toward the sky.

Kieran and I would listen attentively in the matching beds Pa built for us. Mine had a little heart carved into the headboard and Kieran's had a star. Ma would sit on a stool between us, her face illuminated by a flickering golden candle as she told us about the Bards of Montane. *By Telling, the Bards can lure luck into being. Their words can whisper away your heartbeat and show your deepest secrets to the world.*

It was a happy time, before the myth of Gondal was deemed profane. Before the Bards began the raids, removing any stories or iconography of Gondal from homes and gathering places, and the very word was banned.

Gondal is nothing more than a fairy tale, albeit a dangerous one. As a child, I might not have understood that fully, but I do now. Such tales are treacherous and have no place amidst reality.

She never should have told us those stories, I think angrily. *If she hadn't, Kieran would be alive.*

My fingers itch to take up my sewing to calm myself, but instead, I take a deep breath to dispel the poisonous thoughts from my mind as the village of Aster comes into full view at the other side of the pass.

Of all its citizens, Ma and I live farthest from the village proper. It was deemed necessary by the constable after what happened to Kieran. The day Ma took my hand and we made the trek into the mountain valley where we've been ever since is still vivid in my mind. The memory of the constable's hammer pounding as he nailed a blackened plague marker above our door—the shape of a death mask, its mouth and eyes empty—a constant reminder of what we'd lost. The good people of Aster don't have to worry about our misfortune infecting them if they stay away. Not that it matters. Ma already hasn't been the same since Pa's heart failed him. Since Kieran's death, she hasn't strayed from the house, except to tend the land.

From the pass, I can just make out the cluster of rooftops below on the windswept plains. Here, feral horses run in packs, attacking anything foolish enough to draw close. Before the Blot, this barren stretch of countryside was some of the best farmland in the region. Now, the flat, dusty earth stretches for miles, dotted sparsely with long-dead trees. To the west, a dried-up river cuts a jagged line through the ground like a raw, gaping wound. The bridge across was stripped for firewood during a particularly cruel winter, leaving behind a skeletal path of cracked stone and mortar.

The village of Aster is a huddled group of small houses, shrinking every time another band of highwaymen find it. It sits alone on the dusty plains, shadowed from behind by the unforgiving peaks of the mountains. In recent decades, a wall and watchtower were erected, looming over the houses. The investment was sound; Aster became much safer when it stopped being such an easy target.

The simple wood and stone houses were whitewashed after the Blot ended to give the appearance of cleanliness. The paint is graying, peeling off to reveal the dirty material beneath in a drab patchwork. Little bursts of color try valiantly to peek through: a line of shutters once painted a bright red but now ruddy and worn, a wall covered in withered ivy, and window boxes full of dead weeds. You can see how Aster was a beautiful town once, before poverty and plague raced through its narrow dirt streets.

A hundred years ago, when the Blot first ravaged Montane, bloated, blue bodies littered the streets. But the family of High House cured Montane of the worst of it, and for a few decades, the Indigo Death disappeared entirely. Yet people did not heed their rules. They smuggled ink into their towns, invited the Blot inside their homes. And so the sickness returned in waves.

It still could, if we are not careful.

The Bards keep us safe and blessed. Despite the

harsh punishments, we owe them our lives. Their Tellings can pull the breath from your lungs if you speak words that might conjure the Indigo Death. But they can also breathe life back into those on the edge of death, if the people are virtuous enough.

Kieran was not so lucky. Many others were not either. There are some things that even High House cannot do. But I would never dare to say it aloud.

The outskirts of town are nearly deserted. As I walk between rows of worn clapboard houses, all I hear is the sound of a howling cat nearby. Everyone must already be gathered in the market.

Music drifts from the center of town, but the lively tune sends a ghostly echo through the empty streets. I follow the hollow sound, wrapping a shawl around my face to hide my features. My teeth clench at the thought of the crowd recognizing me—the glaring eyes, the muttered curses—but still, I pick up my pace toward the market square.

Turning a corner around the abandoned blacksmith's shop, I see the first signs of the crowd preparing for the Bards' arrival—their *inspection*, though no one dares call it that. Grandfather Quinn is playing his rusted flute, his wife conducting. The town's children sing along to the music. Directions are shouted over the melody as a group of young men hang thin banners from the windows. The colors are dull with age and the cloths threadbare, looking likely to blow away at the first sign of a stiff breeze.

Beneath the banners, Aster's most prosperous

families have arranged various stalls and booths to showcase the best of their wares. Fiona's father is among them, tall and fair like his daughter, hastily erecting a weathered canopy over a cluster of modest vegetables, which have been propped upright against an overturned basket to give the appearance of bountifulness. My heart twists with pity—and fear. Even Fiona's father, the most blessed among us, is struggling to produce food. Soon, all will be loaded onto a cart and sent to High House.

Unless the Bards are displeased.

On the other side of the street, girls my age are hurrying toward the square in their finest clothes, each bearing platters of fruit and pitchers of precious water. My throat aches for it. I recognize a few of them, though I hope they won't know me. The elders escorting them fuss over their hair and dresses, barking, "stand up straight!" and "be sure to smile!" The prettiest are pushed to the front of the crowd—where they are more likely to catch the Bards' attention. One of the elders comments loudly about Fiona's absence, sending a cold shiver up my spine.

The town's excitement barely masks its desperation. It's only a shroud to conceal the drought, our lack of offerings for High House. I wonder if it will be enough to fool the Bards.

Keeping my head low, I use my elbows to break through the crowd and inch closer to the square. I pull the shawl tighter around my face, but most of the townspeople are too transfixed by what's happening to notice me.

The air is tense, people's faces tight beneath forced smiles. Aster has had a bad run, even before the current drought, but Constable Dunne told us things were looking better this year. According to Fiona, he assured us that this season we'd be granted a Telling. Our woes would be over. The starvation would end.

I dare a glance at my fellow villagers, many in rags, their faces as gaunt and carved-out as my own. The knot in my gut cinches tighter. From the edges of the town square, people are packed so densely that I can't even see the center.

I frown and try to elbow my way farther in. The crowd is hard to maneuver through; I remain trapped far from where I wish to be. I lurch onto the tips of my toes, barely making out the scene over the shoulders of the man in front of me.

Constable Dunne stands alone at the bottom of the town hall steps, his lean figure stiff with worry. Shingles and oak panels—once fine—have been stripped from the building. Dunne directs his gaze toward the square. Dunne has been Aster's leader as long as I can remember. He's tall and strong for a man of his years, but there is a tinge of weariness behind his eyes as he keeps a lookout for the Bards. A few minutes pass before he hurriedly squares his shoulders, smoothing his worn coat and lifting a hand in the air.

The music grows louder and the people in the

street grow utterly silent. On the other side of the square, the crowd parts.

The Bards have arrived.

My heart leaps, and it takes me a moment to find the word for the feeling that floods my chest. *Hope.*

Three imposing figures enter as a hush falls over the crowd. Their long black coats are accented with gold, the colors of High House, and are tailored perfectly, accenting sharp lines and perfect posture. Upon each of their right upper arms is the crest of High House, a shield and three swords. The finery of their uniforms stands in stark contrast to the rabble surrounding them. From what I can see under their dark hoods, their expressions are fixed and impassive.

Constable Dunne greets them with a deep, reverent bow that the Bards ignore. He rights himself awkwardly and signals again, this time for the procession of girls with their baskets.

The music picks up: shaky at first, but growing steady. A light, festive melody fills the air as the procession files in around the Bards. First the girls, dancing joyfully and tossing pieces of painted fabric that mimic flower petals into the air. They smile tightly at the Bards and fan out, each taking a spot that tactfully conceals anything that might look less than perfect. One moves her thinly slippered foot over a dark stain on the ground. *Blood,* I realize, spilled during the Bards' last visit. My stomach lurches.

Next, the merchants and tradespeople push their

carefully prepared goods through the square. They form a line, each bowing to the Bards before stepping back. The three figures in black share a look before walking to inspect the town's offering. The whole town seems to go silent, holding its breath, as the Bards make their way from cart to cart.

After what feels like an eternity, they turn to confer with Constable Dunne while the crowd watches. Dunne's jaw is set uncomfortably. His broad brow furrows, shining with sweat.

The crowd begins to murmur softly, the sound moving from the front to the back of the crowd like wind over grass.

"Did you hear anything?"

"Perhaps they'll show mercy . . ."

". . . the lowest-performing village in the region," I hear a woman nearby say to her aging father. "The Bards will refuse their blessings again."

Another sobs, handkerchief clutched to her mouth. "We're not worthy."

The constable is pleading with the Bards, but they don't even seem to hear what he says. Desperation is mounting in the crowd with every passing second. It's strange to see the esteemed Constable Dunne, usually a measured and reliable man, cower so powerlessly.

If the most important man in town can't get them to listen, what chance do I have?

My frantic thoughts are cut short as one of the Bards, a tall man with shoulders even broader than

Dunne's, steps forward with his hand in the air. A call for silence. The crowd obeys immediately.

"Good people of Aster," he addresses us. Although his voice is not raised, I hear him clearly—as though he's standing right beside me. It's a deep, resonant sound, tinged with a faint, sophisticated accent I've never heard before. "As always, High House is humbled by your generosity. It pains us greatly that your tithe is not equal to the spirit in which it is given."

My insides twist. Another rush of voices begins to rise from the people, but the Bard cuts them off, raising his hand higher. His eyes pinch in anger. "Sadly, this marks yet another visit wherein Aster has disappointed. By the grace of Lord Cathal, High House can only offer as much as you provide us in return."

He approaches Fiona's father's cart and picks up a shriveled turnip. The carefully placed display falls away, revealing the overturned basket beneath that props everything up. Another Bard picks up an apple and turns it over, revealing a bruise that shadows the fruit's skin. The Bard clicks his tongue and shakes his head. Fiona's father stands stock-still, his face ashen.

"Where other villages beyond the plains have offered bountiful harvests, here, the crops are meager," the dark-haired Bard continues, delicately placing the turnip back on the cart. "We want to help you. Truly. But clearly there is something amiss here. Aster will benefit little from a Telling."

Constable Dunne clears his throat. "It's the drought. Nothing will—"

"Please show mercy! We'll never survive without a Telling," the woman next to me wails, cutting off the constable's speech. Tears are streaming down her face.

The Bard signals for silence once more, and the crowd complies, the air thick with their unspoken pleas.

"As I said." The Bard's voice is firmer. "There is a reason that Aster alone is experiencing such hardship. A responsible party." He pauses, looking over the gathered faces. I'm certain his eyes meet mine from beneath his hood—and I let out a ragged breath when they sweep past me to continue surveying the crowd. "I encourage anyone with information to step forward. Has someone you know spoken a forbidden word? Used or kept ink? Withheld banned objects?"

The woman next to me inhales sharply.

Constable Dunne steps forward, nodding weakly. "The time to divulge is now. The fate of Aster depends on it."

The crowded square falls into silence, but the people of Aster are not looking at the Bards—they are looking at one another. Their eyes are wide and fearful. Cruel, even. I should know; they are the same stares that forced my mother and me from our home. Could they be searching for someone I know?

A frost creeps through my core. Could they be searching for me?

A small boy steps into the center of the square, walking silently toward the Bard. I recognize his mop of dark tangled hair. Grandfather Quinn's youngest grandchild.

The towering Bard leans down to allow the child to whisper in his ear. A thunderstorm overtakes my mind.

Is he whispering my name?

My heartbeat echoes dully in my ears, growing faster and louder as the Bard stands upright again. He sends the child away with a gentle pat on the shoulder.

"The village elder known as Quinn hereby stands accused of spreading stories of Gondal," the Bard says, folding his hands neatly behind his back. "Step forward, please."

My fists unclench. Sounds of a scuffle rise from the back of the crowd, punctuated by pleading as Grandfather Quinn is grabbed roughly by the nearest townspeople and dragged forward. He is deposited with a shove at the Bard's feet where he cowers, his aged body trembling violently. Bile rises in my throat—but I can't avert my eyes. I believe it, yet I'm still in shock. At his betrayal. That he could be so foolish. That he would risk us all.

"Please, good Bards . . ."

"Silence!" The Bard's voice is edged with anger.

"Do what he says." I can't help but wish for it under my breath. Thankfully, the old man falls quiet.

"For the crime of uttering forbidden language,

you are hereby sentenced to a silencing. Your tongue shall pay the debt owed to High House."

The expression on his face unreadable, Dunne nods to the group who brought Quinn forward. They hesitate, throwing glances at one another—until the broadest of the group pounces on Quinn. The motion reminds me of a cat digging its claws into a mouse. Quinn throws a watery smile at his grandson over his shoulder, but remains quiet as they drag him toward the decrepit town hall.

It isn't until he disappears into the shadows of the building that his scream pierces the silence.

Constable Dunne rushes to close the doors. With a *bang*, they separate Quinn from the crowd as firmly as a sharp blade slices meat from the bone.

Eventually, Constable Dunne turns to the Bards, hands pressed together tightly. "Surely, noble Bards, the removal of this stain will be enough to lift the blight from our town and earn back the favor of High House?"

The Bard regards Dunne impassively. "Aster has shown impressive loyalty to High House today," he replies. "It took great bravery for one so young to come forward. For your efforts, we shall grant a Telling."

This news is enough to completely transform the tension in the air. A cheer surges from the crowd, along with promises of abundant harvests, breathtaking festivals—and vows to root out traitors. The Bard nods briefly in approval before stepping back to prepare the Telling.

I draw a deep breath into my lungs, rising up on my toes to see them—and to stop myself from fainting in the close press of bodies.

There's a charge that moves through the air as my eyes linger on the Bards. The three black-and-gold figures stand facing one another, their fingers tented in front of their chests. They are so still that they look as though they could be made of stone. But their lips move wordlessly in unison, raw energy corralling in the space between them, pulling toward them through their voiceless chant. The wind tightens around us. It feels as if the fabric of the world is being drawn closer with every passing second. The pull grows stronger as their lips move faster.

A booming clap of thunder issues from overhead. Hundreds of awed faces look up at once, their mouths open in wonder at a dark cloud newly overhead.

Then, a precious drop of water, gleaming like a jewel, falls on the village of Aster. In the span of a breath, the drop is followed by another, and another, and another.

Rain.

3

The crowd erupts into joyful cheers. We stare up into the sky, letting the blessed rain pour down on our cheeks. I feel as if I am weeping—perhaps I am. I've known the greatness of the Bards' powers all my life, yet I have never seen it like this. So pure, so life-bringing.

The townspeople start to dance, their skin glistening with new rainfall, and I exhale an awed breath, hope flooding me. With the crowd distracted by the rain, I may have a chance at an audience with the Bards once the Telling is complete.

Suddenly, a hand yanks away my covering. *"You."*

The heat of being recognized moves through me in a wave of nausea.

My old neighbor—a kind man who once pressed a basket of strawberries into my hand—glares at me. Heads turn, mouths falling open as the villagers register who I am. The girl touched by the Blot. "How dare you show your face here? Just when we've *finally* earned a Telling?"

A younger man glares at me venomously. "They ought to drag you off with Grandfather Quinn!"

"Scourge," a woman hisses.

Someone shoves me hard onto my knees in the

wet dirt. Another spits at me. Before I can fully pick myself up, a storm of limbs, hisses, and taunts pushes me back, away from the Bards. It's all I can do to scramble over the street and out of the way.

Despite my trembling, I manage to stumble to my feet, pull the shawl over my head, and flee, trying hard not to release my tears.

I want to run home, curl up beside my mother, and dream of her singing me a lullaby. Dream, even, of Gondal, that beautiful toxic lie. The myth my brother and I lived by, and the one that, in the end, might have killed him . . .

That cost Grandfather Quinn his tongue.

But there is no going back—not when the darkness is waiting for me every night, the ever-growing certainty that something is consuming me: the curse, the Blot, the mark of one who is doomed, or doomed to hurt others.

Finally, I emerge at the edge of the crowd, panting. In the chaos, no one has followed. They are too distracted by the rain. I grit my teeth and brush the mud from my clothes. My heart is pounding, and the lump in my throat feels as if it's choking me.

Breathe. *Breathe,* I remind myself. There has to be something I can do to get the Bards' attention.

I cast my gaze toward the wall of people, still cheering and celebrating, mercifully oblivious to me now.

A flash of light down a small path between houses catches my eye. Then another. Squinting in the direction of the distraction, I see it: a grand horse tossing its head, causing light to glint off its golden bridle.

My breath catches. Suddenly, I'm eleven years old again, weaving Kieran's death ribbons into tree branches.

The Bards' horses paw the ground impatiently, like they've just stepped out of my memory.

I slink away as quickly as possible until I reach the edge of the square where I can skirt the side of the building toward the horses. Their owners will have to come back to them at some point.

The three elegant creatures are not even tied to a hitching post; they simply wait for their masters obediently where they were left. They are black mares, almost fearsome in their beauty, nothing like the old nags I've seen in town or on the farms. Their dark, intelligent eyes watch me as I approach, almost as if they are assessing me.

The closest one even cocks her head, curious.

"Hello there," I whisper, and the horse bobs her head, as though in greeting. A wave of calm washes over me, and for the first time since leaving the pasture—since lying to Fiona—I can breathe evenly. The light catches the mare's golden bridle, and the motion tosses her mane from her forehead, revealing a small white star.

I place the basket of wool I've been clutching tightly the whole time between my feet and slowly hold out my hand. After a curious sniff, the mare lets me run my fingers over the marking on her forehead and down her ebony face to her soft muzzle. She whinnies, lowering her head to allow me to scratch behind her ear.

Up close, the incredible detail in her bridle is striking; it shimmers in the rainfall. The gold brow band and nose strap are engraved with a delicate filigree of shapes that I don't recognize, and set with small, white gems of some kind. I don't need to know what they're called to understand that just one of those sparkling stones is worth more than the entire town of Aster twice over. My free hand runs its fingers over the engraving and jewels, half-expecting such finery to vanish at my touch.

A firm, gloved hand suddenly circles my wrist and pulls me back. Spinning around, I choke on my breath as a storm of black and gold takes over my vision. Shaking, I find myself face-to-face with a Bard of High House.

He is no longer expressionless—fire seems to dance against the dark of his eyes, making them flash beneath his hood. His voice is low and dangerous when he whispers, "Hands off, thief."

When feeling returns to my limbs after my initial shock, there is a dull pain in my wrist from the Bard's grip. Not enough to leave a mark, but enough to remind me that it could get worse if I try anything foolish. My gaze falls automatically to the wet cobblestones.

He releases me. "Well? Nothing to say for your-self?"

His voice leaves a charge in the air between us. It's deep and resonant, but there is a strange, other-worldly reverberation that carries beneath the surface, a separate sound woven into his words, that keeps me rooted to the spot. I remember clinging to Ma's skirts as Claire, the baker, sang in the market at dusk, her husband playing a stringed instrument I never learned the name of. Now, it's as if the Bard's voice creates its own accompaniment. With each word, I can feel prickling heat on the skin of my face and neck, the air around us tightening and growing heavy like a storm is about to break.

The sensation dissipates as soon as he stops speaking, and I am left cold and wanting more.

I try not to wince as my gaze trails up from the finely polished leather boots standing in front of me. The gold trim on his uniform leads from elegant pants beneath his black cloak to a pristine jacket of the same color, adorned with two rows of shining golden buttons on either side of his chest. He stands unnaturally still, staring into my eyes without blink-ing, even as the rain sprinkles his face. Up close, he seems even more powerful, more extraordinary—and far more dangerous—than I imagined.

"I . . ." Now that an actual Bard is in front of me, I seem to have forgotten my senses. I swallow hard and try once more. "S-Sir . . ." Is he a sir? Sir Bard? Or do

I say lord? In my haste, I never even accounted for how to properly address a Bard. Humiliation washes over me.

The Bard makes a noise that is half groan, half sigh of annoyance. He pulls me out of his way easily, as if drawing back a curtain—as if I were invisible—fixing his attention on the mare.

"And what have I told you about letting strangers near?" He strokes the creature's neck. "You are far too trusting." A softness has crept into his stern voice.

I feel my face flush as a flurry of mixed emotions tangle up in my chest—first mortification at my own clumsiness, then outrage that he would value an animal over the human beside him, and finally fury at myself for lacking the words to say what I need to.

The Bard sweeps back his cloak, reaching for the saddle to swing into it. He doesn't even glance in my direction.

All my emotions harden into one: determination. My opportunity is rapidly slipping away.

"Wait—" The word falls from my mouth, blunt and awkward. "I'm—I'm not a thief." Before I can think better of it, I reach out in desperation to grasp the hem of his cloak right as he pulls himself astride the horse.

The movement makes his hood fall to his shoulders, revealing his look of surprise and affront. It doesn't help my racing heart to see the Bard is actually quite handsome. His thick, raven-black hair is striking, swept neatly back from his forehead. His skin is pale, and his features are soft, offset by high, angular cheekbones and a square jaw.

His mouth twitches, and I think of the words stored in his throat, how they are like snake venom—each with the power to cure or kill.

There's a sickening tightness in my gut, but I push on. "I'm sorry, but I must ask a favor—"

"A *favor*?" He repeats the question back at me with deliberate slowness, as if he is not sure I understand what I have asked.

Help me, I want to say. But the look on the Bard's face makes it painfully clear: I'm nothing. How foolish was I to imagine that the towering figure before me would lower himself to help a peasant like me? That he would care?

I think of Grandfather Quinn being dragged into the shadows of town hall, the sting of the blade as it pressed against his tongue. If I am sick—cursed—I must fix it. Before anyone else gets hurt. It's the right thing to do.

"I'm . . . I believe I'm cursed by the plague," I whisper. "I humbly ask your blessing for a cure."

The Bard's expression remains the same, as his eyes move downward to where my fist still clutches the tail of his coat. I quickly release it.

To my surprise, he dismounts with an irritated sigh. Turning from his horse, he reaches for me, this time taking my arm in his gloved hands. He turns my wrist over so that my palm is facing the sky, pushes back my sleeve, and begins to trace his eyes over my skin. *Looking for the Blot?* I wonder. With his teeth, he tears the glove from his hand, shoving it into a pocket within his cloak. His bare fingers gently press against my flesh. The warmth of it shocks me. I swallow thickly.

"And precisely why," he asks quietly, eyes searing into my skin, "do you think that you're cursed by the Indigo Death? Have you been sharing forbidden stories? In possession of ink?"

"No, sir." My heart falters before racing faster than I thought possible. I wonder if he can feel the pulse in my wrist. "But my brother—" I stop abruptly when a voice cuts in from around the corner.

"Ravod!" I can only watch, slack-jawed, as the other two Bards appear and stride toward their companion. The Bard drops my arm and takes a step back. It takes me a few long seconds to realize that *Ravod* is the handsome, dark-haired Bard's name. "Should have known you'd gone off to find some young thing to chat up."

The speaker takes down his hood, revealing a man slightly older than Ravod, with a tangle of bright red hair and stubble on his white cheeks. He has a weathered look about him, like some shepherds who walk the earth with their flocks—this Bard has probably seen all of Montane. He was the one who addressed the crowd.

The third Bard does not take down his hood. But as he approaches, I gasp.

For he is not a *he* at all, but a she. A young woman, perhaps only a few years my elder, with dark skin and hair and with amber eyes glowing beneath the shadow of her hood.

I have never heard of a female Bard before, let alone seen one. It is rare for women to possess the gift, they say, and rarer still for a woman to be able to control it. She must be particularly powerful. But before I have time to parse what this means—the awe and confusion of it—her hand moves in warning to her belt, where her knife glints.

Ravod leans in toward me. "Don't come to us again," he whispers.

My thoughts scatter at his nearness. He's easily more attractive than any of the boys in Aster. *Including Mads,* I think guiltily. He's looking right into my eyes, and up this close, I detect the faint scent of cedar on his uniform.

"But—"

"I said *go*," he hisses before mounting his horse once more in a single, swift motion.

The horse rears, and I stumble back, confused, but I know better than to press my luck.

The three Bards unite and exchange a few more words before turning their backs on me and galloping away in a blur. I look around, blinking, dazed, and filled with more emotions than I have names for.

They are gone. The spot where Ravod was standing is vacant, the earth undisturbed, as if he were never even there.

Even the rain has stopped. The blessing granted to us by the Bards has departed with them, leaving me alone in the street with no answers, and nothing to show for my efforts. With no proof that the Bards had ever arrived in Aster at all, save the damp clothes clinging to my skin.

Ma is at her spinning wheel, her back to me, hands moving dexterously over the fibers she's working while I prepare dinner. On any other night, this would feel comfortable. The sounds of her wheel turning, the steady chopping of my knife on the cutting board, and the wind against the walls of the house would slide together into a natural rhythm. But this evening, the spinning wheel creaks too loudly. Ma's silence cries out even louder.

Does she know where I went today? Did one of the villagers inform her? Am I just imagining things?

Maybe it's only the rain. Now that it's gone, we don't know when, or if, it will return. Many others in town are probably wondering the same thing.

Over the years, I've come to realize Ma's silence speaks its own language. I wince, hoping Grandfather Quinn's family figures out the same. But now my mother's body is saying something I can't decipher. There's only the heaviness in her shoulders and an agitation in the way she taps the treadle. Her long fingers have slipped three times tonight. She never slips.

I worry that she senses what's happening to me too.

Time passes in this stiff, punctuated silence: the creaking of the wheel, the chopping of the vegetables, and the wind on the wooden walls of our home. The silence keeps my thoughts returning to the Bards. To High House. To Ravod's dark hair, the softness with which he spoke to his horse, and how abruptly he changed, harshly making me go. Confusion floods me, pierced only by anger—the Bards are meant to protect us. He should have helped me.

No matter how many times I remind myself not to, I wonder if the answer is waiting for me to find it, somewhere far from here. Maybe I am not meant to stay. Not if I could bring the plague back to our village. Or end up like Grandfather Quinn.

I glance over and the hunch in Ma's back reminds me that she cannot manage the farm on her own. We struggle enough together.

Back to work, Shae. I pick up the chopped carrots and carry them to the big black pot bubbling over the fire. With a practiced toss, I launch them in and avoid splashing myself with boiling broth. At least I can make a decent stew.

As I stir, I watch Ma, her attention fixed entirely on her spinning. The sight is an added weight on my heart. I taste the stew to see if it's done. Bland and watery, as usual.

I crouch to search one of the lower cabinets, hiding my face to brush the tears away while I look for the salt sack, which is near empty. We can't afford more. If we run out, we'll have to go through next winter without any dried meat; there will be no salt to preserve it.

Then—a familiar hand on my shoulder. A gentle squeeze. *I love you.*

I turn around and face Ma, who is cupping a pinch of salt in her palm, a tiny, familiar smile tugging the corner of her mouth.

I sometimes forget that Ma can understand me the same way I understand her. She hears what I don't say. What I *want* to say.

She wraps me in her arms, and I let go of a sob—short and fierce—muffled against her chest. After a tight squeeze, she pulls away. Her free hand brushes a wisp of sandy brown hair from my forehead, her fingers lingering lovingly on my freckles. She thinks they're beautiful, but we agree to disagree.

"I know, I know." I can't help smiling, repeating what she always told me as a little girl. "They're kisses from the fairies."

Ma gestures for me to follow her back to the wooden chairs by the fire. She sits, motioning for me to do the same.

When I was much younger, we used to sit like this after dinnertime. Pa smoked his pipe and Kieran played with the toy Bards he sculpted from clay. Ma would braid my hair. Like those old bedtime stories, it was a time of warmth and safety. The tradition tapered off after Pa and Kieran died, but every so often, Ma rekindles it with only the two of us—when she knows I need it most.

The agitation in her fingers is gone as they gently comb though my hair. It isn't particularly pretty like Fiona's thick waves, but it's long enough to twist and shape, which I think Ma enjoys. When I was young, she'd weave wildflowers into my braid.

The fire warms us both, her hands gathering my hair, and the images come—not dreams, exactly, but more than memories. Hungrier, somehow, and scarier, bursting through me like a storm of darkness—the sound of hooves, a pack of horses on a dusty road. A little boy weeping. Blue veins.

I sit against Ma's knees, eyes squeezed shut, until the fire burns down to embers, and the stew is no longer steaming. A soft snore behind me reports that she has fallen asleep. I sit up and pat the elaborate braid she left in my hair, careful not to wake her.

Reclining in her chair, she appears peaceful in a way she doesn't during the day. The crow's feet and fine lines by her brow are softened, making her look more like the woman from my childhood. I pull the blanket off the back of the chair and drape it over her, pressing a kiss to the silver streak of hair at her temple. She snores gently, but doesn't stir.

Strange as it sounds, that snore is the closest thing I've heard to her voice in years, and I wait in case I hear it again. Instead, Ma turns her head and her breath quiets.

I feel a pang of sadness in my chest. She deserves better than this. She deserves to know what's happening to me, but she can't.

But I'm not the only one in the house keeping secrets.

One night, when I couldn't sleep after Kieran's death, I watched from under my blankets as Ma gingerly removed a small item concealed beneath her bed and cradled it, before hiding it once more. Her faint candlelit shadow spread over my bed as she looked me over, and gently kissed my hair before she lay back down and fell asleep.

Now, I quietly step over to her wooden bed frame and reach below, my fingers searching for the small hole in the mattress. I withdraw a cloth pouch the size of my palm. There are strange symbols skillfully stitched into the cloth, but it is otherwise plain. I tip out the contents, and a small but heavy stone talisman slides into my other hand.

My mother's secret treasure: a small, golden ox, a central figure in the stories of Gondal. It was Kieran's. I don't remember the day, but one morning he came home with it, claiming that a trader passing through the town had gifted it to him. Ma wanted to throw it away—it was only a year later that the Bards started raiding towns, hunting for banned items like these to destroy them once and for all. When she told us she'd burned it, Kieran was inconsolable. But he snuck over to my bed one night, opening his palm to reveal the ox. The strange material wouldn't catch flame, he said. Instead, the gold only shone brighter.

Now Ma hides the figure, keeping it despite the danger.

I gently turn the figure over in my hand, feeling its weight. Upon closer inspection, I can see tiny greenish-gold veins in the stone, shimmering without the need for light. Stone like this cannot be found in Montane. Kieran said it was made in Gondal. He may as well have said it fell from the sky. Gondal is a lie, nothing more than a pretty story.

I close my eyes and an image of Kieran lying in bed flashes before me. He's in the early stages of the disease, his brown hair plastered to his forehead with sweat. The larger veins in his neck are only beginning to darken. He gasps for air after every coughing fit, each one more brutal than the last.

"Don't worry about me, Shae. I'm strong as an ox," he told me before I was whisked out of the room, never to see him again.

For a long time, I can only stand in one place, squeezing my eyes shut until the stinging pain in my chest subsides. No matter how much time passes, the loss of Kieran has remained a brutal squeeze to my heart.

Gingerly, I put the ox back in its hiding place, close the front door behind me, and step past the wooden porch onto the road. I make sure to dust the iron death mask that hangs over our door—just in case.

The air smells crisp after the brief rain. In the dark, it's easier to imagine Aster as it once was—shadows obscure the dry cracks in the earth, the barren fields, and the dull-eyed animals whose bones jut out at sharp angles. The moon is bright overhead, illuminating a sky covered in twinkling stars. The sprawling blackness reminds me of the stories of Gondal, bordered on one side by a vast body of sparkling blue water, said to be endless, beautiful, and deadly. It sparks fear in me, but also another feeling I yearn to be able to understand.

The dry grass crunches under the thin soles of my shoes. The sound of sheep rustling in their sleep follows me as I pass the barn.

At the edge of a grove of pine trees, I climb the massive boulder where Mads and I used to come to count the stars. The trees in the area are long dead, leaving behind only the contorted skeletons of their former selves—and plenty of space to see the sky. Their skinny, blackened branches are just another reminder that the land in our village is dying, that we could be next if we aren't careful. I draw my knees to my chin, gazing out over the valley.

It looks bigger in the moonlight, an orb of faintly shimmering lights above. Below, heading west, a wide field is hedged by patches of bluish grass. Everything is ringed by the snow-capped mountains, on the other side of which lies the village of Aster, out on the plains through the pass. The moonlight is bright enough for me to clearly see my house farther down the hill, and the road leading to Aster's center. On the other side, the pasture stretches beyond the dried-up pond and the dwindling forest where Pa used to go hunting.

My fingers reach for the needles tucked into my pocket. I try not to think about the shabbiness of the cloth or thread as I pull out my latest work, and soon, my needle is racing through the fabric, matching the speed of my thoughts. Unbidden images keep slipping into my mind every time I think I've chased them away. My fingers move of their own accord, the tulips I was stitching turn into exploding suns, followed by jagged mountain peaks, then the golden shapes inscribed on the Bards' horses' bridles, and yet more forms, these resembling fangs. I shudder, remembering something at the edge of a dream I had, but can't quite see.

A rustle in the trees.

I gasp and nearly drop the thread. I scan the darkness. The trees stand watchful to my left. I search for movement—a wolf in the tall grass, the fangs of my stitching come alive.

"Freckles? What are you doing out this late?"

Not a wolf, then. For a wild moment, I imagine Ravod's slender figure emerging gracefully from between the trees. My breath hitches a little, remembering the light shimmering in his black hair, the perfect curve of his shoulders, and how his eyes locked onto mine.

But there's only one person in the world who dares call me "Freckles."

"Mads?"

Mads steps into a patch of moonlight. His hair,

which looks almost silver in the light, falls messily over his face. Sweat beads on his forehead, and his shirt is open at the neck. Years of grinding lumber at his father's mill have given him a wide, muscular physique with broad shoulders and big arms. He has nothing of Ravod's grace—more like a hulking gait. According to Fiona, he's not the handsomest boy in Aster, but he has a nice smile. I think I agree with her assessment.

It's difficult for me to clearly define how I feel about Mads. I'm really not sure if I love him or just want to feel that way because I think I should. I don't have the luxury of picking and choosing a partner like Fiona does. Mads is the only boy in town brave enough to come near me.

He does have a nice smile though.

I bite my lip, embarrassed. Ogling boys is more Fiona's purview.

"I heard what happened at the marketplace," he says.

"Grandfather Quinn," I murmur.

"No. I heard what happened to *you*," he says, leaning forward.

I wince, remembering the hands pushing me to the ground. Mads continues, "I went by your house to check on you. When you weren't there, I had a feeling you might have come here."

"I didn't want to wake Ma," I say, quickly stowing my needlework back in my pocket. Mads has never understood my fascination with embroidery, or the images I weave with needle and thread. "Too strange for me," he's always said.

Mads has been by my side for as long as I can remember. When we were younger, we used to play together with Kieran. After my brother's death, he was one of the only children who would come near me, other than Fiona. The other boys in town ridiculed him for it—tracing the sign of the Blot in the dust everywhere I went, the same one that hangs above our door—but Mads never cared. He could never make others accept me; though *in spite* of me, he became well loved. Mads never speaks ill of anyone, much to my frustration at times.

"Wolves have been sighted in this area. What would you have done if one spotted you?"

"Make noise, throw rocks, and stand my ground," I reply readily. "Like you taught me."

He chuckles. "Well, I'm glad I can be of some use to you. This seat taken?"

I move to make room beside me. He climbs the boulder with ease and takes a seat, leaving a hand's length of space between us. Close, but respectful. It can be exasperating how courteous he is. When I think of Fiona and her pack of suitors, it makes me wonder if Mads has feelings for me. But why would he keep his distance? Is it because I'm not pretty like her? Is he only being kind?

When I look back up at his face, his smile is tender and a little shy. My breath hitches. Mads and I haven't been this close in ages. And never this late at night. When we're so alone.

There's a weighted silence between us as Mads's large hand covers mine.

He clears his throat. "Your hair looks nice."

My free hand touches the intricate braid Ma made. "Thank you."

Mads glances away briefly, chewing his lip. After a long exhale, he turns back to me, his face altered in a way I can't quite identify. "I *was* worried about you," he says quietly, leaning closer. His nearness sends a warm shiver over my skin. "Freckles," he says, his eyes searching mine. "Something's going on. I can tell. What's wrong?"

I shake my head. "Nothing." It's not true, but I don't know how to explain it. Not with the heat of his fingers resting on top of mine. Not with all the pressure and fear of the day building up inside my chest, making it hard to separate it all into the right words.

His brow furrows. He's not convinced. "You know you can talk to me, right?" he says. "If there's something bothering you?"

"I know, Mads." I manage to smile at him.

"Listen." He takes my hand properly in his. "The drought is over. We earned a Telling from the Bards. The future isn't as bleak as it seems."

He pauses, and I try to drink in his hope. The safe feeling of his hand clasping mine. There's a lightness in his eyes that hasn't been touched by desperation, or blight, or death. I long to see my reflection in them—but I can't, no matter how hard I search.

"Have a little faith, Freckles." Mads smiles, the tips of his callused fingers tilting my chin as he leans closer.

His breath is warm on my lips, and my heartbeat is racing as fast as my thoughts. The tip of his nose brushes mine. His lips find my cheek. It's not unpleasant.

Maybe it's just not enough. I turn toward him, and our mouths meet. For a moment I feel as though the boulder has begun to spin rapidly and my arms reach around his neck. I'm just not sure if I feel that way because it's Mads I'm kissing, or because I'm being kissed at all. I'm pretty sure I'm doing this all wrong. I tentatively open my mouth.

Mads inhales sharply and the furrow in his brow returns as he shifts back. The night air suddenly feels a little colder, replacing the warmth of his lips, and my half-lidded eyes open wide in surprise.

"What?" I frown, but in the pit of my stomach is the constant fear that he's suddenly realized I'm not worth paying attention to. That everyone is right and he should stay away from me.

I don't want that. I like having him around. He's important to me, even if I'm not entirely sure of my feelings about him.

My arms unwind from his neck, thoughts tumbling wildly. I cradle my knees to my chest, a barrier between us.

Mads shakes his head. "I want to do this right. Not fast. Not without trust. You're too important to me."

I take a deep breath and release it slowly. It's not Mads I'm frustrated with. Not really.

"It's okay," I reply, sparing him what I hope is a reassuring smile. "You're important to me too."

"Then what's really going on?"

I already lied to Fiona today. My mother too. Perhaps it really is time to confide in someone. And who better than Mads?

"I . . ." I swallow hard. "I may have . . ." His eyes darken with concern. "I asked a favor from the Bards today. To cure me." I force the words out quickly.

"You're serious?"

When I say nothing, his frown deepens. I only confessed my fears to Mads once—on the night he kissed me for the first time. He assured me that I was imagining things; the Blot would never touch my family or me again. That he would never *let it* touch me. "What were you thinking? You can't just—"

"I *know*," I interrupt. Disappointment at Mads, and at myself, fills me, leaving an acrid taste in my mouth. I take a deep breath, but even that suddenly feels exhausting. "I know," I repeat, quieter this time. "It was foolish."

"That's not like you," Mads remarks, the disapproval in his voice apparent. "What's gotten into you, Shae?"

Mads never uses my real name unless he's upset. Disappointment turns into a hot fire in my chest.

"I don't know, *Maddox*." I yank my hand from his and climb off the boulder. "I only wanted to find some answers for myself."

"What answers? There's nothing wrong with you. You only fear the Blot because you lost Kieran. But the plague hasn't been here since. It's been *years*. You're *fine*." Mads looks down at me, pity in his eyes. "Why not trust what you already know?"

"Because I don't know anything," I reply hotly.

"Your life is good. You have a home to live in and clothes on your body and food on the table. Your mother loves you," Mads says, irritatingly calm as he climbs down to stand next to me. He puts his hands on my shoulders. His warm palms are the only thing that keep me from crumpling to the ground. "*I* love you. Isn't that enough?"

Shock smothers my anger and frustration. "You love me?"

His smile answers my question.

But all I can do is stand with my fists balled tightly at my sides. He doesn't understand the grief of losing someone to the Blot, of having a single event taint your entire family. Or the fear and uncertainty of knowing that there is something deeply wrong with you, and not being able to talk to anyone. He doesn't know what it's like to live with someone who is so broken by sadness that she won't even speak. That is my reality, and he can't imagine why I would want to do something to *fix* it.

He loves me.

But he doesn't know me.

Mads must see the hesitation in my eyes, because he takes a sudden step away, fixing his gaze on everything but me. "It's late, and we both need some rest. Let me walk you home."

"I don't want to go home, Mads." It comes out sadly, a poor substitute for *I love you too*. A tear falls down my cheek and I wipe it away with the back of my hand. "I can't stand the thought of it right now."

"You can't stay out here alone all night."

"You could stay with me?" I look up at him, hopefully. He is probably the only person I can stand to have around at the moment.

The tips of Mads's ears turn red and he lets out an awkward, shy laugh. "I can't," he says, his voice rough. "I need to get home. Important work tomorrow."

A sigh escapes me. I try not to feel choked with hurt. "Do what you have to. I'm going to stay here a bit longer." His eyebrows rise in concern. "I promise, I'll head home soon."

"Be safe, Freckles." He presses a soft kiss on my forehead before turning and heading down the hill into the valley. I watch until I lose sight of him in the darkness.

I can't sit still anymore, but I can't go home either. My exhaustion is bone deep. But I'm too afraid of what will come when I sleep.

Instead, I walk up the slope in the opposite direction of Mads. With every step, the rational part of me says to run back to Mads and give him the response he wants. But something stronger pulls me forward—the night sky, the darkness burned with a message in the shape of stars that I can't decipher.

I'm not sure how long I walk for. The moon is high overhead as I enter a small clearing, deeper in the woods than I intended to venture. My feet ache from the uphill climb and I half-collapse onto a rare patch of moss. My hand reaches into my pocket, fingers running over the furious needlework. The feel of the thread where I stitched the little yellow tulip petals exploding into suns calms me.

I stare at the sky above, willing it to be a mirror, or even a door into the future that Mads described. But as my eyes flutter open and shut, all I can distinguish is a sea of black, the answers sparkling in its depths slowly burned away by fire on the horizon.

My sleep is deep and dreamless, heavy as a cloak thrown over me. When I open my eyes, it's to squint at the early morning sunlight that's peeking through the gnarled, empty branches of trees overhead. I don't realize I've fallen asleep until I feel the crick in my neck when I try to lift my head.

I should head home before Ma thinks I've run off, I think, brushing a few leaves from my skirt. I only hope she hasn't awoken yet, or noticed I'm missing. If I hurry, I might even have time for a quick breakfast before I have to let the sheep out to pasture.

I turn toward home when a flash of color catches my eye. A patch of yellow tulips, sprouted determinedly from the arid ground. My heart is loud in my ears as I pull my needlework from my pocket. The pattern is the same, down to the detail. One of the flowers is even ill-formed, petals bursting outward from the stem as though exploding.

My jaw trembles, and I shiver. My gut feels like it's been shackled in cold irons.

Needing to be certain—and desperately hoping I'm wrong—I pull the fabric from the embroidery hoop and grip it with my hands. I tear it over and over, until the shreds fall from my desperate, shaking fingers.

In front of me, the flowers droop, then wither, crumbling into dust, until all that's left of the bright yellow petals is my memory of them.

Then, a cry echoes across the valley—an animal scream, familiar though I can't place it. A wolf?

The sound fades, but it leaves me uneasy. I break away from what I've done, my paces turning into a run down the uneven path that leads home. My shoes slip several times in my haste downhill. I hurry over loose rock, falling and skidding through the dirt. My dress and arms are filthy, down to my blackened fingernails. Hastily, I scramble up and keep running with more care. The ground is broken beneath my feet, instead of solid, as if recently turned over, and I recall the passing spell of rain brought on by the Bards. Could it have caused the slope to erode?

Urgently, I press forward, passing the boulder and heading through the valley and up to the road. Something feels *wrong*. I need to get home. To Ma.

I skid to a halt as the house comes into view, my heart and breath pounding discordantly in my chest.

The door is ajar, a smear of something dark, like ink, in the dust of the entryway.

The front door sways slowly on its hinges.

Each step toward the house feels slower, heavier, until I'm standing in front of the door and peering into the darkness within. I swallow hard before pushing it open farther.

"Ma?" I call out, waiting for my eyes to adjust to the dim light. I know she won't answer, but I still expect to see her over the stove fixing breakfast. Instead, I'm knocked back by a potent, unfamiliar scent. My hand instinctively covers my nose and mouth as I step through the doorway.

I barely recognize my home.

The furniture that hasn't been smashed is over-turned. Pots and broken plates litter the floor. Yarn and wool. Pieces of Ma's loom and spinning wheel. Almost everything I see is spattered in dark red.

Not ink. *Blood.*

I stand amidst the wreckage, too shocked to move. When I finally break free, my legs shake beneath me. I only manage a couple of steps farther into the house before I see her.

For a few moments I expect to awaken, either back in the wooded grove or in my bed.

This can't be real.

But the longer I stare, the more the realization sets in.

Ma.

She isn't going to move.

The blood isn't going to vanish.

Things aren't going back to normal.

I'm not going to wake up because I *am* awake, and this is real and—

I tear my gaze away, my entire body trembling violently. I lean against the nearest wall to keep myself upright. If I crumble to my knees, I'm not sure I'll ever be able to get up again. My eyes dart back and forth, trying to find anything else to focus on.

That's when I see, at the back of the room: the pallet mattress of Ma's bed, her hiding spot, is torn open. Like it exploded.

I lurch forward, stumbling over toppled chairs and around the remains of the spinning wheel. My fingers accidentally graze some splattered blood on the wall.

A dry sob issues from somewhere in my chest as I reach the bed.

When I left the house, the last thing I remember doing was shoving the ox into its pouch and back into the secret hiding spot. Then I'd polished our plague mask on the way out. And I closed the door.

Didn't I?

I finally collapse, not even feeling the impact against my kneecaps as my hand reaches desperately into the hiding spot. Nothing. No matter where I touch or how I contort my arm, all I feel is the rough straw inside of the mattress.

No.

Another wave of sickness washes over me.

The pouch and the stone ox within are gone.

Pulling back, I search the area around the hiding spot, trying not to drown in the panic that has consumed me.

Someone found the stone ox.

That's why this happened.

My thoughts blur.

Did I leave it out where it could be seen?

I rack my brain, but I can't recall.

This is your fault, Shae.

The Blot. The curse. My plea to the Bards.

I swivel toward the front door and vomit onto the grass, my entire body breaking out into a cold sweat. I can't breathe. I no longer know if the moisture on my cheeks is tears or sweat. I can hardly bear to turn back to my home—my heart clenches—*everything is ruined.*

My mind refuses to focus on the one thing I know is true:

Ma. Sprawled on the floor, soaked in blood, a dagger driven through her chest.

What have you done, Shae?

Stars blaze out at the edges of my vision, seeming to screech through the sky. My thoughts are a chaotic swirl of dark clouds, wolf howls, and cold wind. I'm shivering so hard, I don't even realize I've fallen to my knees in the yard. The rough gray of early dawn is blurring everything together into a fog. My breath won't come. I can't breathe. I'm going to die. I'm going to die right here.

"Shae! What's happened?"

A man's distant voice reaches me, followed by the snarl of dogs. But worse still is the shrill, high-pitched ringing, growing louder and louder.

I clutch my head as I rock softly on the dead grass.

Ma. Seeping blood. Her glassy eyes. Her too-stiff limbs.

The ringing continues.

I can't move. Can't breathe.

A hand circles my upper arm, pulling me forward and into reality. I struggle before his voice breaks through the ringing. "You're safe. It's okay. I've got you."

Suddenly, the ringing stops. My throat aches. I realize with a shock that I've been screaming. *That* was the terrible, echoing sound.

Constable Dunne's face comes sharply into focus. His broad forehead is slick with sweat that catches the morning light in small, white beads.

"Good. I need you to take a deep breath. Can you do that?" His voice echoes slightly, but sounds much closer now. I nod.

My breath rattles as I draw air into my lungs. It feels cold and harsh and . . .

Ma.

The shaking starts all over again.

Constable Dunne sighs and drags a hand over his face. "You stay here, got it? I'm coming right back." Dunne gets slowly to his feet.

Stay here? Where else would I go? I nearly laugh but my body is too weak. I slump against the side of the house.

Dunne's heavy boots cross the threshold, his dogs not far behind. My fingers go numb remembering what lies within.

My mother, broken and bloody on the floor. The dim light glinting off the hilt of the ornate dagger lodged in her chest.

I clench my jaw to keep from heaving once more. My eyes shut tight.

When I open them, Constable Dunne is emerging from the darkness of the house. He holds the golden dagger, turning the bloody instrument over, examining it. The light flashes blindingly from the engraving on the hilt. I squint at the strange symbols etched into the side. *Are those letters?* Dunne's gaze also lingers on the symbols before he wipes the blood off and secures it safely on his belt. The dogs gather around him, growling and sniffing.

Dunne approaches me, his face ashen.

"What a tragedy," he mutters.

Tragedy. The word reverberates through me. I'm afraid I'm going to be sick all over again.

"Who could have done this?" I can barely make out my own words.

Dunne clears his throat, crouching beside me. "Seems like the work of bandits. Whoever it was, they're gone," he says. "In a hurry, too, by the looks of it. I was close by at the Reeds' homestead when we heard the screams up the pass. I came as fast I could." He curses. "I'm just not as fast as I used to be, Shae. I'm sorry." He removes a handkerchief from his coat and offers it to me.

I take it and press it to my cheeks, expecting more tears, but there are none. I'm too shocked to cry. It's as if I've fallen from a great height, all the wind knocked out of me.

The handkerchief comes away filthy, and I remember skidding and falling down the hill. I must look wild to the constable, like an animal come in from the woods.

"What happens now?" I ask. The words hurt my throat, still raw from screaming. I blink up at him dizzily. The sun is piercing the horizon, too bright.

The dogs are running in circles, sniffing the grass and barking like mad. I can't think straight, can't think at all. I'm having enough trouble remembering to breathe.

"Now . . ." Constable Dunne's stubbly jaw clenches as he glances back to the house. "I'll escort you to town. You're friends with Miss Fiona from the shop, right? I'll explain the situation to her father. You can stay with them until everything gets sorted." He waits for me to assent.

"You want me to *leave*?" I ask, dumbstruck. "When there's a mur—" I can't say it. Fear winds itself snug against my heart. *Murderer*. A forbidden word. I shake my head. There's too much I must do. Fix the wreckage of my home. Clean the blood. Prepare the funeral ribbons. Bury Ma.

The look on Dunne's face stops me from uttering another sound. "I have to be blunt with you, Shae. Leaving you here doesn't look good for me or for you."

I stare at him. "Doesn't look good?" What can look worse than what has already happened?

"I mean, what with the way people talk," he hedges, giving me a sideways glance. "What they say about, well . . . you. You and your family."

That we're freaks. That we're cursed. That *I'm* cursed . . .

Suddenly, I understand, though the darkness of it is so horrifying, I nearly faint. "Are you suggesting that *I* . . ." Words fail me and I flail my hand toward the door. "That I did this?"

"Of course not, Shae," he says, and I let out a

shaky breath. "But there are procedures." He loops his thumbs into his belt. "We can't control what *others* may think. These are rules for your protection. Surely, you can understand." He extends a hand. "We'll get you settled. And I'll report the death. We'll figure this out, Shae. Justice will be served."

He reaches for my arm.

"No." I stumble backward, away from him. "No, I can't. I won't leave. The sheep . . . the farm . . ."

"Shae," he says, warning in his voice. I've never argued with the constable before, and the edge in his tone frightens me. I freeze, staring at him, feeling like a trapped wild animal. All I want to do is bolt back inside my house and slam the door. Back where it is safe.

Except it isn't safe there.

My mother's body lies strewn across the floor.

He sees my hesitation and lunges toward me, going for my arm again. The dogs pick up their barking, and in the chaos of the noise, I panic.

"No! Stop!" I don't know what's come over me, but I won't be dragged away. Tears run down my face, uncontrollable. "You can't take me away. You can't make me leave her!"

Vaguely, I realize he has wrestled my arms behind my back and is holding me in a sort of half embrace, even as I keep struggling. Even as the sobs wrack me harder and harder.

"Don't do this, Shae. Don't fight me," he's saying, quiet, close to my ear. I can hear the whisper of a threat mixed in with the kindness. "I'm doing this for you," he says. "For Aster. For justice." And he's pulling me away.

I try one last time, a wail launching from my throat as I heave my weight against his arms. "Ma!" I cry out, but it's too late. He's got me by the waist and is dragging me away, and it's all I can do to stay upright as we stagger like that all the way downhill, until I can no longer see the house or the farm.

Everything I have ever loved, gone.

Days blur together in a haze. I've been installed in Fiona's home, and they've welcomed me with open arms and sympathetic words, but I can barely hear them. Words are too hard. They keep me busy—with mending and darning and other mindless chores—but there is no salve for the dark, festering pain that lives in my head. Time either passes too slowly or too quickly depending on how much I think about Ma's death. The images replay in my head—her body on the floor, the blood on the walls. My conversation with the Bard in the marketplace—with Ravod, who briefly had seemed kind. Is that what put us in danger in the first place? My conversation with Mads, our kiss. Falling asleep while Ma was home alone. I could have done something. Could have stopped it. Beneath everything is the image of the Gondalese ox.

Did I leave it out?

The constable would have known if my mother's

death was an official punishment for possession of contraband—unless someone else wanted to rid the town of my cursed family, taking it upon themselves to do the job. Every time I arrive at this thought, panic threatens to consume me. I'm not safe here. It could have been *anyone*. We are trained to report one another, to turn our backs on those we love.

But worse than all of it—the terror, the endless theories, the guilt, the wondering—is the ache in my chest. My heart physically feels like it has been broken.

Perhaps it has.

I pour my energy into helping Fiona's family in the shop to keep from dwelling on my grief, but the pity in their faces is too much to bear. And no matter how hard I try, come nightfall, the dreams always find me, feral and full of horror.

The only activity that calms me is my needlework— unspooling the strange and haunting images of my dreams into the thread. But even this feels sinful, like it is part of the curse. I'm afraid of what it means.

Which is why, when I hear Fiona awaken— I've been granted a bedroll near the hearth in her bedroom—I hide the needlework beneath my pillow where she can't see it.

She sits up in her bed and smiles. It hurts to look at—painted on, forced. "Can you stomach a bit of breakfast today?"

I make myself smile back. "Sure." With the exception of Fiona, and her father, who offers a terse nod in my direction when I sit, her family completely ignores me as they chat happily at the table.

It's a little jarring hearing so much noise during a meal. I became so accustomed to eating in comfortable silence with Ma over the years. Sometimes I'd remark on my day or update her on the sheep, only for us to lapse back into the usual quiet. Fiona's family is the opposite—jokes, arguments, stories, and gossip get shared right along with the food. It reminds me of a time so long ago that it is only a fragment of a memory, tugging at the furthest reaches of my mind. Before Kieran's death, when Pa was around, and Ma was not silent. A memory of a family I used to know.

Morning after morning, I grow more distant—detached—from it all. I wonder if I'll ever feel normal like them. It seems more and more like I've never been normal and I never will be.

It is good of Fiona and her family to let me stay, I know. But I'm reminded constantly that I do not belong here. Fiona's kindness cannot change that. As long as I remain, I am useful. That is all. The rest is up to me.

The bulk of my chores keeps me from the front of the store where Fiona works as the clerk, so I barely see her over the course of the day. Her father likes to keep her up front because she is pretty and friendly. He thinks it makes people more comfortable and they will buy more. He may be right. Fiona does have a way with people. Many of the "customers" are handsome boys from the village who stop by only to talk with her.

Though my mind is terrorized with darkness and doubts, one question burns through—where is Mads? Why hasn't he come?

I hate that I don't know. I hate that I keep wondering—it is all I do. I love Fiona, her gentle sweetness, her sunny smile, her endless confidence— but Mads is the one who has always made me feel anchored.

But Mads is nowhere to be found. He has not come by the shop, yet he must know where I've been staying. Someone must have told him what happened. In a town like Aster, secrets have a way of coming out.

Somehow, I can't fathom the idea that the rest of the world hasn't been altered forever the way I have. That my mother's death didn't split the skies apart, cause birds to swim and fish to fly.

I take a shaky breath as I carry a heavy bag of prairie flour into the back of the store. I'm mostly relegated to the stockroom, taking inventory and measuring provisions so they can be brought to the front and sold. On the rare occasion I'm allowed into the shop proper, it's to shelve things. I'm not supposed to talk to anyone, not that they are particularly hasty to strike up conversation with the local outcast, but I have explicit orders to stay out of sight and keep out of trouble.

My one lifeline is the hope that Dunne finds Ma's killer and punishes them. I cling to it when everything else seems bleakest. At the very least, I'll have justice. *Ma* will have justice.

"Shae," Fiona's father, Hugo, greets me as he enters the stockroom. "When you're done measuring the rice into containers, you can go ahead and shelve them."

I nod, watching as he and his eldest son, Thomas, set today's delivery down and leave without another word. Each day the deliveries are smaller, and they weren't very big to begin with. The hardest job so far has been keeping the shelves full.

I pour the last bit of rice out of the bag and into a smaller container. Once it's gone, the town will be out of rice. After, it won't be much longer until we're out of grain.

Aster is slowly starving. I shake the thought from my head and gather the rations of rice into my arms.

Morning sunlight from the large front windows fills the shop. I blink, letting my eyes adjust. The store seems larger today, as merchandise is sold and little replaces it. More of the dusty brown wood of the floor and shelves are exposed as customers drift in and out, picking at everything little by little. Hugo makes a valiant effort to keep up appearances; the place is meticulously clean and tidy, but I wonder what will happen when he has nothing left to sell.

My thoughts halt when I see Mads's father across

the shop. Immediately, my heart begins to race. He's placing his meager purchases in his rucksack and doesn't notice me approach.

"Excuse me, sir," I venture, tapping him on the shoulder. He turns and does not look pleased to see me. The cursed girl his son spends too much time with. "I was wondering where . . ."

"Maddox has gone to the Bards."

A tiny gasp escapes me. "Why?"

His father scratches his beard and sighs. "For you, I think."

Me? Before the word leaves my mouth, or I can ask when he'll be back, Mads's father abruptly turns and leaves.

I stand there in shock until a customer nudges me roughly out of the way. I snap out of it and place the rice on one of the shelves.

"What's *she* doing here?" I hear the woman hiss over the counter to Fiona as she pays for a small bag of prairie flour. "Hasn't this charity gone on long enough?"

"Shae is our family now. This is her home too."

The woman pays Fiona with an irritable sniff and leaves. When Fiona catches my eye at the door to the stockroom, I look at the floor. Shame burns my face. Because it's true—her family has treated me like I am one of them, even when the rest of Aster wishes I had been found dead too.

But Mads went to the Bards on my behalf. I grow giddy at even the small promise of hope. Perhaps there exists some possibility for justice. If I wait only a little longer, everything will turn out right.

It's certainly a noble thing to do. Perhaps I've been seeing him in the wrong light all along.

I could fall for a man who goes in search of justice on my behalf.

Suddenly, all the awful feelings that have been suffocating me begin to lift a little, making room for something else: a small fluttering in my chest. A wisp of faith.

"Shae, come look at this!" Fiona's face brightens as she waves me over from behind the counter. In her hand is a delicate silver hair comb inlaid with colored glass. It looks like a butterfly caught in flight and catches the light when Fiona tilts it in her hand. That same wisp of faith allows me the simple joy of appreciating its beauty. "Miss Ines just traded this for a bag of prairie flour. Said it was in her family for six generations."

"She must have already traded her manners," I mutter, and Fiona giggles. My fingertips ghost over the comb. The delicate design is nowhere near as fine, but it reminds me a little of the bridle Ravod's horse wore. I can't help imagining what it would look like adorning my hair.

"Pa doesn't like it when I trade for something purely decorative," Fiona says, "but I couldn't resist. It's too lovely."

"But it's clearly expensive. Worth much more than a bag of flour."

Fiona rolls her eyes and imitates Hugo's deep, businesslike voice, which always makes me laugh. "People need things that are practical," she says. Then, growing serious, "We can't resell it. Anyone will look at this and say it's not enough silver to make anything useful out of. They won't care how beautiful it is."

"You should hold on to it," I say.

Fiona smiles quietly to herself as she admires the tiny comb. "Maybe just for now," she says. "Even if there's no occasion to wear it, it's a nice reminder. We should hold on to beautiful things while we have them."

Her words make me think of Ma. Her smile. Her gentle hands. Her warm embrace. The beautiful things I could not hold on to.

What would Ma do if she were here?

I take the comb from Fiona and fix it in her hair. It catches the light brilliantly from amongst the golden waves, like it was meant to be there.

I manage a smile. "Perfect."

At the end of the day, Fiona is sweeping the shop floor before closing up. I stretch, my body aching from standing hours on end—it's different work than farming but exhausting in its own way. I hide a yawn behind my hand as Fiona finishes dusting the counter and moves on to the shelves. I'm already fantasizing about curling up on my bedroll, closing my eyes and blocking out the rest of the world, when the shop door opens.

My stomach plummets to the ground.

"Constable Dunne, always a pleasure to see you!" Even I can hear the strain in Fiona's voice as she steals a glance at me. Is this what I think it is?

Dunne tips his broad-brimmed hat to us. "Good evening, Fiona." He doesn't bother to turn to me. "Shae."

This doesn't bode well. I set my broom aside and approach him.

"Is there news?" I ask. "Did you find Ma's killer?"

He fiddles with his hat, and I count the seconds until he finally looks at me. "That's a dangerous word, Shae. We don't *know* what happened that night. We can't be leaping to assumptions."

"Leaping to assumptions? I saw the dagger! There was blood all over the floor!"

"Now, Shae . . ."

"I don't know what you've found or haven't, but you need to keep looking." My mind starts racing. Fiona comes to my side, putting an arm around my shoulder. "What about the tracks on the road? Or the dagger? Surely there must be . . ."

"Shae." His voice is calm, but firm. "It's over."

Fiona squeezes my shoulder, but I wrench myself free, my eyes glistening with my unleashed rage. "I don't understand. You promised me, Constable. On that day. You assured me." False words. "I thought you were a man of your word. Or is *that* not the truth?"

Fiona gasps.

"Tread carefully, young one," Dunne says through his teeth. "Perhaps our kindness has made you forget your place. You need to put this behind you." Dunne places his hat back on his head. I reach for the broom handle so I can have something, anything, to hold on to. My knuckles flush bone white. "I know it's hard. And it's not what you want to hear. But nothing more can be done." He turns on his heel to leave.

"So 'justice' in this town means giving up?" I call out to his back. "To simply lose hope?"

To pretend Ma and Kieran never existed? To forget?

"It's been nearly two weeks with no new leads. There's nothing more I can do," Dunne says. "It's time to start moving ahead with life. You've got a lot of it ahead of you. It's what your ma would have wanted."

I nearly break the broom, I'm gripping it so hard. "How dare you assume what she would have wanted," I hiss under my breath.

"Leave him be," Fiona says as she watches the door swing wide and shut once more. When she's sure he's gone, she rubs out the tension in her shoulder. "Shae, you can't go throwing around accusations like that."

I throw the broom to the ground and cradle my

throbbing head in my hands against the counter. I can't get Dunne's infuriating words out.

The walls of the shop feel like they are converging on me as I drag my hands through my hair.

"Why not?" Even though my eyes are open, all I can see is the dark. "I've got nothing left to lose."

As soon as I say it, I wish I could take it back. The flash of hurt on Fiona's face almost makes me want to apologize.

But that's the thing about words. Once you've said them, there's no going back.

We don't speak the rest of the evening.

My dreams are plagued with nightmares. Whispers in the darkness and watching eyes, trained on me like a predator about to strike. My body is heavy and sluggish, powerless to flee or fight. I can only struggle feebly, but the more I do, the closer the darkness creeps, its claws sinking deeper into my skin until I'm submerged in the inky blackness.

I push myself onto my elbows. My racing heart slows as I ground myself. I'm in the bedroll by the hearth in Fiona's room. The flame has burned down to soft embers; it must be long past midnight.

Sitting up properly, I rub my eyes. My forehead is slick with cold sweat, and my hands ache from clenching my fists in my sleep.

It's what your ma would have wanted echoes relentlessly in my mind, yet I know it's not true.

Without thinking, I throw the threadbare quilt off my legs and rise to my feet, grabbing my clothes and shoes. I wait until I'm safely on the other side of the door before I pull them on and head quietly down the stairs.

I need to go home; I have to see it for myself. Maybe I can find some clue that Dunne missed.

I hurry into the shop, heading for the door. I'll be

back before dawn. They will never even know I was missing.

"Shae?" I freeze when I hear Fiona's curious voice behind me. "Where are you going?"

I turn toward Fiona, her face visibly clouded with worry even in the dim light. I don't know what to say to her. The days I've been at the shop feel like a hopeless blur. I'm wandering blindfolded in a storm.

Fiona has been the only thing keeping my head above the merciless waves of grief that threaten to destroy me. I'm selfish to make her worry.

"I . . ." I lift my chin to meet her gaze as she steps closer. "I wanted to see my house."

A sob escapes my throat, and Fiona wraps her arms around me as my tears free themselves.

"Shae," she says, gently stroking my disheveled hair, "there's nothing for you to find there except more heartbreak. Don't punish yourself like this."

In the darkness of the store, she holds me a long time before letting go. I wipe my eyes with the heel of my palm.

"I feel so useless. I can't stand it," I say finally. "Nothing about this makes any sense."

"That's understandable." Fiona's voice is comforting. "None of this has been easy, or fair. But nothing can change it. All you can do is move forward."

I feel a sting of indignation at her words. So like the constable's. Someone walks into my house, stabs my mother, and vanishes, and I'm supposed to forget about it and move on with my life?

"I can't." I shake my head. "There's more to it than this. There's a *person* out there, and they had a *reason* for killing Ma."

"Even if that were true, isn't it all the more reason to stay away? You should be thankful your own life was spared."

I stare at her, coldness washing over me. "What is that supposed to mean?"

"Nothing," she says quickly. "Only that I'm relieved you're safe, and I want it to stay that way."

"Because you think the curse on our family is real, don't you?" My voice rises.

"Shae, calm down. I'm not saying . . ."

"Aren't you though? What if this happened to *your* mother?" I've never raised my voice with Fiona before. Frustration and guilt twist inside me, gnawing at my heart.

A foreign emotion glimmers in Fiona's eyes. *"Don't."* Her voice has gone flat. "Don't talk like that. It's dangerous."

"You think I don't know that? My mother was murdered!" My fists ball at my sides, the tips of my nails digging into my palms.

She gasps. *Murder.* It's a forbidden word. I've *thought* it—many times over the past weeks. But never, ever, have I said it aloud. As soon as it's out of my mouth, I wish I could take it back. It hangs in the air between us, ugly and invisible, and I shiver, suddenly feeling sick. Maybe she's right.

Maybe I'm a danger to everyone—including her.

"I can't do this anymore," Fiona says into the stunned silence. "Not if you're going to put me and my whole family at risk."

I stammer. Words fail me completely. "I'm sorry. I didn't mean . . ."

"No, Shae. You *did*," Fiona fires back. "You're behaving like a petulant child. Is this how you thank us for everything we've done for you?" Her eyes are cold as she glares at me. I've never seen Fiona like this. I barely know how to react.

"I'm not trying to hurt anyone. I just—"

"Maybe not intentionally," Fiona cuts me off. "But that's your problem, Shae. You never think things through. You're too insistent. Your anger is burning you alive. You'd set this whole town aflame with it. And I can't stand by and watch it happen."

My breath grinds out through my teeth. "If you want to sit this one out, *fine*. But don't complain that I am doing what I think is right. There are things more important than meekly obeying the rules."

"More important than your life? Your safety? Your happiness?" Her voice breaks. She looks like she's going to cry, the unspoken question in the tremble of her voice, asking: *More important than me?*

"I need to know what really happened," I say softly.

I turn away, darting into the darkness, and leave her behind.

———

The air is crisp and cold tonight. I hug my arms halfheartedly, for what little good it does. The chill distracts me only momentarily from my fight with Fiona.

Aster looks ghostly in the pale light of the full moon, its residents sleeping peacefully behind the darkened windows of their homes.

Anger crackles in my chest as Fiona's words wind to the forefront of my mind. I'm cursed, and she knows somehow. I'm a danger to her. She doesn't want me around. No one does.

When I finally crest the hill and my house comes into view, a low gray shape in the darkness, a mix of emotions rushes up into my chest, sickness and dread coating the usual feelings of safety and home. And piercing through it all, a pang that hurts the most—I miss my ma. I miss her so much, I am afraid the feeling will tear itself through the walls of my rib cage and burst out into the night like a feral beast.

A loud rustling sounds behind me, and I gasp, fearing I've somehow conjured a feral beast at the thought. I spin on my heel.

"Is someone there?" I call out, prepared to scream as I picture Ma's murderer leaping out at me from the darkness.

For some stupid reason, I step away from the edge of the road, toward the woods.

Another crunch of branches.

I stand on guard, my entire body rigid. If someone

is here to finish the job, I at least want to see their face before I die. To know.

"Damn . . . Damn it!" Mads stumbles through the branches. Twigs and leaves adorn his hair, and his cheek is scratched.

My anger and fear swiftly become relief. Mads dusts himself off. The tips of his ears are bright red.

"Freckles." He grimaces sheepishly. "Sorry I was away so long, I—"

I rush forward and wrap my arms around his waist like my life depends on it. His surprise soon melts away, and he draws me closer, gently kissing the top of my head.

"You're back," I say, disbelieving. I study his face, trying to see if he has changed in some way, if he has found news from the Bards that will help me. The thought reignites the hope in my chest. "Your pa told me where you'd gone, but I wasn't sure I could believe it. Did you find them? Did you go all the way to High House? What happened? And what are you doing out here in the middle of the night?"

"One question at a time," he says, a soft laugh escaping him. He clears his throat. "Yes, I went to the Bards—they were still stationed a few towns away."

He looks strange in the darkness—a combination of the Mads I know but with a layer of secrecy in his eyes. He seems nervous, his eyes darting around us, as if someone could be watching from the trees. And yet, he seems excited too. His smile keeps trying to quirk up at the corner of his mouth.

"And? What did you learn? Do they know the truth? Do they know who the killer is?"

"The . . . killer?" he stammers, looking genuinely confused.

"Of course! Who else? They must have been able to help, right? They know everything. Surely they had a record of what happened? Do you know who murdered my mother?"

It's the second time I've uttered the forbidden word—*murder*—in one night, and Mads looks like I've slapped him. I step back, hoping the space will encourage him.

"I'm sorry, Mads. I'm rushing over you. Please, take your time. I want to know everything."

"Well," he begins. And suddenly, panic reverberates through me. Maybe he didn't find out the truth and doesn't want to disappoint me. Or maybe he knows but fears the truth will break me. But I must know.

Before I can interrupt, he fishes for something in his pocket and takes a step closer. "I went to the Bards. To ask for their blessing."

"Blessing?" I'm confused. They already granted our village a Telling.

For the millionth time tonight, his expression changes, and I wonder if he's going to laugh or cry or kiss me. "Their permission, really. Which they granted."

I watch, stunned, as Mads gets down on one knee in front of me.

He holds out a small box. Inside is a simple engagement brooch, in the traditional shape of a raven. It shines in the moonlight.

My fingertips graze along its polished edges, catching on the outstretched wings. There is a fable of the raven that flew over the lands of Montane and brought news to the Bards, of the plague that ravaged our lands. It's a symbol of new beginnings.

The meaning of Mads's choice is clear before he says it.

"I'm sorry I wasn't there when you needed me, Shae. I want to make it up to you. I want to spend the rest of my life by your side. As your husband. And I promise . . . I will shield you from everyone who might hurl stones or curses. Anyone who might speak ill of you. Anyone who looks at you the wrong way. I'll fight for you until I die." Crickets screech in the silence. "Will you have me?"

An uncomfortable minute passes as I stand there, wordlessly. One minute turns to two.

You're standing too long without saying anything! Answer him! But I can't move. I can't find words in the maelstrom of feelings that has overtaken all rational thought.

Mads, on bended knee, is waiting expectantly for my answer. His soft blue eyes are full of warmth and hope. His smile makes the moonlight look even brighter, somehow.

I had not dared to consider this outcome. There was always a reason not to. We're too young. My family's curse. Taking care of Ma. Me being the girl in his life for the moment, but never forever.

And yet, he is proposing. This is what I had hoped for.

Isn't it?

This is my chance to put everything behind me. I could marry Mads and live in the town with him, no longer shunned as an outsider. It would be hard, but we could work together and build a future. We could have children. *We could be a family.* In time, I'm sure I will fall in love with him properly, like he deserves.

But I'm not in love with him.

And that's only part of the problem.

Hazy images of Ma, Pa, and Kieran drift in front of me. Pa falling to his knees in the pasture, gasping for air as his heart failed him. The dark blue veins on Kieran's neck. The ornate golden dagger jutting out of Ma's chest. The home I lived in, soaked in sickness, blood, and death.

Can I simply turn my back on all the unanswered questions and pretend nothing is wrong?

"I can't." My voice comes out a whisper. Disappointment cascades through me. He didn't go to the Bards for answers. He thinks he is helping me, but he isn't. He can't. He doesn't understand. Just like Fiona.

Mads's eyes widen for a split second, but his gaze doesn't waver from me. His smile slips from his face, and I so desperately wish I could transfer his hurt and place it on my own shoulders. The more I try to summon the words to help, the more I come up short. In the end, it is Mads who pays the price.

"I'm sorry, Mads," I say. "But there's so much I haven't figured out yet. I must find out what happened to Ma. I need answers."

He lets my words sink in before slowly replacing the box in his pocket and getting to his feet.

"Answers. Right," he whispers. "Forget I said anything. I was only trying to help. Pretty stupid of me, wasn't it?"

"Mads, please. Please stop." Tears sting the corners of my eyes.

He looks shaken. Destroyed.

"I'm sorry, Mads."

He turns his gaze away, toward the ground. His breath is coming heavy, as if he's been running. "Don't be. I—I understand."

Except he doesn't. He shifts his weight from foot to foot, as if desperate to escape me. To Mads, problems like mine can be shoved away, kept at a far enough distance that they can't hurt anyone. But they are still there. I can't simply act like Ma's murderer doesn't exist. That my life wasn't touched by the Blot. That my embroidery doesn't haunt me and play tricks on my eyes. But I know how Mads thinks: Why fix anything when the problem can be ignored or fended off with brute strength?

To him, the truth doesn't matter enough to fight for.

But it *matters*. It has to.

"Mads . . ."

"Don't." He takes a small step back, followed by another. "You don't have to explain anything. I should have known better."

This isn't what he wanted. He went to the Bards thinking their approval would please me. He thought we'd be making plans and promises. Instead, we're standing on opposite sides of the dirt road in uncomfortable silence. Neither of us wants to give away how much we feel the ground crumbling beneath our feet.

I tell myself not to apologize again; it won't help.

"I'm sorry," I say anyway.

"Yeah." He sighs. "Me too."

Without another word, he turns and walks away. I watch him disappear into the darkness before covering my face with my hands. How did I manage to lose both Fiona and Mads in the same night?

Without Fiona's comforting words, or Mads's warmth, or Ma's gentle hands to braid my hair, I've never felt so alone.

Thin, gray light crests the mountaintops. *Dawn.* Somehow this interminable night has come to an end. I feel a sigh of relief escape me. Cold air fills my lungs, solidifying my resolve.

I will not conveniently tuck the past away. Today, I follow the course I've charted for myself.

Swiftly, I cross the threshold into my old home. I look at the narrow rooms, the low walls, the tiny beds, the darkened hearth. The rooms have been cleaned. There is no trace of the violence that occurred. Who did this? The constable? Did he neaten things up out of kindness or to make it all vanish as if it had never happened?

Hardly breathing, I quietly move around the room, touching each surface, as if hoping some trace of Ma's spirit will still be hovering here. The stillness feels ready to swallow me whole.

Finally, I step back out into the early light and head up the hill toward the north pasture. The entire flock of sheep is gone, as if it never existed, though I can smell the familiar scents of the barn. Wool and hay and worn leather. I realize with a start that the constable must have sold them off. It hadn't even occurred to me to ask what he had done with them. Or whether those earnings should have been mine to collect. Worst of all, it never struck me to say good-bye to them.

One by one, I recite their names aloud into the dusty air of the barn. When I'm done, I close the barn door behind me and stare out over the town and to the nearby woods beginning to stir with the calls of birds.

"Wish me luck, Ma," I whisper into the placid new morning. Wherever she is, I can only hope she's listening.

8

By the time I reach the watchtower, sunlight has begun to break out over the roof, making it look like a torch burning away the darkness.

Aster only has a small volunteer militia, and they revolve reliably around two shifts, the morning and the night watch. Dunne likes being easy to find in case anyone needs him and sticks to a rigid schedule. If I squint, I can see the outline of his office, perched at the top of the watchtower.

With the streets empty, I am able to pass through town undisturbed. But even in the hour before the town awakens, I feel the weight of their eyes upon me. I pick up my pace, hurrying down the main street to the very edge of Aster.

Guards pace at the town limits, not more than fifty feet from the tower, monitoring the only road that leads in and out of town. I shiver and wrench open the iron door at the tower's base. Inside is a narrow vestibule with steps leading upward; a few cobwebs and a half-full crate of supplies for the militia rest beneath the stairs. The air is dry and a little stale. I look up the spiral to the top. The watchtower seems even taller from the inside.

My fingers brush the wall to steady myself as I

climb. Each time I round the corner, convinced I must have arrived, I find another twist in the stairs. There's a small window slit for archers and crossbow-men at every level. When I venture a look outside, diz-ziness sweeps over me, along with an eerie feeling of power. This place is like the High House of Aster, watching us from an eagle's perch.

Dunne must be able to see all the way to my house from the top, I think. My legs begin to ache, and sweat coats my neck from the heat inside. I'm beginning to wonder if the tower has a top at all, when I find myself deposited on a small landing.

I take a deep breath and knock on the door.

"Come in." Dunne's voice issues from inside. I push on the heavy door and it creaks open.

Dunne's office is small and cramped, lit by four large windows, facing each cardinal direction. The eastern window is practically blinding from the newly risen sun. I squint as I enter. I can make out shelves and crates, a glass display case, and a few framed pictures on the walls.

"Well, this is unexpected." Dunne's brow furrows, and he rises from his seat. His weathered desk looks dull in the sunlight.

"Constable, I apologize for my intrusion," I say, blinking rapidly until my eyes adjust. "I've had a few more questions since our . . . talk yesterday."

Dunne's lips press into a thin line. I half-expect him to refuse me.

"Yes, of course. It is my duty to dispel any doubts

you may have." Dunne gestures to a chair in front of his desk. "Please, sit."

I take my seat and Dunne does the same.

"Now," he says, leaning forward on his elbows, "what troubles you, Shae?"

"Well . . ." I trail off, finally getting a better look at my surroundings. The pictures on the wall are not pictures at all. I feel my skin crawl, like it's ready to run out the door without the rest of me.

They're paper, covered in ink.

Writing.

My gaze flies over the room, finding the same strange symbols on nearly everything. The display case is full of bottles of various shades of blue and black liquid. The shelves are packed with thin rectangular leather boxes. Cold terror creeps through my bones as I try to make sense of why Constable Dunne is stockpiling dangerous items.

"Shae." Dunne's voice makes my eyes snap back to his. My knuckles have turned white from gripping the wooden armrests of my seat. "Focus."

"What . . . what is all this?" My voice is a shaky whisper.

"It's contraband, Shae. I keep it on display so I know what to look for, and to help others identify writing if they claim they see it."

I nod slowly, the ink on the walls tangling my thoughts. "How often do you find contraband?" The question escapes me before I'm certain I want to know the answer.

"Mercifully, less and less," he says. "The Bards make a sweep every few months to claim the more dangerous items and destroy them. But you didn't come all this way to discuss the contents of my office, did you?"

"No, sir." I shake my head, forcing myself to concentrate. "I need you to reconsider closing my mother's case."

"I see." Dunne steeples his fingers. "What happened to your mother was a tragedy. But I think it's fairly open and shut, don't you?"

I frown. "I beg your pardon?"

"These things happen, Shae."

"These . . . *things happen*?" I repeat, dumbfounded. "Someone—" I almost say *murdered* again, but stop myself. "Someone wanted my mother dead!"

Dunne levels an unreadable look across the desk at me. "Shae, what are you talking about? Your mother was killed in a landslide. No one wanted any such thing, believe me."

All I can do is stare at the constable, my jaw opening and closing as my thoughts collide chaotically. Ma's bloated face, forever painted red, blurs in front of me.

"Landslide?" I'm reeling, unsure what he's talking about. "There's been no landslide."

"Of course there has. After the gift of rains brought to us by the Bards' Telling, the dry soil at your northernmost pasture gave way. Your mother, in her weakness, must have fallen into the rocks by the far wall, at the base of the slope."

I'm stunned and confused. I recall the Telling, the brief spell of rain. I try to remember the landslide, but I can't. Has my mind completely erased it? Or is this further proof of my curse?

"I don't . . . I don't remember anything like that. And my mother wasn't found outside—she was in our home. She—"

"Shae. You've been through a lot. When I found you, you were screaming at the top of your lungs and extremely disoriented. You were covered in filth. Perhaps the trauma is causing your memory to play tricks on you? Painting the picture of a weapon to make it easier to point the blame at someone else?"

Point the blame at someone else? As if it were my fault. *Is it though?* A dark fear slips into my mind and I can't shake it.

"You must be mistaken," I manage. "Constable, you heard a scream from the Reeds' homestead. You saw me running to the house, and you went in after me. I watched you remove the dagger, *the murder weapon,* from my house!" My anger sends me to my feet. "Don't you remember the dagger?"

Dunne is silent, his narrowed eyes fixed on me.

"What dagger?"

"It was gold! It had engraving on the hilt! There were symbols on the blade." I point to the parchment on the wall. "Just like these! It . . ." I pause, at a loss. Nothing about Dunne's expression has changed. "How do you not remember? Why don't you believe me?"

"I believe that *you* believe it," Dunne replies evenly. His words are a knife twisting in my gut. "Shae, maybe you need to think your ma was murdered in order to cope with the reality of her death."

I shake my head. "No," I say. "I *know* what I saw."

But even as I say it, I remember how loose the soil was beneath my feet when I ran home that morning— how I fell, right before I reached the part of the hill where you can see my house. The door was ajar . . . I saw it, I swear . . .

I recall, suddenly and horribly, how I'd been completely covered in dirt—it was caked under my fingernails, clinging in the folds of my messy braid— when the constable had found me.

"That's impossible, Shae." Dunne rises from his chair. He looks at me like I'm some small creature left to die on the side of a road as he points to the window behind him. "Take a look if you need to."

I step to the eastern-facing window. Outside, the entirety of Aster sprawls below me across the plains. My eyes follow the main road up to the pass, the familiar pathway that leads to my home. It threads around the old well and uphill past the familiar landmark of the Reeds' homestead.

Above it is the hill with our north pasture, where, sure enough, there is a strange streak of brown, a pile of rubble and stones below—clear evidence of a small landslide.

My jaw hangs open as I try to reconcile what I'm seeing with what I remember. No, it's not possible. I know what I saw. Don't I?

Dunne approaches me from behind and puts what I'm sure he thinks is a comforting hand on my shoulder. Like he did right before he dragged me from my home.

"Aster is flawed." Dunne's voice is grim. "We try our best. We work hard. We obey the rules. But there's a deep-seeded wickedness here. It's why misfortune follows us, why the crops fail and the Bards won't show their favor."

I feel a twinge of anger. *Misfortune follows us.* What he means is: misfortune follows *me.* The Bards offered a Telling to help the town. That same Telling is what caused the erosion on my land. It can't be a coincidence, can it?

"My ma was murdered," I whisper fiercely, unable to let go of the memory—as crystal clear and harsh as the moment it happened. It was *real.* I know it was, no matter what he says. Tears prick the corners of my eyes. "It's the truth!"

"And I'm saying that's simply not possible." Dunne pinches the bridge of his nose. "Besides, if what you're saying *were* true and a dagger engraved with writing was involved, High House would have taken care of it. Lord Cathal takes these matters very seriously."

I pause, letting his words sink in.

"High House would have . . ." I take a deep breath.

There's so much wrong that it takes a minute for my thoughts to settle into place, but when they do, I only feel more disconcerted. My mind travels to the forbidden idol in my house. The dagger that killed Ma. The contraband collected in this very room that the Bards pick up every few months.

"Shae?"

What I'm saying is true. I know it. Every instinct I possess is screaming at me that something is wrong . . . Which means: The constable is lying. He's hiding something. For someone.

"It's time to put the past behind you." I turn my head to Dunne. His eyes are narrowed sharply, making the lines in his face more severe. "It does no good to have one of my townspeople parading around with such a disturbing story." Dunne's words lace around me, tightening in threat. "Do we understand each other?"

"Yes, Constable Dunne." I need to get out of this tower, down on land where I can breathe, where the world will make sense again. I turn to go when a firm hand grabs my wrist. Dunne pushes my sleeve back slightly and inspects my wrist.

No dark veins.

"Let Hugo know I'll be stopping by to check in," he says, a dark undercurrent in his voice.

I fly from the room, air growing lighter the farther I

get from the cursed objects cluttering the constable's office. The journey down the endless tower stairs is much faster than it was during my ascent, and soon I'm bursting through the door, ignoring the guards' confusion as I rush past them toward the center of Aster.

Things are starting to piece together. There's something bigger going on here. And if Constable Dunne can't be trusted, we're *all* in more danger than we think.

I need to find someone, *anyone,* who will listen.

The general store is busy by the time I rush in, flinging the door open so forcefully that the little tin bells nearly fall off. I ignore the strange looks I get as I approach Fiona behind the counter. One of the boys from town is standing there, chatting her up, but he startles and moves away when he sees me. I must have a wild look in my eyes; even Fiona raises an eyebrow, but she says nothing to me.

"I need to talk to you. Alone. It's very important."

I'll lay everything out for her. No more secrets. No more lies. I have to trust her. If anyone will understand, it's Fiona.

But still Fiona says nothing.

"Ah, Shae, there you are." Hugo's voice comes from the entrance of the stockroom. There is an edge in his voice. "You had us worried."

"Sir . . ." I glance to Fiona, hoping she'll help me out, like always. Her gaze is fixed on the floor.

"We need to discuss our arrangement," Hugo says, joining his daughter behind the counter, his tone unfaltering. "While I'm grateful for your assistance these past few weeks, we think the time has come for you to find new accommodations."

"We?" I repeat quietly. For a second, I forget why

I rushed into the store to begin with. "Fiona?" *Please look at me.* "Fiona, I know we had a disagreement, but . . ."

"It's nothing personal, you understand," Hugo cuts me off. "But my family's well-being must come first."

"I would never do anything to hurt your family," I shoot back, watching Fiona dip behind the counter.

"Then you understand why we must ask you to leave." Hugo nods as Fiona reappears. She sets my old rucksack of possessions in front of her, carefully avoiding my eyes.

Complete silence has fallen on the store. I let out a shaky breath, realizing acutely how much I took Fiona sticking up for me for granted.

"Fiona, please, you have to believe me . . ." I begin, but she moves away.

I take a deep breath. Maybe her father will listen. "Hugo. Sir. I have concerns about the safety of Aster. There's been a cover-up, a mur—"

"I will tolerate no such words in my establishment!" Hugo's face is red and his fist shakes at his side. "Shae, it would be wise of you to leave immediately, before I am forced to report your behavior."

Stunned, I take the rucksack. The last thing I see as I back out of the store is Fiona's face, terror brimming in her eyes. Fear hammers through my chest.

No one wants to listen. The truth is too great a risk to take over stability.

The sun is high in the sky, and people go about their day, busy and purposeful. It's almost impossible to believe that only a few short hours ago the street was dark and deserted. The noise from the bustle of town makes it difficult to think through the haze of hurt that's settled uncomfortably on my shoulders.

I need to get to Mads. Part of me would rather disappear into a hole in the ground for the rest of my natural life than face him, but he's the only other person left who I can trust. Surely he'll understand if I explain.

The closer I get to Mads's home, the tighter the knot in my stomach becomes. My ears begin to ring from nervousness.

The mill stands beside the dried-up riverbed and looks like a large house with no walls. The creaking of the apparatus that moves the enormous shafts of wood through the saw reaches my ears long before I see it. I make out Mads's father up on the platform, so Mads must be out back, manually turning the mill. Without the flow of water to work the wheel, they have to do it by hand. When he's not needed at the mill, Mads and his elder brother go hunting to provide for the family.

A different choice last night would have made this my new home. I swallow the thought, which turns heavy in my throat.

I pick my way down the side of the riverbed. Mads is at the bottom, rotating the large wheel by pulling the slats that would normally be caught in the current of water. A ring of sweat around his neck darkens the collar of his linen shirt.

I stay rooted in place, mutely grappling with saying hello or running away. I don't want to see the disappointment in his eyes. Images of last night flash through my mind—the look of hopeful uncertainty on his face. His eagerness as he knelt before me. The way his shoulders seemed to crush down on him in the darkness after I took that hope away.

I don't know which of us was more disappointed in the end. I had believed he went to the Bards to expose the truth about my mother's death, to bring justice to my family. He *had* wanted to help me, but not in the right away. I ache to think this means he never understood me—not the way I needed him to.

Mads shifts his position at the wheel and spots me. He hesitates, using a hand to shield his brow from the sunlight. He must see the state I'm in, because he calls up to his father, "Taking a quick break, Pa!"

"Five minutes," his father grumbles.

Mads straightens his collar before facing me. The hurt is plain as daybreak on his face. I bite my lip, trying to keep from running away as fast as possible. He's my last hope.

"What do you need, Shae?" He swipes sweaty hair out of his eyes. His voice is blunt. Direct.

Shae. Not Freckles. I wonder if that part of our

lives—our friendship—is gone forever, along with his nickname for me.

I take a deep breath. "I need your help. I'm sorry, it's just . . . I don't know where else to go."

His eyebrow twitches, but the rest of his face remains impassive. "Are you serious?"

"Of course I am. I wouldn't ask otherwise."

A rueful laugh escapes him. The sound he makes when he doesn't quite believe what he's hearing.

"No, are you *serious*?" he repeats, his blue eyes narrowed at me, flashing with cold light. "You remember last night, right? Why in the world would you . . ." He sighs, running a hand through his hair in frustration. He mutters to himself, "Should have known better."

"I have no right to ask anything of you, I know that," I say, "but something terrible is happening to the town, and Fiona doesn't believe me, and Constable Dunne refuses to hear reason, and I think it could mean that he—"

"Look. I understand that you're hurting, Shae. I really, really do. Believe me. I just wish . . ."

He thought I was here to reconsider his proposal, I realize with a sharp pang. He has loved me a long time. This hurt is not fresh.

"Mads—"

"No, let me finish. Chasing answers and not liking what you find doesn't mean you can uproot *my* life," he says.

I blink, taken aback. "There's more to it than that. A *lot* more. Constable Dunne—"

"Shae. Stop. I understand your search for meaning in life is all-consuming, but I have work to do." He scoffs, a wounded animal lashing out. An excruciating silence stretches between us before it dawns on me: He might *believe* Constable Dunne. He might think I'm crazy. Or making this up. That her death was a tragic accident—terrible, yes, but not a crime.

"I wasn't lying when I said I care about you," I say, trying hard to keep my voice from trembling. "You're important to me. You're still my friend." He flinches at the word like I poked an open wound. "You have to understand. This isn't something I can ignore. I can't settle down with this hanging over me."

"There are factors you don't understand, Shae. I have other obligations. And I think we could both use some space right now."

Other obligations. His family. His farm. Until two weeks ago, these were my first loyalties as well. I can't fault him—or Fiona. I never saw before how loyalty can do this—keep people living in a fog of lies, separated from the truth, from what's right.

A tear hits my cheek. All I can do is watch silently as he turns away from me and goes back to work.

My feet lead me out of the riverbed and back to the road. I don't know what to think anymore. Everything that's ever been important to me is gone. Not just my family and Fiona and Mads, but my beliefs: that if I kept my head down and followed along, everything would turn out okay. The Bards would bless us. That the world was not safe or easy, but . . . *right*.

I walk aimlessly at first, but once I catch a glimpse of the path leading into the mountains, I chart my course more decisively. Thoughts of death and darkness fade, and I focus on putting one foot in front of the other.

I reach the edge of the landslide I saw from the constable's tower. With a deep breath, I climb atop the rubble and keep going. The walk is more arduous here, and I nearly fall several times—each stumble, picturing my mother cascading to her death. *But that never happened.*

A cold breeze blows through the mountain pass and I shiver. My hands dive into my pockets, and I feel a jolt of surprise when my fingers connect with a familiar item. Happy tears sting my eyes as I pull my embroidery hoop free. The small handkerchief I couldn't bring myself to start.

I set down my rucksack and sit on the ground, turning to the comfort of my needlework. My fingers move of their own accord, threading my needle, and pulling the colors through the fabric. I work slowly, with purpose, my body relaxing into the movement. Small red flowers bloom like beads of blood, one after another.

If no one in Aster will answer my questions, I'll find someone somewhere else who will. The thought scares me. Everything I've ever known is in this town. I may disagree with them, but I have people I love here.

Even if those people have turned on me. Whatever course I take now, I must accept that I'll be taking it alone.

I think back to what I learned at the constable's tower.

The Bards come here clandestinely every few months to collect contraband from Dunne. Ma was killed with a dagger inscribed with writing—a forbidden item—and a contraband Gondalese ox figurine was stolen from our home. The murder, and the constable's memory of it, was replaced with this landslide—covered up, the same way the mud and rubble have covered the tiny shoots that had begun to peek up from the small garden at the base of the hill.

Only one place exists that possesses the kind of powers that have been at work here.

High House.

The Bards will know who killed my mother.

A thought, far more sinister, follows closely, like a snake in water: *What if it was one of them?*

When I finally look up from my embroidery, the pass has been filled with red flowers springing from the dead, brown earth. I watch the blossoms tilting in the breeze beneath the warm glow of dying sunlight, identical to the image in my embroidery hoop.

How fitting that it all circles back to my curse.

I never found the answers I need about that either. And I sought them from the same people.

That settles it, I suppose.

If High House is the only place that has answers for me, then that's where I have to go.

I've never set foot outside of Aster. Few ever do, except to hunt or engage in trade with neighboring towns. We know to stay in place. And the back-breaking demands of our work mean we can hardly imagine leaving anyway. One day of lost labor could cost us our livelihood, or even our lives.

But I have nothing to lose.

I glance around town as I make my way through, wondering if it's the last time I'll ever see it. The late afternoon is waning into sunset as I pass the mill and then the general store where Fiona lives. Mads is probably finishing up his work. Fiona is sitting down for dinner with her family. I feel a stinging pain deep in my chest. I'm going to miss them.

I hope they miss me too.

I double my speed, making my way to the watchtower for the second time today. The sun casts the tower's long shadow over the street. The large wooden gates leading out of Aster loom intimidatingly before me. My whole life I imagined those gates keeping the rest of the world out—now it feels like they are trapping me in.

I dig my nails into my palms to keep my hands from shaking. The guards eye me sternly as I draw close to the gates. I force myself to look the nearest one in the eye.

"What do *you* want?" the guard asks. He clearly recognizes me in some capacity, which will make this easier.

I take a deep breath. "It's your lucky day," I say, surprised by how even my voice is. "I'm leaving."

The guards share a look of confusion. "What do you mean 'leaving'?"

"Are you crazy, or do you just have a death wish? There's wolves and bandits out on the roads," the second guard admonishes.

I plant my feet and refuse to let my glare falter. "If you recognize my face, then surely you know I'm cursed by the Blot. I have decided to sacrifice myself for the betterment of Aster." It's not exactly untrue. Aster probably *will* be better off without me. And if my hunch is correct, the town will be better when the truth is exposed.

If I am able to expose it.

The second guard glances at his companion. "She's that shepherd girl, the one whose brother got the Blot."

"I *know* who she is!" the first guard hisses. "And never mention the damn thing by *name,* you idiot."

I never imagined leveraging the villagers' fear of me against them, and it gives me a small rush of satisfaction. I watch them shift nervously.

"You know . . ." I smile. "I bet as soon as I leave,

there will be a downpour. Rain for *weeks*. You two will be heroes."

The second guard concedes first. "This one's probably the *reason* we've been suffering."

"It's your own fool head that's made *you* suffer," the first chimes in. "But," he sighs, "not like anyone's going to miss her."

"Right. Thanks, I guess." I grimace, watching as they step to either side of the gate and in tandem begin turning the wheels that open it. The gates groan apart, revealing a long stretch of road that disappears into the darkening horizon.

The guards cast me a look of pity as I give a small shudder and step across the boundary of town.

So this is what it feels like, I think. *To be free.*

I did not account for the night becoming dark so quickly. It's as if a great breath of wind snuffed out the sun as soon as I lost sight of Aster. The gray-black blur of land, air, and sky opens like a hungry mouth around me. The faint canopy of stars looks so distant. It reminds me of the stories of Gondal—a land where the stars each have a name. People follow the shapes they form in the darkness and never get lost. Maybe, in some other form—a breeze or a sprinkle of rain or starlight—my family found their way into that other realm. A place without danger or fear.

The stars overhead have no story and do little to illuminate the path. I have barely enough light to see a few feet ahead of me. It's as if I'm constantly on the brink of walking straight off the edge of the world. From what I've heard, the nearest village is far enough that you wouldn't see it from the narrow mountain road anyway, even in daylight. In between are open fields—littered with rocks and low trees, skeletal in the darkness.

High House is impossibly far. Days, even a week on foot. I move forward only because there is no going back. The only option is justice. I'll have the truth even if I die trying.

My legs are aching, my jaw clenched against the cold. A howl in the distance echoes across the barren land. I shiver, pulling my vest a little closer around my chest, as another follows. Soon it has become a cacophony. Coyotes? Wolves? I pause to gauge how close the sound is.

They say the only thing faster than wolves is the wind, and the only thing that ever traveled faster than the wind was the First Rider, who rode his black stallion across the empty world and spoke it into existence, tree by tree, mountain by mountain, until there was Montane.

Hurriedly, I crouch and fumble in the dirt for a rock large enough to use as a weapon.

Like Mads taught me.

I squeeze my eyes shut, willing the image of his face and the hurt in his eyes away. After another moment of grappling in the darkness, I find a jagged stone slightly larger than my fist and grip it tightly at my side.

I really could have planned this better. Or at all.

That's your problem, Shae. You never think things through. I push away Fiona's voice. Hearing it only brings me more heartache.

Another howl sounds upsettingly near. I consider finding shelter—a large boulder or tree to climb—to keep me at a safe distance from whatever predators might be lurking in the sloped plains. But there's nothing.

Then: a movement of shadow on shadow. I start to run.

My breath is coming heavy, and the howling has gone strangely silent. Are they on the move? The road curves near the jutting ledge of a steep cliff, and as I hug the side of the road, I see it: a wink of brightness.

At first, it looks like a fallen star, tiny and trapped in the underbrush of the slope. I quicken my pace along the road as it continues to bend, heading downward again, feeling the decline under my feet, and wary of stumbling on loose dirt and losing my balance.

I didn't imagine it. It's a small cluster of buildings. A little town, even tinier than Aster. More of an outpost, from its look of abandonment. There are no town guards, and I realize, crestfallen, that it is likely a deserted army station. I wonder if Bards ever camp here. But the squat little lean-tos look like they're about to collapse, and I nearly choke on another gasp when a mangy-looking animal—it could be a cat, but is so bony and damp-looking it might be a weasel—skitters across my path.

At the end of the grouping stands a somewhat larger building. Unlike the others, a light emanates from inside. A single burning candle. Hope and dread wage a war inside my chest as I creep curiously forward like one of the moths battering into the windows.

There is no marker, but it must be some sort of inn; it appears to have a chimney poking out the top, and it's too large to be a store or home. With a panicky sense of hope raging through my shaky arms, I try the handle on the door and it yields, opening into a dusty entry hall. I squint to make it out. The floor is lined with a weathered rug, woven in patterns of horses and swords. Off to one side is a dormant fireplace, charred black like a burnt-out wound in the wall. And there, around the corner, behind a table littered with stained, empty cups, sits a man.

I startle before realizing he's upright, but asleep in his chair, a stream of drool trailing down his chin. The candle I'd seen from afar burns low at one end of the table. It's an odd sight, as if the man has been waiting years for someone to arrive. I suddenly have the chilly, irrational thought that he's been waiting for me. Like some kind of savior.

"Sir?"

The man gives a snort and settles back into sleep, and I wonder if I even spoke aloud.

"Hello?" I try again, as much to test the reality of my own voice as to wake him. But he's an even heavier sleeper than Ma ever was.

Behind him are rows of shapes against the wall—hooks, each bearing a simple iron key hanging in its shadow. I move away from the sleeping innkeeper—that's what he must be, I reason—and toward the wall. It would be so easy to take one and sneak into a room . . . maybe I'd find one with an actual bed. I could leave in the morning before anyone was the wiser. My limbs and head feel heavy. If I could only rest for a few hours. Just until dawn . . .

I reach up and feel the dulled points of the hooks, plucking down one of the keys. It slips into my palm with a tiny jingle, when . . .

Howling breaks through the silence. It's right outside the door.

I spin around in alarm and freeze, my back to the wall, the hooks pressing into my neck.

It's not howling. Not exactly. Howling and *hooting* . . . and raucous laughter.

It is not wolves, but men.

I cower in the shadows, the key tight in my fist, as the door bursts open.

"What! What!" The old man at the table startles awake at last. "What is this?"

Three burly men in dusty, disheveled clothes and patchwork armor have sauntered in, the first carrying a swaying lantern in his giant fist. Each one is heavily armed with a startlingly vast array of blades and crossbows. At their heels are a pair of massive, snarling dogs much bigger than even Constable Dunne's back home. They look practically feral.

"Settle down, sir," the second one says with a laugh. He plants a meaty hand on the old man's shoulder and grips.

The man struggles, and before I know what is happening, the traveler has brandished a rusty-looking knife, slashing it across the old man's throat. The innkeeper chokes, body shuddering, a glassy, surprised look on his face. A spray of blood arcs from the wound, and he topples forward onto the table with a sickening thud.

I let out a scream. Time slows, and they all grin nearly in unison. Their teeth are various shades of the same murky yellow. My skin wants to crawl off my body and run away without the rest of me.

I'd only heard stories and rumors about the bandits and thieves that prowl the open roads. I never thought I'd come face-to-face with any, and I certainly never imagined they would be this truly terrifying.

Run! You need to run! I think, but my feet are rooted to the floor.

"Well, look here, boys!" the man in the middle who seems to be the leader drawls. "Maybe we'll have some fun in this little backwater town after all!"

"Who are you? What do you want here?" I ask, trying to sound braver than I feel, which is not at all.

The leader chuckles, a drawn-out, terrible sound from deep in his throat. "Who, us? We're humble *tax collectors.*" He leans menacingly toward me; a grin nearly splits his grimy face. "And your old pa here's behind on his *payments,* you see. Can't have that, can we?"

They know I'm scared. They know they have the upper hand. I look around frantically, and my gaze falls on a small wooden lockbox tucked under a tufted old chair in the corner.

If they take the money, they'll leave. My heart thunders as I gesture to the chair.

"There. That's where he keeps it," I say, hoping I'm right. "Take it and go."

"Smart girl," the leader says, easily finding the lockbox and handing it to the lackey on his right. "Nice doing business with you."

I feel a wave of relief wash over me as they turn and head for the door. Feeling begins to creep back into my fingertips. I release the breath I was holding.

Then they stop at the door. The leader grins at me over his shoulder.

"Burn it down, boys."

Bright flames lick the torch, lighting up the cruel joy on their faces. Without a second glance, the one holding it drops the flame onto the carpet. It ignites instantly and covers the floor in red heat. The men disappear out the door, lost behind the rising wall of fire, and I think, *The stories were wrong.* There *is* something that travels faster than the wind, faster even than the First Rider. And that is flame.

I cover my nose and mouth with my arm as the smoke starts billowing toward me. I move deeper into the room, my eyes stinging as I rush away from the flames, and discover a second door. I throw myself shoulder first against the sturdy door. It doesn't budge.

I center myself and channel all my weight into my leg. My foot connects with the door, just beside the handle, and the latch bursts open.

The fire engulfs the space I was standing in only seconds before I make it into a kitchen. There's a resounding crash as the roof collapses over the main room. I hurry to the back of the kitchen where a small back door deposits me out into the rubble and dirt.

The cold night air outside stings my face, and I gasp it in desperately, falling to my knees, taking huge gulping breaths.

But beneath the crunching sound of the inn burning and beginning to collapse, I still hear the sound of the dogs barking and howling.

My blood runs cold. Shapes shift in the dark nearby. I can make out the silhouette of a man with a crossbow.

My legs trip over themselves as I turn to run. Up ahead, I see the first hint of gray morning light on the horizon. I push myself in that direction, my heart slamming against the wall of my chest.

"There you are."

There's a sharp, shooting sensation in my scalp, and the horizon retreats in front of me. Someone has grabbed my hair, pulling me backward. My feet slide out from under me as I wince in pain. My head is twisted roughly. I'm brought face-to-face with the leader. He sneers at me. Sour liquor lingers on his breath.

"Willful one, aren't you? I like that." He laughs.

I grit my teeth and struggle, using every last ounce of strength I possess to free myself from his iron grip. I twist in every direction my body will allow. He continues to laugh at me, like he's a cat playing with a mouse.

He grabs my jaw. With a quick toss of my head, my teeth sink into his hand, into the sensitive flesh between his thumb and forefinger. The coppery taste of blood fills my mouth. His hand wrenches away, and in that one, sweet second, I use my elbow to bash in his face and he screams, but still he hangs on to me with one meaty arm.

Something sharp pokes my hip, and I remember I have my embroidery needles in my pocket, nestled into a small ball of wool.

With a free hand, I manage to loose one, gripping it in my fist. I thrash upward, sending the needle's point directly into his shoulder.

He screams again, calling me a word I have never heard but can only assume is forbidden. He loses his grip on me, and without stopping to think, I run.

They say the First Rider brought light and meaning into a world of chaos and darkness. I wish he could have made it a little less treacherous.

I travel the better part of the day, getting lost in a forest and finally stumbling across a narrow mountain creek, where I frantically collapse to my knees, splashing the cool water on my face and thirstily drinking.

I fight back the thought that Fiona was right as I double over with sudden hunger. If I had stayed, I would not be starving and alone.

I follow the creek, unsure how far I've strayed from the road. Panic rises in my throat, but I rein it in, remembering that the road holds just as many dangers as the wild, possibly more.

It is late afternoon when I catch a flash of movement not too far off—a trio of crows dart from some branches, cawing, and I hear it: the rumble of wagon wheels. I take off running toward the sound, tall dry grass scratching my legs through my torn skirt.

I stop short and duck behind a tree. I've hit upon a narrow country road. Three black horses round the corner, their golden tack shining in the afternoon light. The two in front bear crimson banners, and the third pulls an elegant wagon overflowing with food, fabric, and valuables.

Bards bearing a tithe caravan. My heart races.

I doubt I could rely on their charity to simply give me a lift to High House. I'm a peasant, and one who may carry the curse of the Blot at that. But if I'm swift and *very* careful, the wagon they're escorting seems roomy enough for one impertinent stowaway.

I crouch in the underbrush, not even daring to breathe, until the horses draw level with me. None of them cut a familiar figure. They are not the same Bards I saw in town.

Once again, I'm overtaken by the beauty of the horses and their riders, like I was that day in Aster. It feels so long ago now. Their black uniforms are accented with the most beautiful golden thread embroidering their hoods, collars, and wrists. Their posture is regal, commanding, and somehow effortless. A hum of power seems to hover in the air around them; it penetrates deep into my bones.

Mercifully, they don't notice me. I swallow the nervous lump in my throat. The horses pass; the massive cart follows.

As soon as the back wheels turn past me, I slip onto the road and run. I reach forward, my fingers finding purchase on the locked handlebars at its back, and before the wagon can begin to drag me, I push off with both feet, pulling myself upward. The momentum is just enough to send me over the top of the wagon walls, tumbling inside.

My fall is caught by a soft bed of hay at the bottom.

I manage to squeeze behind a large barrel at the back, right before the Bard driving the wagon glances behind him.

"Is something wrong?" I hear one of the riders up front ask.

"I thought I heard something," the driver replies. "Must have hit a rock. The damn roads out here are rubbish."

I quietly exhale.

The rocking of the wagon steadies my nerves somewhat, but the feeling that the journey isn't over gnaws at me. With any luck, these Bards will be heading straight to High House.

Which means I'll have to figure out the next step from there. How to stay alive. How to find the truth.

I close my eyes and think of Ma. Her hand on my shoulder, the way a single touch could communicate in so many different ways. *Be patient*, or *be strong*, or *be still*.

Ma, who is dead and gone. Killed in secret, her death buried by a landslide of lies.

Who did it? And why? The need to know is a cold fire burning in my chest. I *will* find the person who took Ma from me. I *will* look them in the eyes and make sure they know they won't get away with what they've done. And I'll demand to know *why*.

That person is at High House. I feel surer of that than ever. With every turn of the wagon wheels,

I'm getting closer, and an invisible thread is pulling tighter inside me.

And yet—despite my fear, and even the thrill of knowing I'm on my way to answers—the exhaustion of the journey has finally hit me. My lungs still ache from the thick smoke of the burning inn. My legs are weak, the soles of my feet numb. Evening is coming on; the sky above has gone from a litter of gold and blue between the leaves of the trees overhead to dusty lavender. The air is cooler. The jarring bumps in the road can't even prevent me from succumbing to exhaustion.

I don't know how long I've slept but I wake when the wagon jolts roughly. The ride is significantly smoother after. I listen quietly, but the Bards escorting the caravan do not remark on the change.

I venture a peek over the top of the barrel, shivering at the apparent temperature drop. The late afternoon sun is waning, and the altitude is making it colder. The route ahead is paved with silvery stone leading up into a mountain range taller twice over than the one bordering Aster. The white line draws my eye up a winding path through green pine trees that become dusted with white as the road leads upward and the snow-capped summit comes into view.

At first glance, the sweeping spires and glittering parapets look to be floating high above me, as though perched among the clouds. It's only when the wind changes that I see the mountain and the castle are one and the same. The structure is cut directly from the white rock, more blinding than the sun itself, and accented with exquisite shining gold, most of the upper structure almost lost in the sky. I keep blinking, uncertain how what I'm seeing could possibly be real.

Bridges span between the towers, arcing gracefully over one another. Toward the base, the castle diverts a massive, roaring waterfall in two; it spills over the side of the rock. The closer we get, the more details come into view; statues and engravings and flying buttresses catch the eye, glistening in the dying sunlight.

Something lurches in my chest, and I want to throw myself to the ground and cry. I grew up hearing the stories, but I never imagined anything so magnificent could truly exist.

But it's *real*. It's here, right before me.

The sheer beauty stirs something deep at the core of my being and my eyes burn with tears.

High House.

And my mother's killer may be waiting inside it.

As the wagon draws ever nearer to its destination, I find a more suitable hiding place underneath the reams of cloth near the back. Running my fingers over the fabric, I wonder what village this might have come from. It's certainly finer than any of the coarse wool produced by Aster.

"Halt, in the name of High House!" calls a deep voice.

The wagon rolls to a stop. I huddle deeper into the fabric, covering my mouth with my hand so no sound escapes me. I can't afford to get caught. Not when I'm so close.

"Is this the tithe from Taranton?" another voice asks.

"Valmorn." I hear the driver speak up. "Can't you tell by all this wretched scrap?"

A few of the men chuckle. Even their laughter manages to sound pompous. But I frown, confused.

It takes a second for it to sink in as I look around me at fabric that is finer than any I've seen in my lifetime. My indignation and surprise are quickly replaced with relief—it does not appear they will be personally inspecting the tithe.

"Well, you know how much Lord Cathal enjoys dressing up his little trophies," a voice chimes in. "Soon you Bards will be outnumbered by seamstresses."

"Pretty women, more likely," the driver scoffs. "Not that I'm complaining."

"It's a shame that ladies can't handle the Telling better," another interjects. "It would be nice to have more of them in the ranks."

The men continue to banter as I bite down on my

hand, stifling a gasp. I've only heard the very faintest whispers over the years of Cathal, the powerful and enigmatic master of High House, and by extension, all of Montane. It's strange to hear him discussed so casually. He sounds more like a real person than a mythical figure.

The conversation ends on a light note, one of the Bard escorts making a joke about the tithe from Taranton getting lost. I'm still processing what I've heard—the dismissive, sarcastic way the Bards talk to one another. I would have expected something more elevated. My thoughts are lost as the wagon jerks forward again.

The enormous gates to High House are made of wrought gold and slide open without so much as a whisper. I grip the bolt of fabric that conceals me tightly, until my knuckles are as white as the stone of the castle. I don't have much time before the cart is unloaded and I'm discovered. My heart thunders nervously in my chest.

I venture another look out of the wagon, and the finery of my surroundings is dizzying. My head spins and this is merely the entryway. The courtyard alone is the size of Aster, paved with an intricate, colorful mosaic. Two elegant semicircles of topiary in every shape imaginable line the sides, and beyond are arches and stairways leading to luxurious balconies overlooking the waterfalls.

Along the upper walls of the castle, rows and rows of dashing black-clad figures march in succession.

The Bards.

To see so many at once sends a dagger of apprehension and awe through my gut. I thought three Bards were intimidating, but the air of eminence they possess seems only to multiply by their numbers. My chest clenches a little when I recall the delicate features of the Bard I spoke to in Aster. Ravod, with his striking raven-black hair.

With no time to waste, I quickly throw the cloth off me, shivering from the cold wind, and dart over the side of the wagon as it passes under the shadow of an elegant archway. Landing sloppily on my knees and scrambling into the shadows, I throw my back against a curved wall of cool, white limestone. I glance around frantically—I need a spot to wait out the daylight. There's a door on the other side of the archway; I take a quick breath and hurry toward it. Thankfully, it opens at my touch, depositing me into a vestibule, where I have to blink to adjust to the darkness within.

I make my way gingerly inside, careful to step lightly. The vestibule leads to a large, circular chamber. I blink rapidly several times, disoriented. From my glimpses of the castle as we approached, it had seemed far more massive than it does from the inside. It's much darker than I expected, too. Lit only by a few iron sconces, without the splash of sunlight against the falling water and glimmering gilt railings. Still— clearly there are rooms upon rooms, and I just don't understand yet how they are all connected. Rooms where a killer may hide behind their daily life.

Two staircases wind around the perimeter of the room, meeting at a large landing at the top. As much as it terrifies me, I force another deep breath, steadying myself.

I must find Lord Cathal and appeal to him directly. He'll help. He has to. He's the only one who can.

Frozen and overwhelmed, I let myself think that maybe there's a chance I can someday return home to Mads and Fiona. Not as a pariah, but as someone who inspired the leader of the Bards to remove a danger to his people and restore safety and justice to our land. I have to try.

Swift but quiet, I move up the stairs—I swear more appear with each step I take. I try the golden handle at the top landing, and it yields, but a considerable amount of weight is needed to push open the heavy oaken door.

On the other side, I gasp. I've somehow found myself in the guards' barracks and seventeen armored men are staring directly at me.

12

"Stop! Let me go! Get your hands off me!" I shriek in vain as two strong men drag me squirming back toward the gate.

I try everything in my power to slow them down. I drop my weight, dig my heels into the ground, twist and struggle and kick . . . and still they pull me along with barely any effort. Other Bards have paused their business, looking curiously on at the commotion. They look at me in my simple, tattered clothes like I'm a rat rather than a human girl.

"I demand to speak with Lord Cathal!" I finally shout, and the guards look over their shoulders at me as if I told a fantastic joke.

"Oh, of course. We'll get right on that for you, my lady," one says between bursts of laughter.

I growl, twisting my body to the side and hooking my leg around the guard's, causing him to stumble. The brief interruption allows me the chance to wiggle free and scramble backward toward the castle, my feet slipping on the cold stone floor.

I fall to my knees, crawling on all fours, but a gloved hand latches on my ankle while another pushes me flat to the ground. The sharp ends of my needles, coming loose from their ball of wool in my pocket, dig into my hip. My hands are pinned roughly behind my back and my head forced down. The floor is cold against my cheek, and I cry out in pain.

"What is this commotion?" A stern, powerful voice sounds across the courtyard. The guard's grip loosens enough for me to roll inelegantly onto my stomach. To either side of me, the guards are bowing low.

A pair of immaculately polished white leather boots enters my vision; they are trimmed with gold at the heel and toe. I barely even notice the two beautiful, well-dressed ladies in the background who accompanied the newcomer into the courtyard. This man's presence alone commands the attention of all.

I gulp loudly, my gaze wandering upward to a more resplendent, white version of the Bards' uniform. It is tailored perfectly to his athletic frame, and a rare velvety, crimson fur-lined cape drapes over one broad shoulder. An outfit crafted for looks rather than practicality, unlike anything I've ever seen. My eyes finally rest on the man's face, and I gasp.

Lord Cathal returns my gaze with penetrating gray eyes. He seems possessed of both youthful energy and mature wisdom at once. His hair is various shades of silver. Fine stubble shadows his jaw, enhancing his severity. Much like his home, he's captivatingly handsome, both hard to look at and difficult to look away from.

He cocks his head at me, almost amused, before turning conversationally to his men.

"So, we have an uninvited guest, do we?" His voice is heavy with authority. He has an uncanny way of speaking like he is carefully measuring all his words, his teeth flashing white.

"This peasant wandered into the barracks, your lordship," one of the guards replies readily. "We don't know how she got in . . ."

"That much is obvious," Cathal cuts him off with a dismissive wave of his hand. "Double our security forces at the gates and see that this does not happen again."

"And the girl, Lordship?"

Cathal tilts his head in the other direction, observing me. His expression is completely unreadable. "Dispose of her," he says finally.

"No!" I scream, but Cathal merely signals his men, who haul me roughly to my knees.

This is it. I have come this far for nothing.

That's your problem, Shae. You never think things through. Fiona was right.

How I long for her now. For Mads. For anyone who might have defended me. But it's too late.

My blood is pounding through my body like bolts of electricity, and I may die from fear alone. My fingers, arms, chest, and throat burn as everything I am screams to prevent what's about to happen.

"*Ma,*" I cry out. It's unbidden, a deep call for

someone who I will never have back, at least not in this life.

But maybe in the other. Maybe if it's real, we will meet in Gondal.

Gondal. My last thought, a forbidden one. How fitting.

I hear a blade screeching from its scabbard.

Everything seems to happen in slow motion: the flash of a guard's blade, the laughter of the Bards, the flash of Cathal's finery as he begins to turn away.

In that frozen instant, I am consumed by the memory of the first time I understood what death was—the moment I saw the Bards riding into town the morning Kieran was taken by the Blot. Suddenly, I am not in the courtyard at all, but falling from the great tree beside our home, the only thing in my vision the indigo death ribbons I had woven into the branches, rippling and swaying in the breeze. The too-bright sun and the too-dark ribbons, wild and snapping.

Time unfreezes, if it ever stopped.

A scream rips from my throat, and my arms fly up to cover my face, right as the blade swings down and—

A beat.

I draw a ragged breath, lowering my arms. I can hear nothing but the pounding of blood in my ears. The courtyard has gone so silent that the drop of a pin would echo like thunder.

My executioner looks in confusion at his hand. Where he held a sword aloft, there is no blade.

Only a blue-black ribbon, billowing in the cool mountain wind, like a slender flag. A death ribbon.

Finally, his stunned silence snaps and he drops it. His sword clatters to the floor, returned to its original shape.

My mouth hangs open, drawing in a trembling breath of air.

The guard scrambles to pick the blade up, but Cathal steps closer, putting his boot down on top of the fallen sword. He studies me carefully down the narrow bridge of his nose.

"Well, then. It seems we have business after all," he says. "Rise."

I try to speak, but my voice is so raspy, I can barely push it through my throat. I am unsure of what just happened. A miraculous Telling. It could only have been the work of Cathal, done to save me . . . but *he* ordered my removal. Why suddenly show mercy?

He stares intently, waiting for me to stand, and I stumble to my feet, but between Cathal's gaze and my shaking knees, I'm not sure I'll remain upright for long.

"Your name?" Cathal asks. His voice is perfunctory, but there's an undercurrent of curiosity that was not there before.

"Shae, your lordship." I try my best at an unpracticed curtsy. He chuckles softly—is he laughing at me? I can't be sure. It's a melodic sound, and the ghost of a smile on his face only adds to his magnetism. It's hard to believe that only seconds ago he ordered his men to kill me without any compunction whatsoever.

"Perhaps, Shae, it would be best if we speak in private," Cathal says. His eyes flicker to the gathered sentries and Bards, all gazing on in mixtures of shock and apathy at my brush with mortality. Cathal gestures behind us. "Come," he says, turning on his heel and heading toward the main entrance to the castle. The two beautiful ladies from before curtsy deeply and take their leave at a cavalier wave of Cathal's hand.

Still shaking, I fall in step silently behind the master of High House.

Cathal leads me silently up the stairs. I'm so stunned, I can barely take in the details of High House's interior, though I can see that it is masterfully cold and spare. I have heard the Bards live a life of deprivation and modesty; I wonder if that's why the vast rooms of the castle are unadorned. And yet it seems a strange contrast to the white and gold splendor of its exterior.

Cathal spares a look over his shoulder without breaking stride. "From the plains, are you?"

"Yes, Lord," I reply. "If I may ask . . ." I pause to pull more air into my lungs. "How did you know?"

"You sound out of breath. The air is thinner here," he says. "You will adjust to the altitude with time."

"Ah," I manage to gasp as we reach the top; saying any more might suffocate me completely.

Cathal silently continues down another spare hall, this one with a ceiling made of glass, brilliant sunlight pouring in. Abruptly he turns to a dark wooden door flanked by two guards. They bow slightly, opening it. I follow Cathal inside.

Here, the monastic simplicity of the décor is gone, and it's like we have stepped into an entirely new world. I follow him into a magnificent parlor with large windows overlooking a splendid garden, complete with an intricate hedge maze. Ornate objects adorn the space, along with incredible works of art. Portraits of figures with huge eyes and mouths seem to leer over the room, each with the high forehead and pale hair that Cathal shares. At the center of the room are a comfortable settee and luxurious armchairs framing a mahogany table with a shining golden tea set atop it, polished to perfection. Behind the settee sits a massive white-stone statue of the First Rider. The whole room has a disturbing air of excess, but every individual item screams with value and strange beauty.

I catch my reflection in an ornate mirror on the wall and grimace slightly. I can barely see what part of my face is dirt or freckles. My hair has gone from light brown to a dark, grimy color, caked with mud and dust. I feel like vermin infesting this beautiful place I'm not meant to be in.

"Please, sit." Cathal gestures to the settee as he takes a seat in one of the armchairs. I obey him hurriedly, trying not to cringe at the dirt I will leave behind. "I hope you will accept my sincerest apologies for the misunderstanding outside."

My mouth opens and closes, and opens again, as if someone else is controlling it.

In any other context, I might have exclaimed that incoherently expressing yourself is a misunderstanding; ordering his men to *kill* me is something else entirely. I grit my teeth, looking Cathal over warily. Giving him a piece of my mind might not be the best idea.

"I . . . That is . . ." I stammer. "You're too kind, Lord. I'm just thankful you spared my life. Because something has happened. In my village. And . . ." The words run out. Cathal is watching me very carefully. His eyes hold me in place like he's turning me to stone.

"Take your time. You have piqued my interest." The corner of his lip is turned upward. "That alone is no easy feat."

"I have?"

I cut myself off before he changes his mind. His eyes don't waver from mine. "Shae, was it? Do you know how many Bards I have here at High House?" he asks, disregarding my question. "Hundreds." He leans forward on his knees, steepling his fingers.

"And how many of those hundreds do you think are women?"

"I can't . . ." I shake my head. "I would not presume to know such things."

"Six."

My eyebrows rise. "In all of Montane?"

Cathal nods. "Telling is an unpredictable force, one that is difficult to control and more difficult still to master. For every Bard in the ranks of High House, there are dozens more hopefuls who cannot withstand such power. Their minds shatter." He pauses. "Such occurrences are sadly more prevalent among the few women we have discovered in possession of the gift."

"The gift?" I repeat, unsure why Cathal is saying this.

The other corner of his mouth turns upward. "It starts as a warmth in the fingertips. A small shiver that spreads through the arms and shoulders, reaching a fever pitch in the heart that anchors the body to a moment in time where reality and truth exist together."

I drop my gaze to my hands as he speaks.

My embroidery. My dreams. *My curse.*

I look back up at Cathal, and he smiles sagely, as if he can see what my mind is still attempting to process.

"Is that not why you are here? I think you know what I speak of, Shae."

"I . . . don't. I only came here because . . ." I take

a breath to steel my nerves. "I have reason to believe one of your Bards is involved in the death of my mother."

His expression shifts and his eyes narrow at me slightly, just enough to alter his features from kind to severe. "Is that so?" he says slowly, less a question than a statement.

I give a small nod, my body beginning to tremble. I let out a slow breath. If I want to secure his help, I need to be brave.

His brow has furrowed, but in an instant the austerity has vanished from his handsome face. "How troubling."

Hope pierces me in the chest, and I look up, eager to hear more. "Does this mean . . . Will you help me?"

"Well, as I mentioned to you before, there has been a history of madness among the Bards. Unfortunately, it often happens to those who are most powerful. In the history of the Bards, it has been a documented phenomenon, and one we wish we had the power to change."

"So . . . you think it's possible? That someone at High House is . . . is . . ." I can't bring myself to say it. I don't want to risk the forbidden word again. Instead, I slow down and carefully say, "You think one of them could be complicit, then?"

"We cannot be sure. But I will look into it, you have my word."

I fall to my knees. "Oh, thank you, thank you,

my lord." I want to weep, the burst of relief and joy inside me is so strong. *Finally,* someone who believes me.

His fingers gingerly touch my shoulder. The touch sends a shock of simultaneous warmth and coldness through me. I look up.

"Shae," he says quietly, that echo of a smile hovering on his face. "I have a more important order of business first though."

"Oh." I try not to look as crestfallen as I feel.

"I must set you up with a room. And, of course, a trainer."

"Oh, I . . . what?" *A trainer?*

A full smile graces his face and he laughs. "You still do not see it, do you?"

I sit back on my heels, confused, but suddenly obedient. He is going to help me. He *believes* me. That alone gives me a soaring feeling, as if I can accomplish anything. He has shown me mercy. He has heard me out. Someone has finally *listened.*

I wait for him to explain what he means.

"It is you, Shae. The ribbon in the courtyard. The Telling." Yes. His miraculous act of mercy . . . he's going to explain why he took pity on me at last, why he spared my life. "It was an incredible Telling, for someone so young."

"For someone so . . ." I'm still, even now, struggling to follow him.

"You are one of those rare gems, Shae. Those born with the gift, who simply cannot control it yet.

It is dormant, but emerging. Luckily, you have come to the right place."

What is he talking about? He's describing the gift of Telling, the power wielded only by . . .

"A Bard," he says, finishing my thought. "How would you like to become one, Shae?"

Cathal rises to his feet and offers me his hand. His grip is strong but gentle. "With proper training, you could be a Bard of High House."

"Me?"

I stare at his hand, then into his eyes. All the strange and disturbing events of the past few months—years, even—rush back to me. All the times I felt as if I had dreamed a dark and strange image into being. All those times my needles seemed to show me what to see in the world, maybe . . .

Maybe my hands were *Telling*.

This whole time I thought the Blot had come once for us, and that it was coming again for me. That there was something wrong with me, with my whole family. A curse. I believed exactly what others did, that the shadow of the Blot was hovering over us, waiting to descend.

Could it be that I am what Cathal sees instead?

"You have considerable raw talent, Shae. Hone it, train it, control it, and you will one day become an incredible Bard." He pauses, his eyes narrowing grimly. "An untrained gift is a danger. Your power is not to be trifled with, and you have a long way to go to reach your full potential. The alternative is to succumb to madness—perhaps far sooner than you think."

Relief washes over me. I don't know how to thank him, to be sure this isn't some wild and fantastical dream that will burst back open into ugliness the moment I awaken.

"You really don't make an easy bargain to refuse, Lord Cathal."

"It is one of the perks of my station, I am afraid." Cathal smiles.

A sudden knock on the door jolts me back to reality, although Cathal seems unruffled by the interruption.

"Enter," he calls.

The door opens silently and a Bard steps into the parlor, stopping a respectful distance from Cathal and bowing. My jaw drops when I recognize his thick, black hair, refined cheekbones, and chiseled jaw.

Ravod.

"Exactly the man I was hoping to see," Cathal says as Ravod rises. The Bard's eyes lock with mine.

"Lordship," Ravod says, his dark eyes flickering over me before flitting to Cathal. "I've come to report that my recruitment party is prepared to depart on your order."

"Delay that order, Ravod," Cathal replies. "It seems I have done your job for you this time."

Ravod frowns and cocks his head. For a moment his reaction reminds me of Mads. I wince, remembering him, someone who I hurt so deeply. "I don't understand."

Cathal gestures to me with an elegant flourish, and I watch as Ravod gives me a look of utter apathy. Does he not recognize me after all?

"This young lady is Shae," Cathal says. "She is your newest recruit."

13

Ravod's gait is stiff as he leads me through the cool, echoing halls of High House. The castle only seems to get darker and have more twists the farther we travel.

I follow first through an enormous circular hub with a majestic dome painted in the image of the night sky and lit with candles to mimic the stars. Violent images of horses, swords, and soldiers are scattered across it. We pass through a two-floor basilica, lined with blank-eyed statues, that splits off into a series of cloistered gardens. There, Bards pace with their heads down, a few kneeling and tending to the plants. Within one of the gardens, we walk along a narrow stone path, and I marvel at the vines that wind around the pillars in each corner, bearing remarkable blue flowers that shimmer in the dying sunlight. Unable to help myself, I carefully touch the delicate petals of the one nearest.

Ravod slows his pace, coming to a full stop a few steps ahead of me. With a long, heavy sigh, he turns around completely and watches me with appraising eyes.

"Sorry," I stammer quickly. "I didn't mean to slow us down."

Ravod's mouth tightens, and he takes a step toward me, folding his hands in front of his chest.

"I told you not to seek us out."

He does *recognize me.*

I had almost forgotten the strange, subtle power of his voice. At his words, a small electric sensation travels along each of my ribs, from my sides to the center of my chest.

I smile a little too hopefully. "You remember me?"

"That's not . . ." Ravod clears his throat, but his chiseled face remains unmoved. "Should I assume that you are simpleminded or merely hard of hearing? You clearly went out of your way to ignore a very specific and straightforward instruction."

Fury flushes my cheeks, rising up from my neck. "I came because something terrible happened in my village." My breath is ragged, and I should probably stop there, but I'm too angry at his insinuation that I'm a stupid, silly girl who *followed him* all this way despite his warnings. "This may come as a surprise, but I didn't come here because I *felt* like it. You can't imagine the difficulty I've faced in leaving my home and traveling—"

"I've traveled extensively across Montane, so I actually do." Ravod talks over me, igniting the anger in my chest further. "You—"

I determinedly continue speaking over him in turn. "—*all* this way across unsafe terrain for an audience with *anyone* who will listen to me, and—"

"Very well, I concede. You've made your point."

Ravod raises his hand, cutting me off. He pauses, searching my face. "You're a fierce one, aren't you?" he says, although nothing in his countenance betrays that he found my comments moving. My skin prickles at his tone, and I glare at him.

"My *point* is that I wasn't just in the neighborhood dropping by for tea," I say, crossing my arms over my chest.

To my surprise, he smiles and laughs so softly, I almost don't hear it.

"You're funny too. I guess we'll see how long that lasts."

"What's that supposed to mean?" I ask as Ravod begins walking away. I jog to catch up with him.

"Usually when we get a recruit with a sense of humor, one of two things happens," Ravod says, his dark eyes fixed ahead of him as we continue through the cloister. "Either they break the habit, or they wind up dead."

"Is that a threat?" The garden is starting to feel ghostly and gray in the falling dusk, and it finally hits me how *cold* it is this far up in the mountains. I wrap my arms around myself.

Ravod's eyes flicker to me and away. "Not necessarily." He adds, more quietly, "You must have shown *some* promise. Lord Cathal has a particular talent for sensing these things."

"What do you mean?" I ask, frowning at Ravod who continues to stubbornly not meet my gaze.

"Curiosity. Another trait you should think about

quickly eradicating," Ravod states. We've reached a large, wrought-iron gate at the edge of the cloister. A pair of guards bow to Ravod and usher us through. "I will say only this, and I hope for your sake that you heed me this time." Ravod nods as we pass. "Mind yourself around Cathal. Serve him. Obey him. But be *very* careful when speaking with him."

"Why?" The question burns too hot not to ask, but Ravod shoots me a dark glare that says not to push my luck.

The gate deposits us into a flat, sprawling field, ringed on one side by High House and the other by the edge of the mountain. I've never seen cliffs like these—grand, massive, terrifying, deadly. Distantly, I hear the crash of the waterfalls, and it sounds to me now like the thundering of a thousand hooves.

Ravod keeps to a direct path, crossing the lawn toward the sound, toward that magnificent, horrifying edge. Beyond him, clouds billow and swirl in the darkening sky. Even this late in the day I see groups of Bards paired off in different areas, training. Some hone their martial skills with blades and crossbows; others march in tightly regimented formations. Some sit in quiet meditation. A fourth group is gathered attentively around an older Bard, who appears to be giving a lecture of some sort, but they are too far away to hear.

"These are the training grounds," Ravod explains. "You'll be spending most of your time here for the near future."

I stand awed, taking it all in. The scent of mountain wind and freshly cut grass fills my lungs. When he says I will be training here, I am still struggling to believe it's true. That I have the gift and have been recruited. It's beyond what I could ever have imagined for my life, and as I stare at all these other Bards in training, I wonder if somehow this *was* my calling, the reason for all my suffering—to be led here. It's a strange thought, and it comes with a mixture of hope and fear.

I can't forget what drew me here. One of these Bards, right here on this field, one of these moving shadows against the coming darkness, could be my mother's killer. Perhaps, though I hate the thought, it may even be Ravod. I barely contain my shiver.

"Your days will be regimented and scheduled according to what talents we see manifest in your evaluation," Ravod is saying as I tune in to his words, "and, assuming you pass, your initial training. Each Bard has a place and a purpose, thus order is maintained both here at High House and throughout Montane."

"What's your place?" I ask, genuinely curious. The broad slope of his shoulders under his Bard's cloak is rigid; he is so hard to read, the need to know what he is thinking is strangely consuming.

Maybe he's hiding something.

Ravod glances at me with one eyebrow raised. "I see you've already decided to ignore my advice about being too curious," he says.

"And you're deflecting my question," I counter. "I've seen you collecting tithes from my village *and* mentioning recruitment to Lord Cathal, so I'm going to hazard a guess that you're some kind of envoy?"

Ravod barks a laugh, but the harshness of the sound is offset by the brilliance of his surprised smile. Two dimples appear on his cheeks. I feel red heat rise in the tips of my ears. A few of the nearby Bards glance at us curiously before returning to their duties.

"An envoy. Very well, let's call it that." Ravod's amusement fades as if he's embarrassed to have shown it. But the pleasure of it, like a quick burst of sun, leaves lasting warmth on my skin. I watch his dark eyes pass over the training grounds. "If you simply *must* know, Cathal honors me with the task of watching over the other Bards. I go wherever he needs me, to ensure order is maintained among us."

"That sounds difficult," I say. "If all the Bards know you report to Cathal about them, don't you feel mistrusted?"

"Their trust is irrelevant," Ravod replies. "They know their duty and I know mine."

My brow furrows at the coldness in his voice.

I look around at the Bards on the training grounds. There is clearly a sort of camaraderie that exists. The off-duty Bards murmur with one another and laugh, but somehow there is the same impersonal air between them that Ravod is displaying. Thinking back to when I first saw him interact with his fellow Bards in Aster, it was the same then as well.

"This is the Bards' Wing." Ravod's voice interrupts my reverie as we reach the other side of the training grounds and reenter the castle. Metal braziers light the area inside, and the halls feel older here, as if frozen in time from long ago.

Ravod halts in the center of the main room, pointing at a door to his left. "The refectory. Meals are served promptly at sunrise, midday, and sunset." His finger redirects to a door on the opposite side of the room. "The scriptorium. The only one in all of Montane."

Scriptorium. I have never heard this word, but he says it with complete and total reverence.

As if aware of my uncertainty, he adds, "It's High House's repository for written knowledge. This is where elder Bards learn the art of written Telling." My eyes widen in horror, but he continues, "As a Bard, you will eventually be instructed in the written word. It is one of our many responsibilities in maintaining High House's careful order."

Cold dread knots at the back of my throat. The artifacts Constable Dunne kept in his office flash through my mind, and I can't help shivering. I exhale shakily, realizing that I've surreptitiously stepped away from the door of the scriptorium.

"This is part of how the Bards protect Montane," he says with unexpected gentleness. "We must be familiar with the danger if we are to protect others from it."

He pauses, and even in the dim light of the hall, I can feel the way his eyes move over my face. He is probably wondering what Cathal saw in me, or how I will ever prove myself worthy of studying with him and the other Bards.

To be perfectly honest, I have the same questions. Part of me feels sick, wants to curl up in a ball and make all of this go away. It's too much. I'm not sure which outcome is more terrifying—that I will disappoint them all, or that I won't. Both possibilities feel like heavy rocks strapped to my body, pulling me to the bottom of a dark ocean.

"Follow me," he says finally, leading me through an ornate arch and into a long hallway. "I'll show you to your quarters."

I fall in step behind him, knowing that no matter how afraid I am, I have no choice.

The faint sound of chanting hums in the air of the Bards' Wing. It's a slow, deep monotone that is both beautiful and haunting, and so quiet I have to strain to hear it.

"What is that sound?" I ask.

"There's a constant Telling done by the elder Bards for the protection of High House," Ravod explains. "If you become proficient enough yourself, you'll start to hear it from anywhere in the castle."

"That's amazing," I whisper. "It must take a lifetime to become that powerful."

Ravod does not answer, instead turning a corner into a shorter hallway, lined only with rows of simple wooden doors.

"These are the ladies' dormitories." He gestures. "Because there are so few women, you each have your own room." I stare in wonder at the other closed doors. The other women. I long to knock on each door and meet them. Perhaps then I won't feel quite so intimidated and alone. He walks to one of the last doors and retrieves a small, bronze key from the lock, handing it to me. "I know how bad you are with instructions, but believe me, you do not want to lose this."

I take the key and clutch it tightly. I'm not sure if he's teasing me; the look on his face is his usual—deadly serious.

Ravod opens the door and gestures me inside, remaining on the threshold with his arms crossed over his chest.

"I hope it's to your liking."

It's likely modest by High House standards, but it's the grandest room I've ever been allowed to stay in. Like the rest of the wing, the walls and ceiling are stone, but there's a lovely window overlooking the training grounds and a cozy little bed, laid with crisp white linen sheets. There's also a chest of drawers, a desk, and a chair, all made from rich, dark wood. An adjoining door leads to a simple but elegant washroom. I gasp when I notice my fireplace. I rush to each thing in turn, running my fingers over every surface if only to ensure that it's all real. The room is nearly the size of my entire home in Aster.

"This is all for me?" The words come out in an astonished whisper.

"There are training clothes provided for you in the chest." Ravod ignores my question, tilting his head to the bureau. "You'll be expected to wear them tomorrow when you report in. We can have them altered for you later on. You have a private washroom over there . . ."

"Are you just going to lurk in the doorway to explain all of this?" I ask, turning to Ravod, who has not moved since he ushered me into the room. His face takes on a look of shock at my question, and a faint hint of color rises in his cheeks.

"Entering would be highly improper," he says, his voice somehow even more stern than before. He indicates the fireplace with another nod of his head. "And please don't set the dormitory on fire. It's happened before."

I roll my eyes. "I know how to properly light a fireplace."

"Not by Telling," Ravod corrects me. "Which, by the way, you are strictly forbidden from practicing alone."

My nose begins to twitch in indignation before what he's saying can fully land. *You can do that?* And, quickly after: *You think I can do that?*

"You're at High House now. Those are the rules

and you will obey them." Ravod's eyes flash, adding silently that the topic is not up for further discussion. Before I can ask anything else, he takes a step back into the hall. "Your evaluation begins tomorrow on the training grounds. Report to Kennan in the morning after breakfast." He closes the door. After the latch clicks, I hear his stiff footsteps retreating back down the hall, leaving me alone.

The sunlight is all but faded from the window as I slide my rucksack off my shoulder and take a moment to let everything sink in. At least, as much as I can. I was nearly a captive of bandits only last night. Just days ago, I was in Aster.

My mind launches into circles again, spinning wildly, and I stop it with a brisk shake of my head. I light the torch on the wall with the nearby flint and tinder, before venturing into the washroom.

The mechanisms that allow running water into the bathtub are confusing at first, and I'm further shocked when the water that pours from one of the spouts is *hot,* as if warmed by a fire, though my hearth is currently cold. Is this a work of Telling, or part of the mechanics of High House? And, I wonder, is there really any difference? This whole place seems to be laced with wonders half made, half magic.

I marvel at it until my hand comes away scalded, and finally manage to work out how to fill the tub with pleasantly warm water. Back home, we wash with cold well water from a bucket—or, in late summer, if there was water in the tiny stream that runs along the south portion of the pasture, we might bathe there. It is rarely pleasant, the cold water, heavy with minerals, stinging my chapped skin and leaving me shivering. Fiona, on special occasions, would bathe in fermented milk, which she said softens the roughness of calluses. That's the finest thing I've ever heard of.

Until now.

When I slide into the brass tub, a delicious, soothing sensation overcomes me. I feel my journey slough from my body like a snake's skin. I close my eyes, and for a brief second, I am safe. I'm right where I should be. Fiona and I never fought. Mads never proposed. Ma never died. The curse never touched me.

I open my eyes. Not a curse. A *gift*.

I stare at my hands. How is it possible, that all this time, I have had the power of Telling, the gift of the Bards, and not known it? We hear of the Bards combing the countryside for youths who show signs of possessing this gift. But it is known to be incredibly rare, especially in girls. No one knows if it is carried in the blood; it seems to just be as random as it is rare. It's as common as getting struck by lightning. No one in Aster has ever, to my knowledge, been recruited by the Bards.

The weight of today's revelations—and the journey

that led to them—finally hits me, with a wave of exhaustion so acute, I nearly let out a sob.

It takes several tries before I feel ready to leave the embrace of the warm water. The stones beneath my feet are warm too, I notice with astonishment. There must be a heating system beneath the floor. The large towel hanging on a nearby hook is softer than any clothing I've ever worn. I dry myself off and wrap it around my body, heading back to my bedroom.

My bedroom. The thought is strange. I've never slept in a room alone before. It's exciting and a little frightening all at once.

I empty my rucksack onto the bed, searching for my nightclothes. My mouth twists as I riffle through my few belongings. I imagine Fiona packing them up for me, probably unable to wait to see me gone.

When I find my nightgown, I pull it a little too forcefully from the bottom of the bag, and as it comes free, I hear a faint clatter on the floor behind me.

I turn, casting my frown downward before I feel the muscles in my face slacken.

Shimmering up at me is the small silver hair comb inlaid with colored glass in the shape of a butterfly. The one I placed in Fiona's hair. The tiny reminder of the beautiful things we have; the love of a faraway friend, despite everything.

The first pang of missing Fiona softens as I turn

the comb over in my hand, letting it catch the torch's firelight.

What I wouldn't give to share this with her. I imagine her eyes popping out of her head with disbelief and can practically hear her: *You? A Bard? That's incredible, Shae, I want to know everything!*

Sadness pricks at me, and I turn my head to the window to look out into the darkness.

A sharp knock at the door nearly makes me drop the linen wrapped around me. Frantically, I slip on my nightgown.

Is someone really knocking at this hour? Perhaps they have the wrong room? In an instant, the wistfulness that had consumed me turns into a flutter of fear. I must not forget that my mother's killer could be lurking beyond this door.

Do murderers knock?

Whoever it is knocks again.

I cross the heated floor, padding quietly to the door. My brow furrows as I lean a little closer to the dark wood.

"Who's there?" My voice shakes a little.

"It's Ravod." His voice is muffled through the door, but unmistakable.

The air hitches in my throat.

"Ravod?" I open the door, more than a little confused to see the tall, handsome Bard so soon. His hair and uniform are still immaculate and his face remains impassive when I open the door a little wider. Once again he makes no attempt to cross the threshold into my quarters, and his reluctance to look at me in my nightgown borders on comical. His preoccupation with propriety is equally infuriating and adorable.

"Cathal was displeased that you were not properly fed," Ravod states. "I apologize for the oversight. I brought you this."

He hands me a small linen pouch, inside of which is the reddest apple I have ever seen, a soft piece of bread, and fresh cheese. Even the most common food at High House is fancier than anything I could have found in Aster.

My stomach insists very loudly that I accept. "Thank you so much."

Ravod nods curtly. "I hope the rest of your night is pleasant," he says. "If there's nothing else, I'll take my leave."

"Wait." I stop Ravod with a brief touch on his forearm, and my cheeks flush when he moves his arm away from my hand. "There's something I need to know," I whisper.

I don't know whether to trust him yet. For all I know, he's the killer I've come here to find. But I find myself wanting desperately to give him the chance to prove me wrong.

Ravod says nothing, merely quirking an eyebrow, reminding me what he said about asking questions. With effort, I determinedly keep my eyes on his. "Have the Bards ever killed people?"

Ravod's expression changes rapidly from surprise

to shock to fury and finally something I can't quite determine. He takes a step closer to me in the doorway, careful to keep the threshold between us. I catch the faint hint of cedar I noticed before in Aster.

"I'm not sure how I can make myself clearer. Did you not understand me the first time I told you to quell your curiosity?"

"Please, Ravod, I'm . . ." I pause, unsure how to make him understand how much I need to trust him, and for him to trust *me*. "I need your help. Someone killed my mother," I persist. "I think it was a Bard."

Ravod keeps his eyes locked on mine as he leans very slightly closer and lowers his voice to a whisper.

"You really don't get it, do you?" he says, low and dangerous. The reverberations in his voice are deep, and send waves of hot and cold through me. "Do not mistake my courtesy for kindness. I have no concern for your problems. I don't care why you are here. I am not your friend. You are not here for friendship." He looks into my eyes. They look even darker in the faint light. Dangerous, yet pained. I swallow. "You are here to serve High House, and that is all. Everyone within this place is duty-bound to Cathal, myself included. Our loyalty and our lives belong to High House, and to High House alone."

"But—"

He cuts me off. "I will only say this once. Don't *ever* say these things aloud again, to me, or *anyone*."

He pulls back, eyes burning into mine. The torch in the wall beside us flares up, lighting his face, but it's over so quickly, I might have imagined it.

I don't know whether to be furious or afraid, or something else: the exact opposite of what he wants me to feel. I need to know what he is hiding. I need to know what makes this young man, who rarely reveals a single sign of emotion, suddenly become so intense.

His eyes flick to the torch, and for a split second, horror crosses his face. I'm not sure if it's because of what he said or what he didn't. "I must go."

He takes his leave as quickly as he first appeared, and as soon as he's out of sight, I bolt the door swiftly.

My hands are shaking, and I accidentally drop the bag of food Ravod delivered to me, the apple rolling out and across the floor. The memory of his voice echoes distantly in my ears. I crouch, gathering everything up, only to drop it a second time.

As tired as I am, I don't think I'll be able to sleep tonight. Not with all the questions rushing through my mind—images of the constable and the gilt dagger with inlaid lettering. Images of my past life, fragmented and jarring.

Not with the memory of Ravod's warnings. His dark eyes locking on mine. His words. *Don't ever say these things aloud again, to me, or anyone.*

Later, I lie restlessly in bed, the sheets smooth against my skin, and one thing becomes certain: I'm not going to obey Ravod. Especially not when it's so obvious that he knows more than he lets on. A terrible secret trembles behind his words, behind that piercing, sorrowful look in his eyes.

I'm not here to stay silent and afraid.

I am here for answers.

14

The next morning, I hurriedly retrace my steps through the corridors of the Bards' Wing, still buttoning my shirt. The training gear of the Bards is a simple black shirt, pants, and boots, but the fabric is far silkier than I'm used to. In Aster, this would be considered finery.

My needles are in my pocket. They remind me of home, of who I am, and it makes me feel a tiny bit stronger knowing they are close.

Sleepless night notwithstanding—my dreams were riddled with dark figures lurking in the night, glinting knives, and treacherous landslides—there is a tight determination deep in my chest. If finding Ma's killer means training to be a Bard to blend in at High House, I will be the best Bard they've ever seen.

I only need a lead. The bloody dagger flashes in my mind. I curse myself for allowing the constable to whisk it away. But the memory of it is crystal clear in my mind.

Prior to the murder—chills run through me as soon as I think the word—there were three Bards present in Aster. The weathered-looking red-haired man, the mysterious woman with dark skin and pale, amber eyes. And Ravod. I need to find out which of them the knife belonged to, if any.

It won't be enough to simply discover the killer, I realize. I will need irrefutable evidence. Something Cathal can't ignore.

I'll turn this entire castle upside down if I have to. For Ma.

I halt outside the refectory and take a deep breath before reaching for the large double doors.

The High House sentries to either side of the entrance push the heavy oaken doors open before I can touch them, startling me. I'm not used to people opening doors for me. The confusion must be written on my face; I hear several audible snickers as I stumble into the room.

The refectory is massive. Although similar to the rest of the Bards' Wing, when I look closer, I see it was cut out of the side of the mountain in one piece. The pillars, windows, and ornate carvings that wind into the vaulted ceiling are the same stone. Long rows of dark wooden tables and benches fill the space, and black-and-gold-clad Bards and their trainees crowd each one. They cast dark looks in my direction.

That, at least, I am used to.

I pause, wondering what the protocol here is.

"Go ahead and have a seat, my lady," a smiling girl in a pressed black and white uniform says to me. "I'll bring your breakfast."

I nod gratefully to the servant girl—relieved to see another female face in this sea of men—and try to find a seat far from the other Bards. Their glares make it very clear I'm not welcome to join them.

I look around for the other female Bards, on the off chance they are as isolated as I am. My mouth twists in disappointment when I see two others at different sides of the throng, laughing and dining casually with their male counterparts. One is probably twice my age and half my size, with most of her long chestnut hair shaved off and an intricate red tattoo that looks like branches winding over the side of her face. The other stands out almost immediately because of her shock of white hair, braided elaborately with an assortment of fiery-colored beads. She's much older, possibly than many of her fellow Bards, and the occupants of her table look visibly nervous in her presence. She does not speak a word. She doesn't have to for everyone to know she dislikes being bothered.

There should be four others, including the woman I saw in Aster, but I don't see them. Perhaps they are traveling to Montane, collecting tithes, or somewhere else in the castle.

I take a deep breath. It looks like I'll be taking my first official meal here alone.

While servants bustle by attending to the Bards, I look for a seat somewhere isolated. Luckily, the end of the closest table is vacant. A group of older Bards are clustered about ten feet away and either ignore me or don't notice me take a seat.

I am not your friend. You are not here for friendship.

Ravod's voice reverberates in my head, and I drop my gaze to my hands, knotted in my lap.

The logical part of me knows I didn't come here with any expectation of kindness. But that knowledge doesn't lessen the sting of being looked at and treated with disdain like I was back home.

A plate of food is set before me, with a warm smile from the servant who greeted me. She's quite young, probably a couple of years my junior, but tall. Her head is covered in tight, wild curls, the color of freshly tilled soil, locked in battle with the cord that ties them to the nape of her neck. Her smile is broad, revealing a gap in her two front teeth. It's the first real sliver of affability I've received since arriving in this viper's den.

Suddenly tears threaten to overwhelm me, and all I want is my ma to hold me, and my pa to sing to me. I can't bear it another minute. I cling to the ball of wool in my pocket, my needles grasped between my fingers, the one anchor I have to home, to my past. To *myself*.

"New here, my lady?" The servant sets a fork and knife at either side of the plate in front of me. I nod. Anything else I fear would crack me open. "I've served High House my whole life. I know every face in this room." She leans over to whisper conspiratorially in my ear, "Believe me, each one of them looked like you do right now when it was *their* first day of training."

"Thank you." My voice shakes a bit.

The girl smiles broadly, flashing the gap in her teeth, and I realize just how *young* she actually is. Maybe she grew up here. She can only be about eleven or twelve. A mere child in a place where a murderer hides. The thought sends a chill through me. "Only doing my job," she says with a tiny shrug.

"Do you like it here?"

The girl looks vaguely puzzled by my question, but her cheerful smile doesn't falter. "Well, yes! High House is the most beautiful place in the world, don't you think? I'm very lucky to serve here." She pauses. "I've never left the castle. I've overheard from the Bards that things are . . . bad. Down there." She makes a little gesture with her chin to indicate the outside world.

"It's a completely different world." The words slip out of my mouth. My heart squeezes painfully as I recall the poverty and famine in Aster, the barren dusty roads plagued by bandits, and the towns that were destroyed by their cruelty and barbarism. "But I come from one of the poorest villages. I have heard that much of Montane is beautiful and thriving. Every year, my village would strive to live up to the standards set by the rest of the villages, and every year, we struggle."

"It's a good thing you made it here safely." The girl nods sagely, although it's clear she has no idea how close I came to not being here at all. "This is the first time in a long while I've seen them bring a girl in," she adds, "but I'm sure you'll do much better than the last one."

"What happened to the . . ." Before I can finish, she seems to realize her off-putting remark and scurries away.

I remember what Cathal said yesterday. *For every Bard in the ranks of High House, there are dozens more hopefuls who cannot withstand such power. Their minds shatter. Such occurrences are sadly more prevalent amongst the few women we have discovered in possession of the gift.*

Is this the fate that awaits me?

My hand is shaking so badly, it sends my fork clattering to the floor. The noise causes the nearest group of Bards to glance in my direction.

Keeping my actions quiet and discreet, I duck my head beneath the table. Thankfully the cutlery at High House is as shiny as everything else, and I see it glinting on the floor where it skidded a few feet away.

Bracing myself with one hand on the table, I reach for the fork underneath. My fingers brush the side, pushing it farther away. Groaning, I slip beneath the table before I can think to simply ask one of the servants for a new fork.

Now that I'm on my hands and knees under the table, I exhale a heavy sigh and grab my wayward utensil.

A flash of gold catches my eye.

In an instant, I'm outside my home, watching Constable Dunne carry the knife that killed Ma out of the house. It glints in the sun.

Except I'm at High House. And the glint is coming from the hilt of an identical knife protruding from the boot of a Bard seated only a few feet away.

The ground beneath me feels very cold. I blink several times, but the golden hilt is still there.

I bite my lip hard, scrambling closer for a better look. My fork is clutched tightly in my hand like a lifeline as I crawl beneath the length of the table. I can only see the legs and large black boots of the knife's owner.

I reach out with my free hand. The tiny, delicate engravings are unmistakable. The tips of my fingers brush the cold metal.

The owner of the knife shifts in his seat, and I pull back, gritting my teeth and holding my breath. They're leaving the table. I scramble forward.

Too late. The knife moves from under the table and out of sight.

I sit back on my heels, my mind racing.

Another flash.

I look up with a quiet gasp, noticing another golden knife, tucked into another boot farther down the long table. And another. And another.

From where I sit, I count sixteen identical knives tucked into black boots in two long rows.

I swallow hard, backing toward my abandoned seat.

I may not have found the exact knife that killed Ma, but one fact is inescapable: It was a knife that belonged to a Bard.

It's just a knife, I reason. *Maybe a thief stole it and broke into the house . . .*

No. Another piece clicks into place as I clamber back up onto my seat. The landslide. A thief wouldn't cover up their crime with a Telling. Only a Bard can do that.

I just have to find out which Bard, one who has lost their dagger. And to hopefully not die or go mad in the process.

I take a deep breath, shaking my head to clear it, and deliberately concentrate all my attention on the delightful smelling food in front of me.

Warm buttery rolls, fresh fruit, porridge, eggs, and sausage sit steaming on the plate. In a mug to the side is a dark, hot liquid with a bitter, earthy aroma. Back in Aster, this one meal would be more than I would eat in a whole day.

Intimidated, but excited, I take a sip of my beverage. It lands on my tongue harsh and sour, leaving a slimy texture behind. I choke it down and decide I'll worry about acquiring a taste for it later. I'm too hungry to worry about it. Instead, I shovel as much food as I can onto my fork and tuck in with enthusiasm. The hot food melts on my tongue, rolling over and dissolving into a cold, wiggling mass.

Gagging, I spit a writhing clump of maggots onto the table.

I stare in horror, ready to expel the rest of my stomach's meager contents, until I hear the sound of a low chuckle turn to raucous laughter at the table across from mine. Looking up, I see a Bard, perhaps half a decade my elder, watching me while his lips move imperceptibly. He is surrounded by four others, all gawking in my direction with different variations of the same wicked grin.

I glance back to the table and find only a mass of half-chewed food.

I blink. I can still feel the nauseating, disgusting sensation of the maggots on my tongue. The food looks normal again, but I'm terrified to take another bite.

"She sure is jumpy." I pretend not to hear the remark.

"It's the first sign she's going to snap," another chimes in. "I bet my stipend she doesn't last the month."

My hand goes to my needles, clutching tightly as others excitedly place their wagers on the limits of my sanity. Pretty soon, there's a large sum riding on whether I will last three weeks or a whole month.

I stare at my food, appetite gone. They did this as a cruel joke. *At least no one in Aster knew how to perform a Telling,* I think as the Bards nearby have a laugh at my expense.

"What do you think, Ravod?"

He's somehow entered the refectory without my notice; I was too busy trying to keep yesterday's dinner down. Our eyes catch, and last night flashes back to me: his urgent warning. The way his eyes locked on mine. He was hostile, intense, almost terrifying. And yet I swear there was something else in his tone—an air of protectiveness. The same kind I often felt in Mads, but in a different form. There are layers of anger and hurt in him, and he guards them well. Watching him pass me, something in my chest flutters. Part of me hopes he pauses to speak with me. To apologize for last night or explain himself better. Maybe sit down to keep me company.

Without even breaking his stride, Ravod sails right past and places a few coins on his compatriots' table. "One week," he says.

My horror and nausea turn into painful humiliation. Even Ravod thinks I won't last.

"What about you, Niall?" the others address the red-haired Bard who I remember from Aster.

Niall's eyes flick to me and crinkle around the edges as he studies my face. They are the color of the grass on the training grounds—a brilliant green. His mouth is pressed in a thin line.

I hold his gaze, trying hard not to blink until he looks away.

"I don't waste my time with foolishness," he says before moving farther into the room.

The other Bards jeer playfully at Niall's back before busying themselves with counting their wagers. The money has taken precedence over taunting me at least.

I exhale a ragged breath.

Perhaps this is what High House does to people, strips away compassion and erodes kindness until there's nothing left but duty. I push my plate away and get to my feet.

It would be easy to go mad in a place like this. A place where nothing is what it seems, where even your own senses can't be trusted.

It is only as I stand—unable to risk another bite—that I catch another look at Niall as he's taking his seat beside Ravod. He does not wear a dagger in his boot like the others.

My chest flashes hot.

It could mean nothing.

But he was there the day before my mother was killed. The day before I found a Bard's dagger in her chest.

I have my first lead.

I just have to figure out how to follow it, without getting caught.

The training grounds are bathed in warm sunlight. They are busier than before, with High House coming to life in the new morning. Iridescent beads of dew cling to the grass, rippling like waves as a breeze sweeps over the mountain.

I stop near the edge, looking for any sign of my mysterious new trainer. I wonder what the chances are they won't be as cold and hostile as the other Bards.

"You." A cold, hostile voice barks from behind me. I nearly laugh; I don't know why I bothered hoping otherwise.

I turn around, my breath catching when I recognize her pale eyes and dark skin: the woman who I saw so fleetingly in Aster. She stands a good two heads taller than me, with her gloved hands on her hips and a scowl on her face. Her dark hair is swept into an austere bun with tiny braids running up the side of it. I'm struck by how gorgeous she is.

"You're Kennan?" I ask, my voice sounding smaller than I intended. "I was told to wait for you."

Kennan fixes me with her haunting eyes and gives a tight nod. "That's right, peasant. I'll be evaluating you over the course of the week." Her mouth twists like she's tasted something sour. Raw hatred drips off her every word.

Ravod's wager is beginning to make a lot more sense.

"First, I'll prepare the hurdles," Kennan says. The corner of her mouth twitches in a devious smirk as she looks me up and down. "We'll start with level five."

A nervous laugh escapes me before I can stop it. "Any reason we're doing away with levels one through four?"

Kennan narrows her eyes, clearly not amused. "You have one week to convince me you're worth keeping around. And you don't want to know what we do with those deemed unworthy to stay. I suggest you adjust your tone appropriately."

"Sorry," I mumble, terror streaking through me. What *does* happen to those deemed unworthy? Those exposed to the Bards' secrets, only to be cast out . . . It can't be good.

Kennan looks out over the training grounds as if addressing an invisible audience. "Over the course of the week, you will be tested physically and spiritually to determine your worthiness of the title."

"How do I prove worthy?" My voice is a timid squeak.

"Perform a Telling on command," Kennan answers, waving one of her hands as if it were nothing, and I'm caught by the elegance of her movements, the way her white-gloved hand flutters like a dove.

"The purpose of my assessments is not to teach you," Kennan goes on. "It's to determine if you're *worth* teaching. The tests will recondition you. Establish the baseline."

I try unsuccessfully to swallow. Kennan has already turned her attention to the field. She pulls a small, white piece of marble out of a satchel she wears over one shoulder, and places it on the ground. I stare at her in confusion—is this some sort of ritual? But her brow is furrowed and she is mumbling below her breath. I lean in, and it sounds like she is saying the word "part." The ground trembles, as if vibrations are radiating out from the stone.

"What are you doing?" I ask. She turns to look at me.

"That," she says, gesturing for me to turn around.

The ground has literally *split apart,* leaving a shallow chasm. She has parted the earth.

By *Telling* it to.

I'm so stunned, I don't notice when she pulls something else out of her satchel: a pair of shining golden cuffs. She hands them to me.

"You will wear these around your ankles."

I look from the cuffs to Kennan and back before taking them from her hands. They're solid gold and much heavier than they look.

"I—"

"Now," she instructs.

I grunt, latching them around my boots at the ankles. "Now what?"

"Now—leap," she says. It takes me a second to realize what she is asking—she wants me to leap across the gap in the earth, weighted down at the ankles. It seems impossible, even as it is slowly dawning on me that when she meant hurdles, she meant *literal* hurdles.

As if to explain herself, she adds, "*Telling* is a combination of physical and mental mastery of the body and its surroundings. Only when your mind is in sync with your physical form can you begin to commune *beyond* your body, with the earth. Eventually, if strong enough, your Telling will connect to the energy of the air, the sky, and all things."

I stare at her in awe. "I thought you weren't going to teach me anything."

A venomous glare is her reply. A servant appears and hands her a steaming cup of tea from a tray. She gingerly takes a sip before speaking, ignoring my question altogether.

"We begin with physical tasks just beyond your body's current natural limits," she says. "You're building strength of body and mind. A Bard requires both to reach into the realm of possibility and alter it."

I honestly have no idea what she's talking about, but from the sharp look of her gaze, I have no other choice than to do what she says. Kennan watches me over the rim of her teacup. Her eyes sparkle with brutal amusement.

I take a breath and turn toward the chasm, which

seems to yawn even wider than when I last looked. And with a step backward for momentum, I try to run, to leap, to levitate . . .

It's only been two days, and I can't take much more. I threw myself into an ever-increasingly deep ditch about seventy-five times yesterday.

Training is less a test and more of a method of torture. I'm halfway convinced Kennan is just trying to kill me. I'm covered in bruises, and my legs sing with pain, more so when I slipped into my bath last night. She even blindfolded me, apparently to help me focus *inward,* saying something about how our power comes from our self-control. But the panic in my throat as I slogged forward blindly was worse—I'm sure my screams and groans could be heard all through High House.

Even still, no one came to my rescue all afternoon. I kept hoping, despite the humiliation of the morning, that Ravod would appear and command Kennan to go easy on me, but I didn't catch a glimpse of him all day. We finally quit the test when I was half sobbing and beaten down.

"I give up," I panted, crawling on my bleeding knees, my new black pants ruined. Kennan bent to inspect me, and I instinctively grabbed onto her hands. She looked down at her gloves, covered in dirt, and fumed, instantly dismissing me.

Today, I woke up to new and equally awful challenges. Learning to hold a staff for the first time—which would have been thrilling had she not blindfolded me *again,* demanding I "listen to the movement of the air" around me. All I heard was Kennan's staff thrashing in large arcs around me until I dropped my weapon and crumpled to the ground with my arms over my head, whimpering.

This is not going well.

And worst of all, I'm so busy training that I've had no time, nor any will, to investigate. I've found out nothing more about Niall, who by this point has probably commissioned a new dagger and I'll never know if he was missing his in the first place.

I don't want to bring Cathal into it before I have evidence, but I will if I have to. He said he would help. I just have to prove myself worthy.

But it seems like a lot to perform a Telling on command. To say Kennan is a harsh taskmaster is a blistering understatement. It's as if all the hatred for me that exists in the world has been distilled into one person.

And she really, really hates me.

Which is why, tonight, even if all I want to do is fall into a dark, endless, dreamless sleep, I don't. After my bath, I pull out my embroidery needles and get to work. My fingers ache and sting, rubbed raw from wielding the staff and from falling on them all day yesterday. The familiarity of the thread through my fingertips relaxes me. I try to envision a pattern that Fiona would like. I think of roses.

By dawn, I have made a delicate pair of gloves, in exactly Kennan's size. Vines of delicate roses twist around the fingers. Despite my skill, I'm not sure I've ever made something quite as beautiful. I can only hope that a small act of kindness will soften her.

Perhaps she will take pity on me; perhaps, as a woman, she will understand how badly I need a friend here. How we must help each other, when no one else will.

I wait for Kennan near the balcony overlooking the cliffside, with all of Montane sprawled below. Even the mountains that bordered the wasteland back home did not reach this far into the sky—I can nearly see them in the distance. More likely, homesickness has led me to seek out something familiar to latch on to.

Montane is very brown. Not the dark, rich color of soil but withered and dusty. Low hills are dotted with spindly trees, bisected by winding roads that seem to lead nowhere.

If Gondal existed, which direction would it lie in? Beyond the stark, cold mountains to the west? Or across the desolate sprawl of wasteland to the north? In the stories, it was supposed to be green and verdant. The way all of Montane would be, if we had not allowed the Indigo Death to ravage us. It's hard to imagine such a place.

I should not be imagining Gondal at all. I take a deep breath, in and out, to purge my thoughts.

The cold morning breeze whips up the side of the mountain across the training grounds as Kennan approaches. She halts in front of me and signals for a servant.

"Five days left, peasant," she states, and the air around us grows colder. "Unless you plan to put me out of my misery and give up. As riveting as it's been to watch you fail, I'm eager for more important work."

I take a deep breath, readying the words I memorized the night before.

"Kennan, I think we got off on the wrong foot," I say, pulling the embroidered gloves from behind my back and presenting them to her with a small flourish. "These are for you. Would you consider it a peace offering?"

Kennan's eyes widen and narrow in quick succession as she takes a step closer to me and gingerly picks up the gloves.

"These are for me?" she asks.

I nod eagerly. "I did all the embroidery myself. It's a bit of a hobby . . ."

I trail off mid-sentence as Kennan turns them over in her hands. Like all Bards, she is impossible to read.

She takes a step closer to me, and I think maybe she is going to embrace me, though it would be so out of character that I merely stand there frozen as she approaches.

She flicks the gloves with a lightning-fast motion in her wrist, using them to strike me hard across the face. I stagger back in shock, tears springing to my eyes. One hand comes up to my cheek, tender and probably bruised.

"Sometimes soft things can hurt more than hard things." The strangest part is that beyond the fury in her eyes I see something almost like pain, as she goes on, "The sting is worse when you don't expect it."

Without another word, she tosses the gloves over the balcony, the sting on my cheek returning momentarily as they disappear down the mountainside.

Swiftly she turns and makes her way toward a winding outdoor staircase that leads across several more terraces before descending into the training field. I trip along after her, feeling helplessly humiliated, angry, and betrayed.

Which is, perhaps, exactly her point.

"Today, we're going to test your focus in the shooting range," she says, as if I'd never offered the gloves in the first place. I watch, stunned, as she strolls to the far side of the lawn.

"That's all you're going to say?" The hours I fought off sleep to prepare those gloves burrow a hole in my gut.

Kennan turns to face me, glaring. "I'm not going to apologize for your bootlicking. My time is valuable. Stop wasting it."

"I wasn't . . ." I stop as Kennan marches farther away. I try to force it down, but I can't help the twinge of hatred in my chest.

I won't let myself become like Kennan.

I think of Ma. Of her gentle hands and patient smile. It brings me back to myself enough not to fall out of step.

A staircase in the mountain face winds down from the training grounds to an alcove directly below. I look for a banister or something to hold on to, but there isn't one. I try not to think about the dizzying fall. The staircase is broad and probably perfectly safe. Kennan glides down it with ease.

An archery range is set up here, tucked safely into the rock with a barrier of stone erected to deter the howling mountain winds. Kennan signals to the servants attending the range. They disperse in a hurry.

My jaw tightens, wondering what torture she's concocted today.

Before long the black-and-white-clad servants return, one carrying a crossbow, another holding a quiver of bolts. A third and fourth are pushing an enormous, ornate mirror.

"The previous tests were a measure of your endurance and willpower." Kennan breaks the silence, her voice echoing harshly against the stone walls. "Today we're testing your focus. Your task is to hit the bull's-eye." She nods to the mirror, which has been placed in the center of the range, blocking the target. "You must do so without disturbing the glass."

The servant quickly sets a bolt in place and hefts the crossbow into my arms. It's heavier than it looks. I've never held one before, but Mads and I used to watch the militia's target practice from the hilltop behind the mill. I fumble a little until I manage to more or less replicate the stance I remember. The servant silently adjusts my form before stepping back.

"I didn't know Bards used crossbows," I say.

"Bards are trained to wield a variety of weaponry," Kennan replies. "Versatility is essential in the field."

"Like knives?" I ask, trying to sound conversational.

I watch Kennan's face carefully, but her only reaction is a fractional furrow of her brow. "We're trained for short-range and long-range combat," she says.

"Why?" The question slips out before I can think better of it.

"There are many ways a land like ours can be threatened, both from inside and out," Kennan states. "As Bards, we have to be prepared to face any threat and prevail."

"Like invasions? Uprisings?"

Kennan's glare turns icy. "Does this inane line of questioning have a point?"

"I just noticed that all the Bards have golden daggers." I shrug, hoping it looks casual. "I guess I assumed it was the weapon of choice."

"An audacious assumption." Kennan's voice is darkly patronizing.

I'm pressing my luck. I might be able to get in one last question, but only if I weigh my words carefully.

"Why carry them at all, then?"

Kennan rolls her eyes. "The daggers are ceremonial. Cathal presents them to us upon completion of our training, when we're formally inducted into the ranks. If you want one so badly, I suggest you complete your test."

I nod obediently and shift my grip on the crossbow, letting it dip toward the ground briefly. The action affords me a momentary glance at Kennan's boots. The ceremonial golden dagger is conspicuously absent.

That could be coincidence, I reason, hefting the crossbow upward to aim it. Something twists up inside me. Maybe I was wrong about Niall—maybe wearing the dagger isn't a requirement after all—and I have no lead, and I'm spinning aimlessly. Ma's killer could just as easily have been Kennan—or Ravod. Or someone else entirely that the three of them are protecting.

My breath turns heavy as I try to angle the crossbow. The image of Ravod driving the golden dagger into my mother's chest flashes through my mind. My hands tremble. I don't understand why the possibility of him being the culprit bothers me so much.

The inadvertent action causes the crossbow to fire accidentally, and I gasp, squeezing my eyes shut as the bolt flies free at an alarming velocity. When I open them, the bolt is sticking out of the dirt a few feet away.

"I suppose it was too hopeful of me to think you might hit *something.*" Kennan sneers and signals the servant to reload the crossbow.

I want to explain that the crossbow is too heavy. My arms have started to grow tired simply from holding the wood and metal apparatus upright. A glance toward Kennan makes it clear this would not be a good idea. I swallow my words as the servant retrieves the bolt and rearms the crossbow for me.

I heft the weapon to eye level. The muscles in my arms strain under the weight bearing on them, making it difficult to keep steady.

A Telling. I need to do a Telling, somehow moving the mirror for a clear shot at the target. Or am I supposed to make the bolt fly around it? I bite my lip, trying to fight back my uncertainty before my hands start shaking more furiously than they already are.

I pull the trigger.

The bolt flies faster than my thoughts. I have no time to figure out what to do before it ricochets off the mirror's ornate silver frame and spins harmlessly off to the side of the range. The servant dutifully hurries to fetch it.

I lower the crossbow. My aching arms are grateful, but I grimace. Maybe it's not the power of Telling that drives people mad, but the training.

Hours pass. My arms and legs are numb. Bolt after bolt is expended. Most miss. One cracks the mirror near the top left corner. Kennan sips her tea, brought by another servant.

I take a moment of respite between reloading to stretch my neck a bit. A flash of red hair strikes the corner of my eye. My pulse quickens as I shift my gaze, careful not to turn my head and risk Kennan seeing I'm distracted.

Niall is walking to the back of the range and disappears quickly behind a door that's nearly lost in shadows.

As the servant reloads the crossbow for the hundredth time, I lower my voice to a whisper. "Where does that door go?" I tilt my head.

"That's the men's barracks, my lady," the servant replies in the same hushed tone.

The men's barracks. If I want more information on Niall, that's where I'm most likely to find it. My mind races, puzzling how to get Kennan to free me for the day.

I risk a glance in her direction. Kennan lowers her teacup onto its saucer, glaring venomously. "You're not done until *I* say so." Her voice splits the quiet like the crack of a whip. I breathe in hard through my teeth and pull up the crossbow. The ache in my arms renews itself.

Perhaps I could just make a run for it and hope for the best . . .

You never think things through, Fiona's voice whispers in my head. I nod imperceptibly. I'm at High House. Impulsive antics will not serve me here. I can't afford to take chances.

If I'm to sneak into the men's barracks, I need a plan.

I pull my old white shirt over my training gear and tuck my hair into the collar. It's a rudimentary disguise, but enough to pass for a servant out of the corner of someone's eye. The servants may as well be invisible to the Bards. If they regard them at all, it is in much the same way they look at all commoners, with cold detachment.

The sun has not yet risen as I make my way through the dark halls. Torches have burned low; sentries are switching shifts. The few people I see are too mired in the early morning haze to notice anything amiss with an errant servant. And it's a good thing, because I find myself turned around in the darkened corridors, passing the same sconces and closed doors I passed only minutes ago.

When Ravod guided me to my rooms, the layout seemed vast, but logical. But now, alone and in the dusty quiet of early morning, the walls seem to waver and shift around me, and worry begins to tremble in my gut. Maybe this wasn't such a great idea. Underneath it all is the hum of chanting—certain guards must never rest, because when all else is silent, you can hear their chants no matter the hour.

I try to listen more closely to the rhythm to keep

my mind calm, but the quiet sound of sniffling breaks through the chanting. A soft whimper. A cry for help, almost inaudible, as if muffled by a door somewhere far down the hall.

Kieran. It's Kieran crying. He's all alone and he needs me. It's foolish, but I can't shake the thought.

I hurry along the hall and push open the door where the sound is coming from, but no one is there. The sound vanishes, and I'm by myself in an empty vestibule. I have to wonder if I imagined it in my loneliness. My brother. Kieran. Dead nearly five years.

What is wrong with you, Shae?

Emotion claws at my throat as I push through another door. I've exited out onto one of the terraces overlooking the training grounds. I heave a sigh of relief and grip the balcony railing, trying to gather myself together.

Below me, the training grounds look like a ghostly, vanished lake at this hour. There are still a few stars flickering in the fading charcoal of the sky.

I slip down the stairs from the terrace and out onto the training grounds, my legs abruptly screaming in protest when I try to run across the field. My body is too sore and exhausted to manage anything more than a light jog down to the archery range, the stairs leading down the cliffside even more treacherous in the predawn darkness. I feel as if I'm descending into an abyss of smoky mist.

I take up a spot I scouted earlier behind one of the targets, out of sight, but with a clear view of the door to the barracks. I steady my breathing and wait. The door opens not long after, and the Bards file out, some alone, others casually chatting with one another, on their way to the dining hall for breakfast, giving me just enough time to look around.

Niall's red hair is instantly recognizable, if a little mussed from sleep. He yawns.

"Heading back into the field again?" another Bard asks him.

"You know me." Niall chuckles in response, adjusting the bag slung over his shoulder. "Can't stay still in the castle too long before I go stir-crazy."

So he'll be leaving High House to collect more tithes or recruits. *Or do more harm to other innocent victims.*

I chance a peek around the side of the target, angling my head to get a look at Niall's feet.

Still no dagger.

From what I've seen, the Bards display the hilt in their boots almost like a badge of honor. That Kennan and Niall both forgo wearing theirs, whatever the reason, is unusual at best—damning at worst.

I duck back into my hiding spot, waiting for the dining hall rush to die down. After the last few Bards have trickled through the door, I wait a few minutes longer to ensure the coast is clear.

The door to the barracks is not kept locked. Getting inside was the easy part of the plan. Now I have to find Niall's quarters, and anything that might suffice as evidence, before someone finds me.

Perhaps he keeps trophies from his doings and conquests. Maybe I'll find a bloodied sleeve, or the Gondalese ox that was taken from our home. Something. *Anything.*

The door from the shooting range empties into a large common room of dark stone. Comfortable chairs and a few tables littered with discarded goblets, wine bottles, and card games fill the space. These quarters are far vaster than where the women are housed, which makes sense, as there are so few of us comparatively. The air in here smells of ash and musk. Stuffed heads of various hunting game are mounted on the walls. Deer, coyote, wolves, even a mountain lion. A buffalo's head is prominently displayed over the mantle of the large stone fireplace.

A staircase leads to a landing at the far side of the room, and I head up, trying to keep my footsteps quiet in case there's anyone still present. When I reach the top, I'm led through another door.

For a second, I'm caught between the immense satisfaction that I managed to reach the barracks and anxious uncertainty as to how I'll ever find what I'm looking for here—there's too much to search. The largest corner of the room is reserved for an array of military bunk beds, shelved three by three in wide rows. At the foot of each are footlockers for personal belongings. Farther down are stone cubicles, each with a cloth divider.

In this instance, I'm glad I'm not a man, I think.

Shaking away my distraction, I start to wander through the rows of bunks. Nerves and frustration coil tightly in my gut. I'm running out of time before I'm to meet with Kennan.

At the far end of the barracks is another fireplace. This one is unlit, and there's a small figure in black and white servant's clothes leaning over it, sweeping vigorously.

My heart hitches in my chest and I clutch my needles tightly, willing myself not to breathe. I step back, but in my surprise, the heel of my boot bumps into the nearest bedpost. The sound might as well have been a horn piercing the air, and I stumble backward onto the floor between the bunks.

I'm too late. The servant is hurrying over. She has a dark smudge of ash on her cheek, but I instantly recognize the younger girl with the dark, curly hair and the gap in her teeth. The one who served my breakfast a short eternity ago on my first day.

"Are you all right, my lord?" she asks, offering a hand to help me up. I accept reluctantly, letting her haul me to my feet. Despite her slight build, she's much stronger than she looks.

"I'm fine," I grumble. "No worse than the rest of this blasted week . . ."

"Oh, my lady! I didn't recognize you!" Her eyes widen with shock, her brow knitting. "You shouldn't be in here! It's not—"

"Not proper, I know."

"I'm only allowed in here to sweep the fireplaces,"

she says. "I could get in big trouble if we're not gone by the time the Lord Bards return."

"I need to find Niall's room," I say, hoping she proves trustworthy. "I'll be in and out, I promise."

The girl frowns, unsure. "Niall? He's the older, redheaded one?" I nod. "Oh, you're in completely the wrong place! But . . ." She trails off, one brow crooking upward. "Why are you going to his room?"

I pause, chewing my lip. My heart begins hammering when I think of the seconds passing by. "It's really important," I say urgently. "I need you to trust me, all right?"

The girl stands back on her heels. Her eyes narrow and she scratches the back of her neck near the cluster of dark, wild curls tied there. Seconds feel like they are creeping into hours as she stares me down, taking my measure.

"Just this once, I suppose," she says eventually. She doesn't wait for me to reply before she starts heading back to the front of the barracks, gesturing for me to follow.

"Wait," I say. "Thank you. What should I—what is your name?"

The girl blushes. "I'm . . ." She hesitates and I wonder if I've done something improper by asking for a servant's name. "Imogen," she says quietly.

"I'm Shae." I give a tentative smile as I walk behind her. "Thank you for trusting me, Imogen."

"We're women—we have to trust each other, right?" She grins over her shoulder, and I feel myself warm to her. It's exactly the thought I had. "I don't break the rules very often. It's a little exciting, isn't it?"

"I suppose so," I have to admit.

We pass bed after bed, and I realize there's another thing I would never admit to; the idea of being so close to where Ravod sleeps has me feeling jittery with nervous excitement. Some of the quarters have small personal touches adorning the space, flowers in vases or paintings on the wall. I wonder what Ravod's room would reveal. Maybe he likes art or collects something odd and obscure. There's more beneath his proper, dignified surface than he lets on, and I ache to learn what it is.

I sharply force my gaze forward. I'm not here for Ravod, even if he somehow manages to infiltrate my thoughts at the least convenient of times.

Imogen has a small spring in her step, and when we've reached the front of the room, her curly hair bounces happily against her back as she turns right, leading me toward the larger row of Bards' quarters.

"Only the junior Bards sleep in the bunks. The older ones get their own cubbies here," she explains, stopping along the second row and pointing to a drawn velvet curtain. "This is Niall's."

"Thank you again," I say, touching her slim shoulder briefly in hopes that I can project my sincerity through my hand somehow. "You should get out of here in case there's any trouble."

Imogen cocks her head. "But what about you?"

"I'll manage. I don't want you getting punished on

my account if something goes wrong." I can't help but feel protective of her.

"I'm nearly thirteen years old, you know. I can take care of myself," Imogen says, drawing herself to her full height, nearly the same as mine.

I sigh, but quickly realize I don't have time to argue. I offer a quick nod and dart behind the curtain.

The space is dim, and my eyes are slow to adjust. Eventually I see a lamp on the desk and manage to light it, sending shadows flickering across the dark.

Niall's quarters are much smaller than mine, with barely enough space for a single bed and a chest of drawers, both immaculately tidy and completely ascetic. They stand in stark contrast to the desk wedged in at the back, cluttered to the point where it's nearly impossible to know that it's a desk to begin with.

I halt in my tracks when I recognize the paraphernalia littering the surface. My breath stops short and my blood runs cold.

Papers . . . quills . . . books . . . *ink*.

I set my jaw, taking a hesitant step forward, remembering what Ravod told me when I arrived.

This isn't unusual. Some Bards are taught to read and write.

With another small step, I'm standing in front of the desk. Spread across the surface of the table is everything I've ever been taught to fear and revile. Suddenly I'm glad I skipped breakfast. I'm not sure my stomach would have been able to handle the sight otherwise.

My hand is trembling as I reach for the pile of

paper. I don't recognize any of the symbols on them, but there are a few diagrams that I can perhaps make sense of.

The drawings in the first pile provide little insight. Many of them look like cross-sections of various organs and body parts, which does not do much to settle my stomach. Many of the words on these pages are crossed out and corrected, but I can't understand anything more by the illustrations.

There's a second stack, more neatly piled and sorted, tucked into the cover of one of the books. I pull at the loose papers, terrified of touching the book itself. I sigh in relief when the pages come free and nothing happens.

I'm shaking so much that I have to sit on the bed to steady myself while I look the papers over.

These are very different, but I recognize what they are immediately: Maps. Delicate symbols cover each page, the detail painstaking, and every landmark carefully labeled. Niall had the look of a traveler about him, but apparently he's also a passionate cartographer. These are sketches of the places he's traveled: rock formations, wooded groves, mountain ranges—each rendered with flawless precision, almost lovingly.

I find myself staring at a picture of a valley ringed by mountains with a dirt road running through it. It reminds me so much of home. If there were only a little house on the path . . .

My hands abruptly grip the paper.

There *is* a house. *My* house. The space it takes up in the rest of the drawing is small, but the details are unmistakable. There's a circle and some words with an arrow pointing right at my home.

The next piece of paper is another map, this one of Aster. I would know it anywhere. I can follow the road through the gates past the constable's tower, through the center of town and Fiona's shop and up the hill to Mads's family's mill. To the north is the pass that leads to my home, marked with a cross in red, like a splash of blood.

Blood pounds in my ears, echoed by the sound of heavy, approaching footsteps. I spring to my feet, folding the papers of my home and pushing them into my pocket and quickly shoving the others back into the book where I found them. I move to the curtain.

I need to get out of here. *Now.*

My hip bumps a small end table as I hasten to leave, toppling an empty brandy bottle. It smashes deafeningly on the stone floor.

"What was that?" a voice booms out from down the hall. I crouch to hide it, trying first to pick up the pieces, before resorting to pushing the broken glass under the bed, wincing as a sharp edge slices my finger.

I rush back to the curtain, my heartbeat reverberating in my ears.

"Good morning, my lord!" Imogen's voice stops me in my tracks. The sound of footsteps outside ceases. "Back so soon?"

"I forgot something." I gulp as I recognize Niall's voice.

I look around, desperate for a place to hide. A cold sweat breaks out on my forehead when I see no options. The desk is too small. The bed is too low. The corner is too exposed.

If only I could perform a Telling. I flex my fingers, trying to force them into feeling the strange sensation that always happened accidentally.

Nothing. The footsteps are coming closer.

"Actually, my lord," Imogen's voice interrupts, "I saw a mouse in the corridor. Would you help me get rid of it? I promise it won't take long."

The silence that passes threatens to crush me into the floor.

"Very well." Niall sighs. "Let's make this quick."

Imogen's and Niall's footsteps disappear around the opposite corner and I exhale slowly.

I slip out of the barracks quickly and quietly. I definitely need to embroider something nice for Imogen.

By the time I approach the training grounds, the sun has finally arisen, and I already feel like I've completed a day's worth of activity from my foray into the men's barracks. I try to dispel my exhaustion with a deep breath of cold morning air. My stomach rumbles irritably, reminding me that I've skipped breakfast.

I slip my fingers into my pocket, touching the papers I stole from Niall's room. I'm one step closer, at least.

I stop at the usual place at the edge of the training grounds where I've met Kennan every day this week. I forget if five days have passed or six. They've all started to bleed together, and I don't know if I'm making progress or floundering completely. Kennan is unreadable, and I feel no closer to understanding my own power—if I truly have any.

"You're still here?" A deep, melodic voice startles me. I turn to see Ravod standing nearby, his arms crossed over his chest, and an indecipherable smile playing at one side of his mouth. I wonder if he realizes that his words have the opposite of their intended effect. The more he taunts or warns me, the more determined I am. I want to see the look in his eyes when I prove him wrong.

"Prepare to lose your bet, Ravod," I say, pleased that I sound more confident than I feel. I'm actually pleased that he's here at all. And curious where he's been all week. "I'm not going anywhere."

Ravod's eyes wander my face, either in amusement or skepticism. "We'll see." His brow creases. "What happened?"

I follow Ravod's gaze to the long cut running along the side of my finger. My breath hitches as I recall the wound I got from sneaking into Niall's room.

"An accident." I clutch my hand, as if pulling it out of sight will somehow cause him to forget he saw it.

"You should probably put something on it," Ravod says. "You don't want it getting infected." Before I can reply, he produces a small vial from a pouch on his belt. "May I?"

I let him take my hand, perhaps a little too eagerly. His fingers are warm through the fabric of his gloves.

"You just carry disinfectant around with you?" I ask him.

"My mother was a physician in—" He cuts himself off abruptly, turning my hand over and applying a few drops of cold liquid to my wound. His dark eyes are steady and focused, more magnetic than usual in their intensity. The medicine stings and my hand flinches in his. He gently squeezes my palm to keep me from disturbing the wound. "I used to help out a little in her clinic. Old habits die hard, I suppose. Hold still so it can sink in."

"Did you want to be a physician too?" I can't help asking questions. This is the first time he's been open with me.

Ravod shrugs. "I probably would have taken over the clinic eventually. But I definitely don't have her bedside manner."

"As your patient, I think you did all right." I smile at him. "Your mother . . . She sounds like a really remarkable person."

The tiniest smile turns the corner of his mouth. "She was," he whispers. "She's . . . gone now."

His hand trembles against mine, like a small,

wounded forest creature. I worry he'll pull away, but he doesn't. His gaze is fixed on the point where our hands meet as though such a thing is completely strange and foreign.

"I lost my mother too," I say softly. "I know how much it hurts."

His eyes lock onto mine, widening fractionally with emotion. I'm not sure if it is because of what I told him the other night, or some other old hurt, but he forces himself to look away, clearing his throat.

"There are fates besides death," he whispers. His voice barely carries over the wind in the mountains. "There are many ways someone precious to you can't be here anymore."

"So keeping medicine with you makes it feel like she's still with you?"

Ravod abruptly drops my hand and replaces the vial in its pouch. I pushed too far. "That should stave off infection and help prevent scarring," he says. "You should try to be more careful in the future."

His eyes flick to the side; Kennan is approaching. He nods tightly to her before walking away, and as I watch his tall, broad form retreat, it takes all my willpower to keep from following.

Even if I didn't find him intriguing, just about anyone in the world would be more pleasant to spend time with than Kennan.

"I've decided to try a different approach today," Kennan says without preamble, as I've come to expect from her. "Come with me."

She scarcely breaks stride, immediately leading me off the training grounds, back toward the main entrance to the Bards' Wing. This time, she leads me past the usual spaces to a large gate at the back that enters into a dark tunnel.

A gust of frigid wind is channeled through the stone, and I shiver. Only dim torch fire lights the path, making it difficult to keep my footing on the uneven ground. After a few dizzying twists and turns, Kennan stops by a second gate and swings it open.

I step down a small flight of narrow stairs. We've been deposited into a corridor cut from the stone behind the southern waterfall that ends in a terrifying precipice. The waterfall is a giant curtain wreathed in white mist, blocking the tunnel off. Torches don't work here because of the vapor in the air. Instead, the space is lit with small, luminescent stones set in a snake scale–like pattern on the walls. Each one is the same pale amber of Kennan's eyes, making me feel like there are dozens of her judging me instead of only one.

"This place is beautiful," I breathe.

"I'm glad you think so," Kennan says. "If today is anything like the rest of this interminable week, we're going to be here a good long while."

I don't want to admit it, but she's probably right.

"You're not going to ask me to jump off the cliff, right?" I ask hesitantly.

"Your task is simple." She nods to the waterfall. "Part the water."

"What?" I ask, turning to the enormous wall of crashing water. "I thought all the tasks were extensions of my natural abilities. You said Telling is magnifying what we already know we can do. But making water separate? That's . . ." *Impossible,* I want to say. But Kennan caused the ground to tremble and part. That, too, was impossible. Still, what she's asking—that should be expert Bard-level Telling, not something for a trainee like me.

Kennan sighs, as if reading my mind. "Water already has the desire to flow, but it also has the ability to take whatever shape you give it, unlike air, which drifts away, or earth, which is naturally shy and resists change. Telling is the act of altering what the world *around* you is capable of. Water is the easiest element to command." She says these things like they are common facts, as simple as the sky being blue. "Even the lowliest of Bards are able to master this." She leans against the side of the cavern wall. "Luckily, you have severely lowered my expectations." She pauses. "Put yourself *inside* the water."

I walk nervously to the edge. Does she want me to dive into the waterfall? The current looks deadly, and I don't even know how to swim . . .

I turn back toward her, abject terror probably obvious on my face, because she laughs. "No, not your *body.* Put your mind inside the water. Feel what it feels. Urge it to part. Urge it to do what it already wants to do—to make space. To conform to your touch."

As Kennan is explaining, her face transforms. Gone

is her usual sternness, and in its place is something else, something that almost resembles softness, as if she were talking about an old friend, instead of a waterfall. But it soon passes and she's back to scowling.

I scowl back, first at Kennan and then the waterfall, but both ignore me. Finally, I take a deep breath.

If the lowliest Bard can do this, how hard can it be?

Time elapses strangely when exhaustion takes hold.

Kennan settles into a nook in the cave when I continually fail to part the water. The simple act of trying to finish a thought feels like I have to drag it up to the surface of a murky bog. Most of the time, it slips and falls back to the bottom, lost in a haze of dark water.

"Again."

Her voice is like nails being driven into the base of my skull; I'm too exhausted to think.

"I'm talking to you, peasant." Kennan draws herself to her full, considerable height. Her lip curls in a snarl that tugs upward. *"Again."*

"You say water is so impressionable." My voice is a whisper as I clutch my pounding head. It echoes with the pulse of the water, a solid beat that I have no power to control. "But just because something is fluid, does not make it obedient."

"Is that so?" Curiosity blooms in Kennan's expression. She maintains her scowl and folded arms, but

I see her knuckles relax. "Challenging my expertise are you, peasant? Do your ten minutes of experience give you a wealth of knowledge I'm somehow not privy to?"

"Of course not." I grit my teeth to keep the pounding from overcoming me. "I just . . ." What if I've been looking at it all wrong? I stare at the rush of falling water, feel its power as it races away from me. Images of Aster flash through my mind: the swell of people clamoring and climbing over one another at the Bards' arrival. Drawn to the graceful force with which their bodies move, closer and closer to the dream of escape.

"If I cannot force the water to change course . . ." I murmur. My fingers grip the needles hidden in my pocket. On the edges of the corridor is a loose segment of large rock, barely hanging against the thud of water running over it. I tap, tap, tap the needle, the pounding in my head matching the pounding of the water as I twist the idea into words. "What if there was incentive for it to move?" I walk closer until I am directly under the rock and let my fingers skim the sting of water. I imagine the great crack of thunder, the life-bringing rain the Bards brought to Aster, changing the entire focus and flow of the crowds as they stopped to look up and witness it.

Kennan gasps, and the next thing I feel is the biting squeeze of her nails clawing into the soft flesh of my neck, jerking me back. I scream as I stagger and fall to my knees.

But the crack of thunder is loud above me. It continues to grow as the segment of rock I was standing under crashes down into the exact spot where I'd been standing, obstructing the water's original path.

I gape in terror as I scramble away and the water rolls down both sides of the rock, changing its course, splashing over my feet.

I *did it*.

At least, I think.

"Are you trying to kill yourself?" Kennan's enraged face breaks my trance. Her cheeks are inflamed, and she's wiping something from her hands. Is that my blood? "You stupid, reckless—"

"But I did it." I make no move to get up from the wet ground. Instead, I relish it, allowing the cool water to soothe the pain in my temples. A laugh emerges as I continue to look up at the gaping hole the rock left. "I . . . I did it!"

"Almost killing yourself in the process." The rage in her voice startles me. "You *must* learn to control yourself. If you can't control yourself, you can't hope to control anything else." She points to the waterfall. "The objective was not to cause a collapse of the corridor. It was to focus on the water."

"Well, doing it *your* way wasn't working." I hold her gaze and stand, feeling brave. Within Kennan's rage is something else, something akin to fear. I dig into it. "Perhaps a new way of thinking is needed around here."

In a breath, Kennan is on me, her clawlike fingers reaching for me, ready to tear out my traitorous tongue. I flinch, readying myself for her reprisal.

The sound of deliberate clapping breaks through our tension and forces Kennan to freeze, her hands centimeters from my neck.

Someone is . . . *applauding*?

A figure steps out from the shadows of the cavern. Cathal.

"Bravo, Shae." He smiles at me. "I am suitably impressed."

Kennan silently curls in on herself as she retracts her hands and bows. Cathal acknowledges her with a scowl. I slump to my knees, too fatigued to stand upright.

Cathal appraises the scene in front of us. His elegant clothes and sharp eyes shimmer in the light.

"I thank you, Kennan, for your time," he says, "but I believe your services are no longer required."

Kennan moves to argue, but Cathal takes a step forward, his attention fully on me. "Now, if you would be so kind, I would like to have a word with my newest Bard in private."

He knows. He knows I snuck into Niall's quarters.

And he heard I'm failing my Bard training. He realizes this has been a terrible mistake. He finally sees the truth—I'm not gifted, but cursed—and I'm going to pay for it. I'll be thrown out, or made an example of.

He'll reconsider having me executed.

I can't stop shaking. I rub my arms, trying to keep calm as I follow Cathal. The castle seems busier the farther we walk, with servants and guards rushing to and fro. They all glance nervously at Cathal as he passes, as though worried he's there to assess their work. Clearly, I am not the only one on edge.

Cathal only slows his stride when a chamberlain falls in step with us, wringing his hands as he speaks. From a few steps behind, I can hear their conversation, but that doesn't seem to bother Cathal. His calm demeanor doesn't falter even for a moment, as usual.

"It's simply *dreadful*, Lordship." The chamberlain is nearly frantic. "In all my years, I've never seen a gallery so dusty!"

"I am sure it is an absolute tragedy. I am more interested in our security issue, however," Cathal replies. "The report I was given mentioned our guards would be insufficient."

"For retinues as large as Ambassador Richter's *and* the archbishop's, yes," the chamberlain replies, growing more flustered, if even possible. "We simply do not have enough security present for a fête of this size!"

"Requisition forces from outside," Cathal states. "The usual candidates ought to suffice."

The chamberlain bows with a dramatic flourish before departing. Cathal glances over his shoulder at me with his customary disarming smile.

"The trials and tribulations of throwing a ball for foreign dignitaries." He chuckles. For a moment, I forget the possibility that I'm in huge trouble.

We arrive at our destination far too quickly, and my apprehension from before crashes over me in a wave. High House has a way of expanding and contracting, or maybe my nervousness is making time rush forward. Well before I'm ready, a massive door is opening in front of us.

"Please make yourself comfortable." Cathal gestures with a flourish as I step inside a different sitting room than last time. The ceiling is an intricate glass dome that seems to beckon golden sunlight into the room. Elegant hothouse orchids, strategically placed around chaise longues, complete the illusion that we're sitting outdoors.

My eyes dart around, attempting to figure out where we are while trying not to be distracted by the splendor.

"Thank you." I bite my lip slightly and gratefully sink onto one of the cushions. It's so soft, I want to melt into it. The clouds have assumed a pink hue through the dome above. I must have been trying to part the waterfall the entire day.

"First things first," he says. "I have a very important question for you, Shae, if you will indulge me." Cathal gracefully seats himself across from me, a serious look in his eyes. I stiffen, bracing myself for the inevitable. *You are a disappointment, Shae. A fake.* "Do you like olives?" he asks. There's a tiny smile playing at his lips.

I am so startled, I'm pretty certain my jaw nearly falls off its hinges. "I'm not sure I've had any," I reply awkwardly.

"We will have to change that," he says. I shiver slightly, unsure how to feel right now. Am I in trouble or not? "Do you have a favorite food? I can have it sent for. You must be hungry."

"Famished," I correct him with a slight grimace, which broadens his smile.

"Do not be shy asking for anything you want. It is my honor to provide it," Cathal says. "Duck, perhaps? Moose cheese? Both?"

"Both?"

"Both it is." He claps his hands twice and another servant hiding nearby scurries away. He grins boyishly at me. "I know you are humoring me, Shae. I appreciate it."

"Well, now I'm curious about this moose cheese," I admit.

"Curiosity *and* a sense of humor?" Cathal laughs. "Rare traits in a Bard. Hang on to those."

My eyebrows shoot up. Ravod said the opposite. I bite my tongue to keep from asking why. Ravod also told me to be careful around Cathal, but I'm beginning to wonder about that too. Cathal's company is the most reassuring in this whole place.

"My lord, why did you ask me here?" I blurt out. I don't know if I mean right this minute, or the bigger question of why he put his faith in me at all, thinking I, of all people, could be a Bard.

A servant appears with a tray heaped with smooth brown almonds, shiny olives, moist cheeses, colorful fruit, and all sorts of delicacies I've never eaten. He bows as he places the tray before us and then leaves.

"Something concerning has come to my attention," Cathal says, and I swallow nervously. I long to devour the food, but my throat is constricting with fear. "I have been closely observing your performance. I am—to put it mildly—displeased."

I'm suddenly so ill at ease, I fear I am going to burst out sobbing. "I . . . I'm sorry," I muster.

"What? Do not be sorry. I am not displeased with *you*. What displeases me is the manner in which Kennan has been conducting your tests."

"My tests? How so?" My pulse is racing. Maybe this meeting is not a referendum on me but on *her*. Is it possible he sees how cruel she has been?

"Her daily reports to me state that your talents are meager at best," he goes on. "I believe this to be false."

I stare at him, speechless. When I am unable to look him in the eyes any longer, I glance away, only to realize Imogen has come into the room and begun to quietly dust a pedestal with an ornate statue on it. A shudder of relief goes through me when I see her face. She gives me a small wink over her shoulder.

Cathal calmly watches me. "In your most recent session, I noticed Kennan went to great lengths to undermine you." *Understatement,* I think. "In the waterfall cave, I witnessed it firsthand. I know what she was doing to you."

I pause, watching Cathal carefully. A tiny, disarming smile continues to play at the corners of his mouth. Cathal is so different from everyone else at High House. He's open and honest while everyone else is closed off, hostile. My eyes sear with unshed tears as I recall the bet against my sanity, Ravod's harsh words when I first arrived, and the hatred in Kennan's eyes over the past week.

"I don't understand." My brow knits.

Cathal waves his hand. Imogen slips from the room, and we are alone once more.

"Kennan was performing a Counter-Telling," he says.

"A what?"

"She used the tea to disguise the movement of her lips, but from where I stood, it was obvious what she was up to. She was performing her own Tellings to prevent yours from succeeding. Quite skillfully, but that is beside the point. It would seem she is threatened by your gift."

What he's saying makes my gut lurch uncomfortably. Cathal may still believe in me, but Kennan hasn't just been cruel, she's been purposefully causing me to fail. In my shock, I don't know whether to be furious at her or terrified of what this means, for either her or myself. I shouldn't care after how she's treated me, but it sends a tremor of worry through me. Will she be punished?

Cathal leans back into his settee. "Relax, Shae. That you were able to perform at all today shows me that you are far more adept with the gift than Kennan let on."

"I know Kennan isn't exactly fond of me, but why would she do that?"

"If someone were to look into it, I would be very interested in knowing the answer to that question as well." I frown, unable to read Cathal's tone. "Nevertheless, I can confirm for you with great certainty that things are going to be very different going forward. You will be provided with a new trainer. Someone who will not be so petty as to sabotage your progress. You have enough to worry about." His tone shifts to cautionary. "Not all the dangers of being a Bard come from without, after all. Some lie within."

"The madness," I say, a low waver in my voice, as if speaking the words louder will somehow bring it upon me. Cathal nods.

"I see a lot of myself in you, Shae. Perhaps it is what compels me to help you reach your full potential. I want you to succeed." He sighs, his eyes piercing into mine. "I, too, understand what it is like to be different. To be cut off from the rest of the world. To be alone." His voice quivers slightly around the final syllable. My body relaxes. I felt the same way in Aster.

"At home, everyone thought I was cursed," I say quietly. "They hated me. I had precious few friends who would treat me like I was a human being."

Cathal gives me a grim smile. "Sometimes being extraordinary is to be extraordinarily lonely."

It's strange to think I have something in common with the Lord of High House. Even stranger that he thinks I am extraordinary.

Cathal leans forward on his knees and watches me, his face serious. His translucent gray eyes search mine.

"The death of your mother must have been very difficult," he says.

Tears spring in my eyes, and I swiftly blink them away.

"I would love to know more about your home," he says.

"I can't imagine how a place like Aster could possibly interest you," I admit. "It's just a small town on the plains. Most of us are simple villagers going about our lives."

The corner of Cathal's mouth curves upward. "Simple villagers do not often leave their simple villages," he points out. "Much less infiltrate my castle and become Bards. I get the distinct impression that there is much more to you than you let on, Shae. I would very much like to hear the whole story." Cathal grimaces. "I do not mean to pry. You need not share anything you do not wish to. I have no desire to make you uncomfortable."

"No," I interject. "I'm not uncomfortable." In truth, my only current fear is that Cathal will realize I'm not as interesting as he thinks and will refuse to help me after all.

"Wonderful." Cathal seems relieved. "My curiosity can be off-putting to some."

"In my experience, curiosity and trouble often go hand in hand." I allow myself a chuckle, thinking back on the mishaps that led me here.

"Indulge me, then," Cathal says. "Start from the beginning."

I take a deep breath, and before I know it, I'm sharing everything from my upbringing in Aster, the accidental Tellings I performed with my embroidery, my assumption I was cursed, to the Telling I snuck out to see. From there, I describe Ma's murder and the strange cover-up. I disclose again my suspicions that a Bard must be involved. I go on to describe how I left Aster and my journey. Cathal listens with rapt attention to all of it.

When I finish, his eyes are wide, twinkling with attentiveness. "So . . . Do you believe me?" I ask.

There's an expression I can't quite read on his face. His dark brows are furrowed, his lips pressed to a thin line.

"Every word." His statement is slow, deliberate. Sincere.

I breathe a sigh of relief. The air in my lungs feels lighter. My indignation from when I talked to Constable Dunne and Fiona about Ma's death fades. It doesn't matter that they chose to think I'm crazy. *Cathal* is the one I needed to convince. His opinion on this is the only one that matters. And he *believes* me.

I feel a sting at the corners of my eyes. This time, I don't blink them away. For so long I'd been keeping everything bottled up and secret because I was afraid. I was so afraid . . .

Cathal gets up when my hands rise to wipe my tears away. He steps elegantly around the table and kneels in front of me, gently taking my hands. His aristocratic fingers are soft and warm as he rubs his thumbs over my knuckles.

Pa used to hold my hands like this, when I was a little girl. If I scraped my knee playing or got in a fight with Kieran. The hands are different, but the feeling is the same.

"Cry if you need to, Shae," Cathal says softly. "You have been through a lot."

I sniff as a tear falls onto my lap. "Thank you," I whisper.

Once my breath steadies, he releases my hands and gets to his feet. He begins to slowly pace the room, rubbing the dark silver stubble on his chin, deep in thought.

"There are hundreds of Bards," he says. "Each would be capable of hiding what they have done. But there *is* a way to discover the truth and bring about the justice you seek. However, it will take patience. And I will need your help to do it."

A flood of gratitude rushes through me. He holds my gaze, unblinking, for a long while before his eyes flick away.

"Why me though?" Surely there must be someone more experienced he can put his faith in.

"I have a bit of a gift for spotting talent." He quirks his head. "What you did at the waterfall is, shall we say, different. Inspired. Same as the day you first arrived. There is something very special about you, Shae. And our task requires someone special."

I *think* it's a compliment, but can't help fearing Cathal is misled in believing in my talent. I have hardly proven myself. But if Kennan really has been holding me back, there's a chance I don't know my own strength, as Cathal says.

"What do I need to do?"

When he speaks again, his voice is barely above a whisper. "You will need to find the *Book of Days*," he says. "And I will teach you how to read it, understand it, and use it."

The quiet, pale dawn heralds a new day. A fresh start. Bathed in the pinkish gray glow of morning, I almost feel like yesterday was a dream.

The *Book of Days*.

I recall Cathal's intense gaze. The conviction in his voice. *It is the repository of all truth, brought to our land by the First Rider. In its pages is the record of everything we know. The fabric upon which all reality is shaped.*

A shudder had gone through me at his words. Of course I'd heard of the *Book*. Who hasn't? It's part of nearly every legend. All of history. All the future. It is existence itself. A product of Telling so great, it is beyond human comprehension.

But no one has ever laid eyes on such a book. It is as fantastical as Gondal.

When I said as much, Cathal simply smirked. "It is safer," he said, "for the world to believe the *Book* is not real, than to realize that such power, such greatness, exists. It is our responsibility to protect it. The people cannot always be trusted with the truth. We would have raids. Riots. The poor and hungry masses trying to get their hands on the *Book*, to destroy it, or worse, to *use* it. Imagine if the entire reality of Montane landed in the wrong hands."

It was a terrifying thought. Could it be true? Why would he make something like that up? This was the ruler of Montane, the leader of the Bards of High House. And he believed in me. Wanted to help me.

The truth about your mother is waiting on the pages of that book, he said.

According to Cathal, the *Book of Days* lives somewhere beneath High House, in a labyrinth protected by an ancient power. Only an incredibly gifted Bard can navigate through the spells of protection, to its heart.

"I have done all I can on my own," he told me. "The Tellings placed upon the labyrinth are unlike anything we currently understand. My last attempt to solve it nearly killed me. I realized during my lengthy convalescence that this is not something I can do myself. I have to place my trust in someone else. Someone who is daring enough to face these obstacles and clever enough to overcome them. Someone extraordinarily gifted. Someone like you."

I scan the grounds, searching for my new trainer, and reeling at the idea that I am, right this very moment, perched above such a profound source of power and truth. Try as I might to focus on anything else, my mind wanders back to yesterday.

Could this book really be my answer? I spent most of the night unable to sleep, trying to imagine such a thing.

Books are evil. Writing is dangerous.

"You're still here." A voice startles me from my thoughts. I whirl around.

Ravod. A tightness in my chest forms, squeezing the breath from my lungs.

"So I am." I clear my throat. "My condolences on losing your bet."

"A shame." Ravod shakes his head. "I was planning to spend the money on something silly and frivolous. I hope you're pleased that your sanity has cost me the fancy hat of my dreams."

"What happened to 'eradicating your sense of humor,' Ravod?" I ask, narrowing my eyes at him with a laugh.

"Who says I'm joking?" The corner of his mouth quirks up and his dark eyes shimmer. Even the barest hint of a smile on his face makes the air feel warmer. Yet before I can relax into the camaraderie, he waves his hand and turns on his heel. "But today we have a different task at hand." Ravod looks over his shoulder, beckoning me. "Ready?"

"Ready?" I repeat, confused. "I'm supposed to be meeting my new instructor."

Ravod nods. "And here I am."

"Wait." My breath hitches. I shake my head, starting over. "*You're* my new trainer?"

"Don't sound too disappointed," Ravod says. "Cathal thought you might be more comfortable with someone familiar to you. He's taken quite an interest in you."

"He approached *me,* for your information." I don't

understand why I feel the need to explain myself to Ravod.

"Spare me the details. I'm familiar with your capacity to follow instructions," he says. "Cathal suggested a change of pace for your next lesson." *How much did Cathal relay to him?* I wonder.

"Where are we going?" I ask, realizing we're not headed toward the training grounds at all.

"You'll see." He gestures me to follow him back into the Bards' Wing.

Ravod is quiet as we walk along multiple passages through the underbelly of the mountain, much like the ones that led to the waterfall cavern. I can hear the distant roar of crashing water.

Our journey concludes before a gate at the back of the main courtyard. The sun has started to crest the mountaintops, bathing the marble in golden light.

"I've requisitioned horses," Ravod says. He comes to a halt near the center of the courtyard. "To take us out to the wasteland by the lake."

"We're leaving High House?" I stop close to his side. Panic grips me. Bandits are out there. What if I lose sight of Ravod and wind up alone and in danger again? It's irrational, but fear overpowers my senses anyway.

The courtyard, while beautiful, begins to feel as if it's closing in on me. The shrubbery looms large and ominous. The empty gazes of numerous elegant statues fill every space, leaving no room to breathe. I gasp, choking for air, convinced my chest is an instant away from bursting.

"Take a deep, slow breath." Ravod's voice is gentle. His kindness is hard to absorb after my ordeal with Kennan. "It's okay to be overwhelmed. And it's okay to take some time to breathe when you are."

It takes a second to remember how to let air in. My heart slows. Air leaves my mouth and the court-yard expands.

"Thanks," I mutter, pushing back sweaty strands of my hair. "It was like everything just hit me at once . . ."

Ravod's eyes linger on mine and I freeze. His expression is open and warm. It almost makes me lose my breath all over again.

The sound of hooves turns my head as two stable hands approach, each leading a beautiful horse. Instantly, Ravod's cold mask slips back in place. He strides toward a large black mare, the same one from when we met in Aster. She whinnies happily when she sees him.

I mount the other horse, a bay gelding. Ravod takes an apple piece from his pocket and feeds it to his mare before he mounts with effortless grace.

"Shall we?" he asks, taking the lead toward the main gate. I watch him, before heaving a sigh and following.

The trip down the mountain takes less time than I remember, but perhaps it's only the shift in my nerves. Ravod and I have slipped into silence; the only sounds are the wind whistling against the mountainside and the clapping of horseshoes against the road.

The sun has reached its peak by the time we fully descend into the plains. I expect them to be much the way I left them: dry and dusty. But I stifle a gasp at what lies before me.

Brown grass and dull rocks scatter the path ahead, uninterrupted but for a few gray, skeletal trees. The emptiness is somehow even more chilling than it was from the training grounds high above.

Ravod turns his horse off the road, and I follow. I watch him intently as he takes a deep, quiet breath and exhales. The deathly expanse doesn't seem to bother him. I begin to wonder if his idea to leave High House was more for his benefit or mine.

Ravod halts and dismounts, and I copy him. My legs ache as I hit the ground.

I had nearly forgotten how vast the plains are. But oddly, High House looks larger than ever from here, shrouded in the clouds above us. Its grandeur in the distance makes for a stark contrast.

"What happened here? Does Cathal know?" Surely if he did, he would have commissioned Bards to come and work their Tellings to make it better. This stretch of land is so close to High House, I'm surprised I didn't see it when I first came. I'm even more surprised that Cathal—or anyone—would be okay with these conditions. It's completely uninhabitable, as if a massive weapon detonated here long ago, withering the roots of anything that tried to grow. It is worse, even, than the desiccated portions of our pastures in Aster. And everyone knows we have one of the poorest villages in Montane. We are a blight upon our great nation.

Or so we were told. What I see now is that this desolation *is* Montane.

"Cathal is aware," Ravod answers, and I struggle to interpret the hardness of his tone.

"How can you stand it?" Anger coils inside me as my horse sniffs the ground timidly, looking for something to eat. But there is nothing but dust. "To live in such luxury while knowing that places like *this* exist?"

"We're not here to discuss me," Ravod says, a frown tugging at his mouth.

"Well, I know how much you enjoy being aloof and mysterious, but do you mind explaining to me what we're doing out here, then?" I ask, facing him.

Ravod's eyebrows shoot up in surprise.

"Mysterious? Really?"

"You're not going to contest that you're aloof?" I raise an eyebrow in turn.

Ravod rolls his eyes. "I can be sociable when the situation calls for it."

"So, never?" I can't stop the corner of my mouth turning up as I tease him. For the first time in a long while, something feels comfortable. Fun, even.

There's even a ghost of a smile playing at the

corners of Ravod's delicate mouth, just enough to cause the dimples on his cheeks to reappear. The sight is a tiny burst of lightning in my chest.

"I wasn't always a Bard. I wasn't even always in Montane . . ." He trails off, his amusement vanishing as his eyes turn distant. He gazes across the ruined landscape into a different time and place, his expression shifting between faint vestiges of thoughtfulness and longing. I watch him silently, wondering where he's gone and wishing I could go wherever he is.

"Ravod?" I step closer. "Hello?"

He shakes his head as he comes back to the present. "Sorry about that," he says.

I have to ask. "Where did you go just now?"

"I was thinking about my . . ." He clears his throat. "About the place where I grew up."

"Where did you grow up?"

Definitely the wrong question. His face snaps back into his usual steel trap of expressionlessness.

"We should focus on the task at hand," Ravod says. "I want to see what comes to you naturally, without prompting from me."

"I can perform any Telling I want?" I ask.

"As long as it accomplishes what I ask, yes," Ravod replies. "Let's see you turn the wasteland into a meadow."

"A meadow?" I take a hesitant step forward. The glare of the sun blurs the plains. "But how? There's nothing here." Kennan always had me manipulate or draw from what was already in place. Is it even possible to create something new?

I close my eyes, feeling the world around me as it is. I think back, summoning all the lessons I learned over the last week to tap into my ability to alter reality.

Starting the Telling feels a bit simpler now that Kennan isn't interfering with Counter-Tellings. The sensation of wading through a murky swamp to find my focus is gone; my thoughts crystallize with greater ease.

The seeds of doubt she planted are less easy to be rid of, however. I start to feel the telltale warmth in my fingers, but nothing more. I can't draw it out further. I'm almost afraid to try, worried that I'm only setting myself up for another failure. I flex my fingers, shifting my weight back and forth between my legs.

What Ravod is asking seems even more advanced and spectacular than parting the water back in the cavern. It makes Kennan seem downright reasonable.

"Focus on what you're trying to accomplish." I hear Ravod's voice and open my eyes. "If you want a meadow, try thinking about something that reminds you of meadows."

"That doesn't seem a little roundabout? Why not just think of a meadow?"

"Too literal." Ravod shakes his head. "That kind of thinking conjures illusions, nothing more. Spoken

228 — DYLAN FARROW

Tellings are impermanent, but still alter the truth of what's around us. Tethering the Telling to something real will lend it a basis in reality."

I consider his words and close my eyes again. My breath slows; my heartbeat shifts and syncs with the current of everything around me. I listen to wind in the dead grass and feel the ground beneath my boots. I anchor myself in the moment before I reach out within my mind for something to tie it all together.

I need to think of something that reminds me of meadows. Living in Montane my whole life, I've never even seen one. The only reason I even know about them is from stories Ma and Pa used to tell.

They used to describe verdant fields, peppered with colorful wildflowers, where birds soared overhead and gallant nobles courted beautiful maidens. Maybe the stories themselves were too whimsical to have a basis in reality, but the memory causes the tips of my fingers to grow warm again.

Then it stops, like before. I growl at myself, frustrated.

"Try again." Ravod's voice is calm and patient. "You can do this."

His gentle encouragement is a welcome change from Kennan's brusque approach. With a little effort, I manage to push aside my irritation at myself and try yet again.

Ravod says I need to think of something that

reminds me of a meadow. I wrack my brain, turning the statement over again and again.

A meadow. Sunshine. Warmth. Beauty.

An image appears in my mind's eye. I recall effortless grace and an infectious smile and the sound of laughter like tinkling bells.

Fiona.

A wave of warmth crashes through me, starting in my fingertips. I open my eyes.

I'm startled when the dull colors around me explode into vibrant green. Flowers of all shapes and varieties burst into bloom at my feet and spread out from me in a circle. Overhead a flock of doves soars through the air.

I had hoped to summon a small patch of green grass and flowers, but new life has nearly stretched to the road. I gasp, turning to Ravod with an exultant grin.

Ravod's eyes are wide, meeting mine unblinking. The wind gently moves his hair back, flicking delicate black wisps over his forehead.

And he smiles.

Joy launches upward into my chest. He is effortlessly beautiful, more so even than the vibrant field newly cascading over the land. There is an ache that penetrates deep into my core.

Feelings rush through me, reckless and chaotic, like jumping down into a ravine without looking. I could spontaneously start dancing but also feel a breath away from bursting into tears. The thought awakens every nerve in my body with an icy touch. The longer I look at him, the deeper the ache in my chest penetrates. There's something uniquely special about him. It is an unsettling energy, unlike anything I felt for Mads.

Mads . . . a pang of guilt pierces me. It has been days since I've thought of him.

The sky darkens, and a flash of pain gallops through my skull as my focus slips. Before I can catch hold of it, a clap of thunder shakes the air, startling me. Dark clouds have massed over the sun, where moments ago the sky was clear.

Something is wrong.

My beautiful field is dying.

The greenery recedes into black, withered stalks. They crumble and fall as another wave of thunder echoes overhead.

Doves screech in pain as they swarm and collide with one another. Their movements are erratic—as if they have gone rabid and are trying to snap their own necks.

Their bodies fall with sickening thuds. Their delicate little bodies lie broken on the blackened earth. I cry out in fear as I try to run. But Ravod holds me in place.

I'm screaming, the image burned into my eyes even as I press them closed. I take one rattling breath after another.

"I'm sorry," I whisper. It's all I can manage.

"There's nothing to apologize for." Under his breath, he whispers a gentle Telling that pulls everything back into place around us. Undoing my mistake. The plains are as they once were. Barren. "I know it was difficult, but you needed to see. There are consequences when we lose control. Any Telling can turn into a disaster if you're not careful. You need to understand that our Tellings have limits. Once the balance has gone too far in one direction, there is no bringing it back."

I swallow hard, confused and so shaken, I'm afraid I may collapse. A wave of dizziness overcomes me and my knees give out.

Ravod awkwardly catches me against his chest, and suddenly, all that exists in the world is the warmth of his body and the muffled, steady beat of his heart against my ear. Proximity to him is like standing in the middle of a fire, both warm and suffocating. He holds me there, seeming unsure of what to do next. His eyes are a storm—lost to something in the past, and I am caught somewhere in the middle.

"What happened to you, Ravod?" I breathe, tilting my face up to his.

My question is innocent, but it's enough for Ravod's walls to lock back in place. He loosens his grip around me, pushing me back to stand on my own.

"We should go back. You need to rest." There's a grimace of pain in the way he averts his eyes instead of looking into mine. A flash of a feeling I know intimately. It's the same pain I felt at Ma's death. I know then that I'm right. He has lost something great and terrible, and he'll never be the same.

The ride back seems steeper than the way there; the horses are harder to motivate. Maybe it's only the exhaustion at my core—the shock of what I experienced. The immense high and low of it.

The clouds billow and the sun sets, glancing off the sides of the mountain in flashes and glares, and I think again about my conversation with Cathal. About the *Book of Days*.

If he's right, if it *is* real, maybe it can do more than give me Ma's killer.

Maybe it can help us fix things like that barren place. Maybe it can help all of Aster. What if we rewrote the world?

The idea is so wild, I am half dizzy with it.

When we pass through the gates of the courtyard, Ravod dismounts first and watches as I follow, his dark eyes tracing my every movement.

I want to trust him. I want it more than almost anything.

I bite my lip when I see the hilt of a golden dagger peeking out of his boot, and I remember the papers I have been keeping close.

Ravod is not my ma's killer. I don't need the *Book of Days* to know that. This truth I feel so deeply, I know I can't be wrong.

But he could still know something about it.

"You should head to the refectory and eat something. You need to keep up your strength." Ravod has already started walking away.

"Wait," I call out. He turns with a slight frown. My heart thuds as I jump headfirst, acting before I can second-guess myself. "Before you leave." My hand reaches into my pocket, pulling out the papers I took from Niall's room. "You need to see this."

Ravod's frown intensifies when he takes the papers from me. His dark eyes scan the contents carefully. After what feels like an eternity, he looks at me.

"Where did you get these?" he asks. His melodic voice radiates anger. It makes the skin on the back of my neck tingle. Maybe he knows what they are for.

There is only one way to find out.

With a deep breath, I reply, "Perhaps I should just show you."

"You went into the *men's barracks?*"

Standing outside the door at the back of the shooting range, I grimace and shrug defensively at the shock in Ravod's voice.

"I needed answers," I say. "And I found them. I think." He'll understand when he sees: the maps, the forbidden writing.

"You should not have been unescorted." Ravod runs a hand through his hair and it flops back into place with a few strands in disarray. That he's so flustered by this is actually a little endearing. "And what you found is *mildly* suspicious at best."

"I'm escorted now, aren't I?" I retort. "So let's go."

With a heavy sigh, Ravod pushes the door open and leads me inside. Like before, the barracks are deserted, with everyone on duty. He follows as I trace the path Imogen showed me to Niall's quarters. My feet remember the way, even as my heart rate notches up in my chest.

"What does it say? On the papers I found," I ask Ravod over my shoulder. I can't look him in the eyes. My hands are shaking.

"Longitudes and latitudes of different locations," Ravod replies. "They're directional coordinates."

"That's it?" Worry tumbles through me. Am I wrong to suspect more? "But why would Niall want directions to my house?"

Ravod shrugs. "Unlike the spoken word, anything set in ink is permanent. It could be a Telling. Or someone consulting Niall's maps was scouting the location for a possible stronghold or safe house for Bards in the field."

"It's *not* a coincidence," I say firmly, anger boiling in my gut. I stop him outside Niall's room with a hand on his forearm. He tenses at the contact and I withdraw my hand; his warmth lingers. I compose myself and look into Ravod's eyes. "My mother was *murdered* in that house, with a Bard's dagger, right after your group left. The killer is a Bard, either Niall or Kennan. If you don't believe me, go and look for yourself."

Ravod holds my gaze, and I could swear fear flickers behind his eyes, before he sighs and disappears through the curtain into Niall's room.

I watch the curtain for several minutes, hardly daring to blink. My nails dig into my palms at my sides and my teeth grind together. There has to be something in there that confirms my suspicions.

My heart jumps when the curtain rustles and Ravod emerges, his face grim. I watch him expectantly. He must have found something . . .

As though he anticipates my question, he shakes his head.

"No . . ." A bad feeling wells inside me as I push past him, past the curtain, and into Niall's room.

It's clean. Pristine. All the maps and books and ink are gone. Nothing remains to even suggest that I found anything there to begin with. He must have gotten rid of it all after he found the broken bottle. I stand in shock, feeling as if all the blood in my body is draining out the soles of my feet onto the floor.

A gentle hand on my shoulder makes me whirl around. Ravod's face is unreadable, like always. "Come on, Shae. It's time to go." He says it as if I'm a fragile child.

Like he pities me.

He doesn't believe me.

"No, this isn't right!" I exclaim. "There were books here!" I try to keep my voice from trembling. "Ink! Papers and . . ." I trail off under Ravod's cool gaze and finally cover my face with my hands.

I can't even summon the will to protest as Ravod escorts me back outside the barracks and up to the training grounds. He leads me to one of the marble benches near the perimeter and motions for me to sit.

My body sways as my knees weaken, and I'm grateful for the seat. Between the horrors of the day and the confusion of Niall's rooms being empty, one thought keeps floating up to me, like a sinister taunt . . .

What if I'm going mad?

The untilled earth in my mother's pastures flashes before my mind. The constable sneering at me. The dizzying way Mads and Fiona turned away from me, certain I was only bringing danger on them and myself.

Has everything I've done been an unraveling of madness within, the corrupting power of the gift, untrained and wild within me?

I don't even realize tears are streaking down my face until Ravod haltingly pats my shoulder. My eyes are anchored stubbornly on my feet. I watch from the corner of my eye as he leans forward on his knees.

"You shouldn't let yourself come undone like this," he says. It's a knife to the gut. He sounds just like Mads. It makes me furious.

"If I shut down and refuse to care like *you* do, my mother will have died for nothing," I say, lifting my eyes boldly to his. "She deserves better than that."

"If I didn't care, I wouldn't say anything," Ravod replies evenly. My anger flips over, tumbling past my heart. "You're my charge. Your well-being is my responsibility."

I blink. My sense returns somewhat. Of course that's the only reason he has to care about me. I take a deep breath. "It's just . . ." I stare at him. I want to make him understand how I feel, how intriguing I find him. I want to put words to the amorphous feelings that overwhelmed me back in the meadow.

"I care about you. A lot," is all I manage to say.

"That's very considerate," Ravod says with a tiny nod as my confession flies over his head.

I look away quickly. My feelings have only just crystallized and still feel raw and new. I force myself to look at him, trying to make him see what I mean with my eyes. He stares back at me innocently, and I raise an eyebrow.

The blank expression frozen on Ravod's face melts into bewilderment, like I've just handed him an axe and asked him to chop his own hand off.

He stands abruptly and takes two deliberate steps away from the bench before stopping. He turns back to me, head cocked. Thousands of thoughts flicker behind his eyes in rapid succession.

I say nothing, frozen in place, as much in shock as he is. He takes a ragged breath.

"I will inform Cathal that a conflict of interest prevents me from continuing your training and request a position elsewhere in the castle so you can resolve these feelings," he says, his voice cold with authority. "I'm sorry, Shae. I appreciate your honesty."

Without another word, he disappears across the training grounds. Every step he takes causes the hollow cavity in my chest to grow larger, threatening to swallow me up inside it. I wait until he is out of sight to finally let my tears overtake me again.

The castle is consumed with festivities by the time night falls. The foreign dignitaries Cathal mentioned arrive by carriage beneath twinkling stars, dressed in stunning suits and gowns, as if they stepped out of one of Ma's bedtime stories.

The flurry of activity provides the small mercy of being overlooked as I stalk back to my dormitory. No one cares to stare at the lone trainee with tears in her eyes when there are other, more beautiful people to ogle.

Distantly, I hear an elegant tune playing. The music is light and uplifting, completely at odds with the hard shell of hurt in my chest. I'm thankful I have no rank and am not needed to participate in the security detail. I don't think I could stand being around people after the day I had.

I only have to keep from falling apart long enough to reach the privacy of my room.

I want to be angry. Part of me wants to find Ravod and Kennan and Niall and scream at them until I'm blue in the face.

Not that it would be any use. It feels like I've been banging my head against a wall since coming here, accomplishing absolutely nothing.

A quick flash of movement catches my eye. I turn my head just in time to see Imogen disappear around a corner.

It's strange that she's not with everyone else attending to the ball. The conversation I overheard between Cathal and the chamberlain made it sound like every last pair of hands was needed at the event.

I peer down the hall after her. She is glancing around furtively as she walks.

I definitely know sneaking around when I see it.

My problems momentarily forgotten, I slip after her, keeping myself at a safe distance in the shadows. High House is certainly a hotbed of secrets. Even little Imogen has some, apparently.

From the other end of the hall, I watch Imogen halt in front of a statue of an unknown Bard. I squint through the darkness, trying to see her better. She's shifting her weight rapidly between her feet and knotting her fingers in front of her.

Faint footsteps from the adjacent corridor herald the arrival of a newcomer.

"There you are!" Imogen sighs impatiently. The silhouette of a muscular figure wearing a guard's uniform comes into view. "Hurry up, before they realize we're missing at the party."

The guard replies, but his voice is too quiet to make out. They don't seem to be exchanging anything but words.

When the guard turns, I catch a fleeting glimpse of blue eyes beneath a square brow. Features that remind me of Mads.

How silly of me. Mads is far away in Aster, working the mill with his father. He probably put me from his mind ages ago. Or at the very least, does not remember me all too fondly. Serves me right. I am the girl who broke his heart.

Fitting, after today, that I'm the one who winds

up rejected. My guilt over Mads was punishing me in the wasteland earlier and corrupted my Telling. Fate must be punishing me now, projecting his features onto some random guard.

There is so much left unresolved. I probably thought of Mads because I'm desperate for something familiar in this huge, unfriendly place.

The music fades and changes. A slow, sad ballad begins, accompanied by singing in a language I've never heard. The guard rushes away. Imogen waits a careful moment before following.

My body sways, much heavier suddenly. Fatigue overcomes all my senses, purging my thoughts until all that's left is the desire to collapse in bed and wake up with some distance between myself and this day.

I take a deep breath and resume my lonely walk to my room.

My dreams that night take me to dark places. Haunted memories. Old hurts.

I wake several times, tangled in my sheets, and I could swear I hear footsteps outside my door followed by a soft knock. I want to answer. I yearn for it to be Ravod with a different response. But I also don't. If he came to talk about what happened earlier, I'm not sure I could control myself. Every time I close my eyes, I see the cold indifference in his eyes right before he walked away, and my limbs tremble.

Maybe coming here was a mistake. I think of the

devastation of the barren fields. Of Cathal's words about the *Book of Days.* Of Niall's contraband items, vanished as if they'd never been. Imagining Mads's blue eyes, wanting so badly to find something familiar in this place.

I think, over and over, of Ravod. The pain he tries to hide and the intensity in his voice that betrays him.

This is a disaster. Female Bards are supposed to be the most volatile, vulnerable to our emotions and desires. I'm standing at the edge of a knife.

Madness. The word haunts me as I toss against the sheets, wishing they were Ravod's arms, wishing I could run away, rewind time, and make the hurt stop.

Finally, I clutch at my needles on the bedside table. It's a strange comfort, holding them close.

I drift back into sleep.

It feels like only moments later that I hear a knocking at my door. Finally, I get up to open it, but no one is there. Yet there are whispers swirling all around me in the still air of the hallway. I turn and run through the halls of High House while they shift and alter, turning in circles. Doorway after doorway. Archway after archway. Stairwells and hidden doors and more hallways.

I shudder, knowing I am lost. I shove open a door, and it is not a room at all but Fiona's store. *No.* I turn and continue racing through the maze of a fortress. In another room, Mads awaits me. He's sitting there in a leather chair, one leg crossed over the knee, whittling a piece of wood. He looks up at me and shakes his head, disapproving. His eyes are indigo, weeping ink down his cheeks. I scream, and he bursts into ash.

Suddenly I'm back in my own home, where Kieran lies dying in his bed, dark blue veins winding over his face. Ma tends to him, and I want to cry out, want to hug them both, want to freeze time and stay here forever, before I lose Kieran. But already the ground is rumbling beneath me, thunderous and terrifying, and through the window, I see an avalanche of rocks and mud. Walls collapse around us, and I watch as they are both swallowed in a landslide. I can't save them. I am thrown back and we are separated.

I scream again, flying rearward but finding no ground.

A hot burst of panic. I try to awaken myself to no avail. The usual trick of squeezing my eyes shut and opening them fast doesn't work. When I try, I'm back on the training grounds.

Ravod stands in front of me, the same way he did this afternoon. Except horror is etched into his beautiful features as he watches me. I open my mouth to speak, and one by one, every Bard in High House appears behind him, staring at me accusingly.

The ground beneath my feet starts to tremble. It's happening again. As if the avalanche, the curse, the *madness*, has followed me.

"Shae," Ravod whispers, somehow louder than the

sound of the mountain quaking beneath us. "What have you done?" he says.

The tremors throw me back over the side of the cliff. I cling to the edge for dear life, but it's too much, and I fall, the rush of the waterfall everywhere, swallowing me whole.

My eyes snap open in the dark. I try to breathe.

I am sitting in my bed, shaking, covered in sweat. I look around my room, so fine and lovely. Now I can't help feeling the walls tightening around me.

"It was only a dream," I whisper, trying desperately to calm my nerves and slow my racing heartbeat.

It is little use. I can still hear screaming and thunder ringing in my ears. I rub my eyes, trying to shake the numbness of sleep off, and that's when I hear it. Piercing screams coming from the outside.

I throw my covers off and rush to pull my uniform and boots on and open the door.

Some of the other Bards have emerged curiously from their bedrooms, listening in the hall. I've seen two of them before: the one with the red tattoo and the older woman with beads in her white hair. I catch sight of Kennan, whose pale eyes are narrowed at the entrance to the hall.

"What's happening?" she says. She looks scared. There are dark rings beneath her eyes.

The mountain quivers with a final aftershock and is still. Kennan has already broken into a run down the hall. Before I can think better of it, I find myself chasing her.

My breath is heaving in my chest as I try to keep pace, but Kennan is almost unnaturally fast. She must be performing a Telling to allow herself to move so quickly. I try to do the same, but my thoughts are too scattered and I'm too out of breath. It's all I can do to keep her slender figure in my sights as I barrel down the halls and skid around corners. She flings the door to the training grounds wide open and disappears outside. It nearly smacks me in the face as it slams shut, but I push through before it can.

I stumble into the light of the full moon and lean on my knees to catch my breath. When I look up, the air I finally managed to recoup is shot from my lungs like a blast.

I've never seen the training grounds so packed. Every Bard in High House must be out here. They are all facing the castle proper with varying looks of alarm and shock.

"The Civilian's Tower . . ." I hear a voice in the crowd gasp.

Another intones, "A tragedy . . ."

"The families of our servants . . ."

I spin around and stare, an overwhelming terror descending over me. An entire wing of the castle has collapsed. Like a massive, invisible giant stepped on it.

"Everyone, fan out and look for survivors!"

I can't move.

My nightmare is fresh in my mind. This is the

consequence of allowing my emotions to get the better of me.

I made this happen.

This is my fault. If Cathal's belief in my power is real, so is this.

The devastation in the fields yesterday comes back to me. This is what Ravod was trying to warn me about.

I do the only thing I can think of. I run for my life.

20

The world goes silent as I take off running, shutting everything else out. The only coherent thought I'm capable of is that I need to get as far away from here as possible. I don't even know where I'm headed, I can only trust my feet to get me where I need to go. Doing reckless things without thinking first . . . That, at least, I'm good at.

I feel hot breath on the back of my neck as I run, stumbling through the gilded halls back the way I first came in. I don't even see my surroundings, only the path ahead. When I glance over my shoulder, figures are behind me, impossible to make out in the darkness. It's as if I'm being chased by the specters of the people who were in the tower when it collapsed. The families of the servants. Maybe even little Imogen's family. I can see her face in my mind, her open, friendly sweetness morphing into grief and accusation. I can't bear it. I never meant to hurt her, or anyone. Fiona was right. I'm putting everyone around me in danger.

The voices calling after me have become nothing more than dull echoes by the time I reach the main courtyard.

Everyone is scrambling. Yelling. Maybe they're

shouting at me, or are just swept up in the chaos of the collapsed tower. Everything beyond my own body feels dark and stagnant, shrouded in death. All I can do is rush forward and hope to escape it.

The wrought-iron gate of the main entrance lies ahead, locking me in. I don't have the dexterity to climb over.

But I do have the Telling.

My body grows warm as I focus. I have just enough awareness of the world around me to channel my fear at the barrier ahead.

"Vanish!" I cry out.

The gate blinks out of reality, and I pass through onto the road. I don't need to look behind me to know that it's there again as soon as I clear the threshold.

The thought of going down the mountain to the wasteland only exacerbates my panic. I can't go back there. I run in the opposite direction instead, up the mountain. The air becomes rapidly colder the smaller High House gets in the distance. A few flakes of snow brush my skin as I ascend higher into the frigid mountaintops. I'm nearly free.

It's a short-lived victory. I trip over a loose rock in the road where the cement gives way to dirt. Panic is all I feel as I lurch forward, losing control of my body.

I tumble head over feet, off the road entirely, where it bends down the mountainside.

The ground slams against my body as I somer-sault down a ledge. The haze of emotions takes the edge off the pain I would normally feel at being bat-tered like this.

I wonder if I will die at the bottom.

A blast of dark cold envelops me.

I've stopped moving. The world still feels unsteady, but I can lift my neck and see that I've fallen into a snowbank, not dead after all.

The rocks are icy, stabbing into me through my clothes, and the air stings against my skin like brittle glass. I'm higher in the mountains here. The waste-lands are far below; I can no longer see them around the jagged peaks.

I don't remember losing consciousness, but I must have; the sun is cresting the mountaintops that encircle me. It could be the next day or any number of days later. Time feels fuzzy and difficult to gauge.

Perched in the snow before me are three white vultures. They observe me with vague disappoint-ment before they fly off in search of a better meal.

I trace their path with my eyes until they disap-pear into the distance. Lowering my gaze, I make out a smaller path winding through the mountains.

My muscles throb as I push myself up out of the snow. The cold has seeped into my clothes, down to my very bones, muting the worst of my pain, but I still feel as if I fell off the side of a mountain.

For a few minutes, all I can do is sit and wait for the world to stop lurching unevenly around me. Behind me is the sheer cliffside I rolled down. A dark smattering of blood remains on one of the nearest rocks, and I touch my temple, grimacing. The tips of my fingers are bloody when I pull them away. Luckily the wound has started to scab, and a little snow is all I need to clean it.

I look around. Going back the way I came is not an option. I couldn't scale a slope like that without equipment, even if I did feel physically matched to the task.

Perhaps it's for the best, I think. They have probably deduced by now that I was the one who caused the collapse. *They would have expected me to head in the familiar direction of the wasteland. They'll search for me there. I have a better chance of escaping if I go deeper into the mountains.*

The small burst of clarity helps ease my nerves. Even so, it takes a couple of deep, steadying breaths to muster enough resolve to get to my feet. My head is pounding, and my body isn't holding together much better.

I gingerly pick my way over the snowbank and onto the narrow mountain road. When I was younger and more travelers passed through Aster, I remember hearing about paths such as these, so treacherous that sometimes only the sure-footed mountain goats that populate the region could traverse them. Back then, it seemed almost as improbable as the existence of Gondal.

I clear my head of thoughts to focus on the path before me. At best, the smallest misstep would send me face-first onto the ground; at worst, I would fall into a chasm between the mountains. The distraction is far from pleasant, but more bearable than the dark, murky void of my mind.

Keeping my head down, I put one foot in front of the other. Some steps are easier than others. I nearly slip on the dark ice several times.

When I pause to catch my breath, I find myself looking back, against my better judgment. The shock wave of heat nearly thaws my frozen body on its own. The cold is getting to me.

High House is clear in the distance, pristine and white against the clear blue sky and golden rays of sunshine. The shining beacon of hope and order it always was.

I can even see the tower that collapsed last night, standing as if nothing happened. My jaw trembles, my teeth chattering, but not from the cold.

The tower flickers into rubble, a cloud of dust and death rising over castle spires, and back into existence. I blink once . . . twice . . . but it doesn't change.

This is it. This is the madness I was always fated to succumb to. It's finally happening.

One thing is certain, I need to get away from

High House more than ever. Before it claims me completely. Before I can hurt anyone else.

Before Ravod finds out and loses what little respect he has left for me.

Before Cathal realizes that his faith in me was misplaced.

I squeeze my eyes shut and turn back to the road. All I can do is lower my head and continue on.

I don't know if minutes or hours have passed when I finally see movement ahead.

Black-cloaked Bards patrol the road. One is on horseback barking orders to another two on foot, but the rest—I count six—are positioned at varying heights up the cliff. They watch in both directions, almost as if they are looking for something.

Or *someone.*

I shiver involuntarily, picking my way quietly up the path, staying out of sight behind a rocky outcropping. Shielded from the leader's gaze atop his horse, I press my back against the frigid stone and try to hear what they are saying.

"—been mostly quiet out here. Not many caravans this time of year," a Bard on foot reports.

"Let's keep it that way," the leader responds, "at least until the situation is resolved."

Situation? I mouth the word silently. Are they talking about the tower? Are these men here to find me? Will they bring me back to High House? Or will they kill me here and leave my corpse for the vultures?

The ground beneath me wobbles a little. With

effort, I plant my feet and rest my head back against the rock, trying to remain calm.

"Word from the village says Crowell's squad has things mostly under control. If we keep traffic to a minimum, they'll only need a day, maybe two to wrap up," another Bard pipes up.

I exhale the breath I've been holding. They're only monitoring traffic. Perhaps there's a chance I can slip by unnoticed. I have to act fast.

Stepping out from the outcropping, I arrange my features into what I hope is a perfectly neutral expression. The Bards finally notice me as I draw closer, but their glances grow dismissive when they see the training uniform I'm wearing.

"State your business," the Bard on horseback orders, gazing coldly down at me.

I clear my throat, adopting the terse tone I've noticed among Bards on duty.

"I was sent with a message for Crowell," I say, sounding more confident than I feel.

"He's up the road overseeing operations at the village. Tread carefully." The Bard nods me past.

I maintain a smooth gait as I pass the others, trying to ignore my heart pounding fearfully in my chest. When the road curves around the cliff and out of sight, I nearly fall to my knees from the exertion of the charade.

If I stop quickly at the village up ahead, I might be able to blend in with the Bards again and scrounge up some supplies.

I lose track of time again as the path winds around the mountains; it narrows dangerously when I least expect. I'm shivering violently by the time I round yet another corner and finally see the village ahead.

The burst of color is unexpected. Bright banners and flags of all shapes and sizes wave at me in the wind. The stone houses, built into the rocks of the mountain, are painted in colorful trimming, and the narrow streets below are busy with a bustling marketplace.

Most tempting of all is the smoke billowing happily from the chimneys, the promise of warmth.

With renewed energy, I trek closer, eager to find shelter where I can stop shivering and collect my scattered thoughts. My empty stomach reminds me loudly that food is also a necessity.

A blast of frigid wind hits me when I approach the outskirts of the town, carrying with it a foul stench that sends me reeling back. I cover my nose and mouth with my hand, trying to wave it away as I make my way through the main gates.

I remember that smell. It was in my home when I found Ma on the floor.

Death has a very distinctive odor.

The colorful banners still wave overhead, but when I swivel toward the narrow dirt road that led into town, I have to blink several times. The festive outcropping of trees and banners and lanterns has vanished.

When I turn again to walk forward, everything

looks different. As if I've passed through an illusion and now I'm in the *real* village. It's frightening. Far worse even than Aster. Groups of filthy people huddle around meager fires or in makeshift tents. Some are injured beyond repair. A few enter and exit a dilapidated building that looks ready to slide right off the side of the cliff. A faded cloth sign hanging outside bears a woven icon of a keg of beer and mugs, proclaiming itself a tavern. Standing vigilantly at either side of the door is a pair of Bards. They seem to be guarding the building, but their eyes flick watchfully over the people out front.

I didn't see this from the road. Could I have overlooked it in my eagerness to find shelter?

Something is very wrong here.

Or else, something is very wrong with *me*.

I shake the thought away, willing myself to focus.

I know better than to ask questions of the nearby Bards and potentially blow my cover. Instead, I stride purposefully up to the door. They permit my entrance with a tight nod each.

My joy at the heat inside is short-lived. Even as I feel sensation creep back into my body through my thawing skin, my throat tightens with renewed trepidation.

The tavern appears to have been repurposed as a base of operations for the Bards. The shutters are closed and bolted. The only natural light comes from the narrow slits in the uneven wood that reflects the motes of dust in the air. If not for the faint glow of a few candles, the room would be cast almost completely in darkness.

Several Bards strategize over a table littered with maps. Another group is gearing up for what looks like a shift change.

Refugees have clustered in nervous knots throughout the room. One larger group uses the bar to perform surgery on a young man who looks like he was struck with a bolt through his shoulder. He howls in pain as he's held down. His cries drown out the hushed whispers around the room. Hardly anyone dares acknowledge the Bards' presence. The Bards seem happy to return the favor.

With everyone's focus on their respective tasks and struggles, I easily slip into a shadowy corner.

My body stinging with much needed warmth, I keep an eye on the tavern. That doesn't stop it from tilting side to side like it's floating out at sea. The movement is slow, just enough to make me sick to my stomach.

I close my eyes, bracing myself against the wall. The splintery wood digs into my palms, grounding me.

The tilting stops. I open my eyes, hopeful that I've staved off the worst of the madness.

As usual, I'm wrong.

Confusion is quickly replaced by cold, biting fear as I see the tavern again. All the shutters are open, casting the space in warm, bright sunlight. Banners hang from the rafters in every imaginable color.

Customers chat at tables while a pretty, dark-haired woman bustles about serving food and drinks. The bar is packed with patrons, singing and toasting together.

This isn't real, is it?

I open and close my eyes several times, as if trying to awaken from a dream—or a nightmare—but the room only changes back and forth rapidly between the two scenes. One moment it's filled with horror and the next with laughter.

Shaking, I trace the wall back to the door and waste no time throwing it open and dashing outside into a blast of frigid mountain air.

I shield my eyes with my arm. I don't want to see anything as I take to the road, running as fast as my body will allow. I have to get away. Somewhere far from here, from the Bards, from High House. I can feel my mind unraveling with every rushed, terrified step I take.

That smell again. The stench of death. I can feel it seeping into my clothes, my hair, my lungs. It's choking the breath from me.

My arm is forced from my eyes when something barrels into my side, knocking me to the ground. When I look up, there's nothing there.

I'm splayed in the middle of the street of the pristine mountain village. No one in the busy marketplace seems to notice me as they go about their lives. Above, colorful banners wave cheerfully in the breeze . . . The breeze that reeks of decay. Now it's laced with smoke but there's no fire.

I get to my feet, rubbing my shoulder where I was hit. It still stings from the impact, but is it real?

My boot crunches as I take a step forward. Looking down, I see broken glass from a window I was passing. I look up to see the window, intact, with a small box of little blue and yellow flowers on the sill. When I glance down, the glass is gone.

I look back to the window. The flowers are nothing but withered black stalks. The windowpane is shattered, dark blood crusted on the edges of the broken glass.

The noises of the market are replaced by screams and panic. The busy shopkeepers and their patrons become mobs of filthy, starving beggars rioting in the street. Fires blaze in the distance. Smoke curls in the air. Bodies lie in the road, stripped of their meager valuables.

Is this where the smell of death was coming from before? Now, I can only smell incense and freshly baked bread.

There's an undercurrent to all of it, the faint sound of monotonous chanting. Black cloaks dart around the corners of my eyes, slipping behind buildings or patrolling rooftops, visible for only a split second before they slide out of sight.

The Bards are performing a Telling here, but I don't know what is real and what is manufactured.

As I glance quickly back and forth across the street, I find myself on the bleeding edge of reality. On one side is the bustling market and on the other are riots and famine, existing at the same time independently of one another. Screams of anguish mix with the sound of vendors hawking their wares. The aroma of incense and pastries mixes with the stench of blood and smoke.

Some villagers go about their day; the others live out a nightmare and are beginning to shove past me as I become grounded in their violent reality.

"Watch it!" someone shouts, knocking into me.

Another, a peasant whose face is smeared in grease, stops in his tracks. "She's one of *them*," he hollers.

Suddenly a frenzy of villagers, all with reeking breath and open sores spotting their hands and arms, crowd in, grasping at me, trying to tear off my cloak.

I try to scream, and maybe I do, but the sound is swallowed up in the chaos of noise and shouts as I'm nearly knocked off my feet.

The ground is shifting. I can't keep my balance as the edges of my vision grow tangled and dark.

I hear my name shouted from far away.

My knees buckle beneath me, and I feel myself falling, powerless to stop it.

"Run! Get out of here!" my attackers cry out to one another as I collapse onto the rough ground.

The violent whinnying of a horse is muted in my ears.

I feel an arm encircle me, drawing me up.

The last thing I see is Cathal, his face creased with worry.

My head is heavy. The rest of me is numb. Lifting my eyelids is a chore, and all I can see is a bright blur in front of me.

I think I'm lying down. Or floating. I could be suspended from a ceiling by my toes, for all I know. Nothing feels right.

"Shae?" Cathal's voice. "Shae, can you hear me?"

I try to take a breath to respond, but all that issues is a low mumble. Cathal's face slips in and out of focus above me. A halo of light dances over his edges.

He speaks again, but it sounds too far away to interpret. The effort it takes to listen is exhausting, and my eyes close.

I can't be dead because suddenly I feel a sharp pain flare from my spine outward. It races along every vein, penetrating deep into my bones. It pulses there before it dies down.

I'm still not dead. Warm water surrounds me. I hear voices. Distant, but growing closer.

". . . glad she's alive." *Imogen*, I think distantly.

"There are worse things than death," another says. "Just look around."

"Where am I?" My voice feels detached from the rest of me.

264 — DYLAN FARROW

"You're in the—"

A third voice cuts her off. "The less she knows, the better. Keep her calm so we can bathe her and get her back to bed like Cathal instructed."

"But . . ." Imogen sounds hesitant.

"Just reassure her already, so we can do our job and get out of here!" the second voice commands.

I try to breathe through the building panic that sparks the pain again.

"Imogen?" I try to reach for her, for something, *anything* that's familiar. I can barely move my finger-tips toward the sound of her voice.

"It's all right, Shae." I see Imogen amid the blurry shapes moving rapidly in front of me. "You're safe. You're going to be fine, I promise." Her young face comes into focus near mine. "You're going to be fine . . ." Her voice is the last sound I hear before darkness swallows me.

When Kieran died, I remember him slipping in and out of consciousness like this. Is that what's happening to me? Am I dying?

Do I have the Blot?

My eyes snap open into darkness, as if I hadn't opened them at all. The pain is gone, replaced by searing heat. A bead of sweat courses slowly from my hairline to my eyebrow.

I'm being crushed under a brutal weight and oppressive darkness, but I can turn my head slightly. The cool touch of a pillow is at my cheek.

Somewhere ahead, I see a small square of light and the vague silhouette of a man behind. It turns and walks away. Faint footsteps recede in time with my eyes closing against my will.

"Shae?" Cathal's voice again. The back of his fingers are cool and dry against my clammy forehead. Ma used to check Kieran's temperature that way.

Perhaps I'll see them soon . . .

"Shae." Fingers snap in front of me.

Fiona must be waking me up so I can go to town to see the Bards . . .

"Shae."

My eyes open. Not to darkness, or Fiona, but Cathal. I can see him more clearly. His brow is knit, but his gray eyes are gentle as ever.

"You are awake. That is a relief."

"I feel terrible." I don't know if I'm talking about the collapse, or my current state, or both. My voice is little more than a hoarse whisper that grates painfully against the walls of my throat.

Cathal grimaces. "That is to be expected, unfortunately. You have been through quite an ordeal. I was worried you might not make it."

"What's happening to me?"

"You contracted a fever. Such things tend to happen when you charge off into the mountains without proper gear. I'm afraid you were pushed too far in your training."

His tone is one I haven't heard in a long time.

Pa and Ma used that inflection in their voices when they were disappointed in me. Before Pa died and Ma went silent. The long lost affiliation is unexpectedly comforting.

"I'm sorry," I whisper.

"The delirium brought you dangerously close to your breaking point," Cathal continues. "Had you remained, you would have died from the cold or gone mad. I cannot say which might have happened first." He pauses his lecture, taking a deep breath and shaking his head. "I suppose it does not matter now. I am just glad you are all right." His chiseled face is stern, as if he is scolding me for almost dying.

"I . . ." My voice trails off. I have limited energy to express myself. "Thank you for helping me."

Cathal moves out of view, and briefly, it looks as if he's writing something. But just as quickly, he's returned to my side.

"I only did what I had to," he says finally. "Get some rest. I will check on you again as soon as I am able."

I nod slowly, my exhaustion taking hold. I fall asleep to the sound of Cathal's footsteps departing. As the sound recedes, I realize I never asked him where I am.

Muffled voices in the dark wake me. I can't make out the words, but it sounds like an argument.

My eyes flutter open; the square of light is less

blurry. There's a small window cut into the door. I see a man's profile, talking to someone out of sight.

"Ravod?"

His delicate features are contorted with rage as he speaks to the other person, punctuating each unintelligible sentence with a pointed finger. When he finishes, he glances through the window and his eyes meet mine.

"Shae! Can you hear me?"

"I can hear you . . ." I try to reach for him, but my arm is too heavy to lift, and I find my eyes are still too heavy to keep open.

It must be a dream, because when my eyes flutter open again, he is not there—only a stretch of longing and grief so great, I fear it will swallow me whole. I dreamed about Ravod because I want so desperately to believe that he misses me. That he wants to be near me as badly as I want to be near him.

That must be it.

The fog does not abate for some time. Periodically it lessens, but my head still feels like it's crammed with rocks and rubble, and when I try to rally the strength to move them aside, I remember the guilt that's beneath them. I'd rather be buried alive than face how I feel. What I've done.

I don't know how much time has passed when I hear the door open. Quiet footsteps pad over to me.

I hear the clink of silverware on porcelain. My stomach churns audibly. I can't remember the last time I had anything to eat.

"Are you hungry?" Imogen is perched at the edge of my bed with a bowl of steaming soup.

"Starving," I reply, mustering what I hope is a smile.

"That's a good sign! My ma always used to say a good meal is the best medicine." Imogen stirs the soup before feeding me a spoonful, and I want to ask about her mother. I wonder if she was anything like mine.

But my voice is too weak.

Still, I notice with a budding sense of hope that she's not as blurry today. But the room is still dark, too dark to see much more than the side of Imogen's face and the soup. The only light comes from the window in the door, and it's faint at best.

"What is this place?" I finally whisper.

Imogen hesitates, chewing her lower lip. "High House," she replies finally.

"I gathered as much," I reply, watching the young servant girl closely. Her normally chipper demeanor is replaced by apprehension. I phrase my next question carefully. "Imogen, *where* in High House?"

The bowl she's holding is quivering, sending ripples over the broth. I worry she might drop it.

"I'm not supposed to say," she answers quietly. "Please don't ask me to."

I drop the question and allow Imogen to finish

feeding me. Like clockwork, as she gets up to leave, sleep takes hold of me once more.

When I open my eyes, I am surprised to see Cathal clearly. He's seated on an armchair beside my bed, illuminated by the dawn sunlight beginning to peek in through an open window, its frame decorated with wildflowers. I can't see what's beyond the brightness of the window.

The room is small but cozy. Almost as if plucked out of a country cottage. The walls are whitewashed plaster with painted blue stencil tulips wreathing the chamber like a garland. It reminds me of something I might have embroidered back in Aster. The wooden door with a small window is painted a cheerful, contrasting red, like a barn. A few paintings depicting pleasant pastoral scenes decorate the walls in simple wooden frames. My bed is carved from pine like it was back home. It's much nicer than anything in Aster.

"You seem to be feeling better today," Cathal remarks.

I try my best to nod.

"Good. Because I need to speak to you about something." *Here it is.* The punishment. The acknowledgment of what I've done.

"Of course," I say nervously.

He sits forward slightly, his eyes growing serious. "Why did you run after the collapse of the tower?"

"I . . ." There's no use lying. He'll see through it.

"I had a dream that there was a landslide, like back home." I swallow the lump in my throat. "I awoke to the sounds of the collapse and its aftermath . . ." I go silent, letting Cathal make of it what he will.

He frowns. "You believed you were responsible?"

"Yes." My voice wavers and cracks. My chest is a tangle of grief and guilt; I don't know how to unspool it all.

"Set your mind at ease, Shae. You did no such thing," Cathal replies. "I already know the identity of the culprit, and justice will be served."

A deluge of relief washes over me. "Oh."

"But I want you to promise me not to be so reckless in the future. You must consider your actions more carefully. Imagine what people would think, witnessing a Bard running loose in the streets, frantic, as if mad."

"I promise," I reply, feeling the weight of his implications. I am being spared, yes, but warned too. "I understand completely. Thank you, Cathal. For everything."

"You need not thank me, I simply want to keep you safe." His voice is quiet and earnest. "I like to think that if I had a daughter, she might be like you." I find myself smiling as he rests a warm hand atop my head and rises from the armchair. "Get some sleep." He stands, looming over me. "You have regained much of your strength, but not all. It will not be long before your formal training resumes. And you have much to do."

"I haven't forgotten about the *Book of Days,* I promise. I will find it, and the truth about my ma's death," I say.

Cathal nods. "All in good time. I brought you something. A gift." He leans forward, placing a small rectangular box on my lap. It's wrapped in beautiful green paper. "Go ahead and open it." He prompts me with a grin. Whatever it is, he seems eager for me to see it. I smile back, gently unwrapping the paper, not wanting to damage it.

"I really appreciate it, but you didn't have to get me anything—" I stop abruptly when a book falls into my lap and a familiar twisting dread grips my heart.

"You hate it. I know," Cathal says. "But I was hoping to help you overcome your fear of the written word by teaching you to read while you convalesce. If nothing else, it will help pass the time." He takes the book, showing me the cover. "That is, if it is all right with you."

I peer at the cover, my gaze floating over the letters and the stylized icon of the Bard's sigil. It's an old book, handled many times, and well-loved. Cathal's smile is gentle, and observing his comfort handling the book helps disarm my defensiveness. He raises his dark brows at me, expectantly.

"Read? Me?" The disjointed words come out in a whisper. This flies in the face of everything I was ever taught. He places the book in my hands, but they are trembling so violently holding the small, rectangular object that it drops into my lap. I instinctively recoil. The book feels like a crushing weight. I can't speak, instead shaking my head mutely. "No, I can't," I finally tell him. "It's too dangerous."

What I want to say, and what I think he can see in my eyes, is that I'm terrified. He takes my hands in his, squeezing gently like he did before when we met in his solarium.

"Breathe, Shae. Look at me."

With effort, I comply. I drag my eyes from the book to Cathal's face. His gaze is unfaltering and that confidence helps thaw the cold fear in my gut.

"Do you trust me?" he asks.

I nod without hesitation. His honesty and support have tethered me. His guidance has been my beacon in the dark.

"I would never seek to harm you, Shae," he says. "If you do not want to learn to read, I will not ask it of you. I will not pass judgment on your decision. I will never bring it up again, if that is your wish. Now, take a breath."

I do as he says, drawing in a long breath through my nose and exhaling slowly from my mouth. I repeat the process, focusing on the warmth of Cathal's hand on mine and the steadiness in his gaze, until I feel my mind clear.

"You think it will help me find Ma's killer? And the *Book of Days*?" I ask.

He nods. "I do. And I understand your trepidation. But I also think you are better equipped to overcome your fear than you believe."

I squeeze my eyes shut for a moment. The book resting in my lap feels a little lighter. Finally, I nod back.

"I'll do it," I say. "Teach me."

Cathal smiles encouragingly. His pale eyes twinkle a little as he releases my hands with a final, gentle squeeze.

"I am very proud of you, Shae," he says. "And it goes without saying that you should not attempt to read or write without me present."

"Of course."

"Normally, only the most Senior Bards are instructed in reading and writing," Cathal says, "but I trust you. I believe in you. You can handle it."

"Really?"

He nods. "I do not impart this knowledge lightly. I do so with you because you have proven yourself. You are the strongest, most tenacious person I have ever met. I want to help foster these traits in you. I . . ." He catches himself becoming impassioned and draws a deep breath. "I believe now, beyond a shadow of a doubt, that you are the one who will find the *Book of Days*. We will right the wrongs of the past and usher in a new dawn for Montane. Together."

His face is earnest. Sincere. He alone believes me as much as he believes *in* me. That confidence somehow makes me want to believe in myself as much as he does, to prove I'm worthy of such faith. I swallow the last of my fear.

"All right." I push myself farther up on my pillow.

274 — DYLAN FARROW

"Excellent." His grin broadens. "This book is the High House Manifesto. We use it as a primer to instruct the Senior Bards to read. I want you to have my copy that I used . . . I won't say how long ago."

I laugh, and Cathal opens the book to the first page, turning it to show me. Hours pass as he patiently introduces me to letters and phonics and the building blocks of reading and writing. My head is swimming with characters and sounds by the time he concludes the lesson. Daylight is dying in the window when he finally lets me drift off to sleep.

My recovery stretches over more days than I can count, but my strength slowly returns. I am awoken each day by Cathal, who sits in his armchair beside my bed. We continue our lessons, taking breaks to chat about my childhood or eat sumptuous food brought in by the servants. During this time, he sometimes produces a small gilded notebook and writes in it. "Reminders," he always says.

I find myself looking forward to his visits, and even the lessons, and sad when he inevitably announces that they have come to an end.

For the first time in a long while, I feel a sense of unconditional companionship, and my heart is full.

Tap-tap-tap.

My eyes open in the darkness to a sound at the window. I turn my head, squinting, attempting to adjust my eyes enough to see.

Tap-tap-tap.

It's louder, more urgent. I sit up, shaking the haze of sleep from my head. I push the covers away, stumbling through the dark toward the sound.

There's pale light in the window. Enough to see . . .

Tap-tap-tap!

I jolt back in shock, suddenly fully awake. Ravod is on the other side of the glass.

"Ravod!"

I lean against the wall, my legs shaking from disuse, before moving closer, pressing my hands to the window and lifting, but it won't budge. And there's no latch that I can find. The glass is sealed.

With lithe grace, he twists around, landing lightly on the windowsill. My eyes grow wide in the dim light. He has rappelled down a line from . . . somewhere.

I can't see anything else through the window but a sheer wall of rock.

Crouching on the sill, Ravod leans close to the glass mouthing the words:

Are you all right?

I nod.

Ravod nods back, looking somewhat relieved as he glances around tentatively. Admittedly, I feel a rush at the thought that he's concerned for me. I'm even touched by his odd way of showing it, coming to my window like this.

Ravod leans back to the glass, breathing fog onto the surface. He uses the tip of his index finger to start tracing a shape.

No, not a shape. A letter. And another. It takes a bit for me to follow along, sounding out the letters the way Cathal taught me. Remembering the difference between upper and lower case letters . . . hard and soft vowels . . . context . . .

When he finishes, there's a single word on the glass.

Danger.

I frown at him, not understanding. What danger? And how does Ravod know how to write? Is this a dream?

The door is slammed open behind me. Light floods the room and obscures Ravod. I whirl around.

There has to be some mistake. This isn't my room. The quaint decorations and comforting atmosphere are gone. There's only a plain bed, a small stool, and a nightstand. The walls are white, padded with fabric. I bring my hand to my forehead, anxious and dizzy.

Is this a prison?

A Bard I don't recognize stands authoritatively in the doorway, silhouetted against the bright light outside.

"You're cleared for discharge," he says.

I swallow the growing lump in my throat, looking back to the window.

Ravod is gone, if he was ever there.

"Let's go, I don't have all day." The Bard's voice is loud, but absorbed by the padded walls.

I step toward the door. The tiny hairs on my arms

and the back of my neck stand upright. I hug my chest over my simple nightshirt. The floor is cold against my bare feet.

The Bard says nothing as I pass him into a long, stone corridor. Metal doors with small windows line the walls in every direction, lit by twisted metal braziers in between. I hear the faint sounds of moaning, muttering. Screaming.

"What is this place?" My voice shakes.

"High House's sanitarium," the Bard replies tersely. "Consider yourself lucky. Cathal doesn't let most people out of here."

He leads me past door after door. Other Bards patrol the hall, periodically stopping to shine a light inside each door and check on the inhabitants.

How many Bards are locked up down here? I shiver the thought away, but one far more sinister replaces it.

The cozy room from before was nothing but a Telling. This is the reality.

Cathal lied to me.

It has been two days since I was released from the sanitarium, but I was told to remain in my room, still requiring rest. The terror of madness has continued to rush through my veins, my fear growing the stronger my body gets and the more clearer things become. My mind *feels* sharp; the haze has burned away. And yet I know with certainty that what I experienced during the collapse and subsequent events were shades of madness creeping in. So I have obeyed the rules and kept to myself. I have tried, truly, to rest, and to contain and steady my thoughts.

I feel more alert—and more acutely lonely too. No one has come to check on me—not Cathal, not Ravod, not even Imogen.

More than lonely, I'm restless. Despite wanting to stay safe and not attract any more negative attention, I can't help my raging curiosity when I turn my mind to everything that's happened.

Cathal said he knew who was behind the collapse. That it wasn't my fault. Except he lied to me about putting me in a sanitarium for mad Bards. But he wouldn't free me if I were to blame.

Who, then?

A plan hatches slowly while I pace the small floor

of my room. *That's your problem, Shae. You don't think before you act.* Well, that's about to change. I've got nothing if not time to think in here, after all.

The collapsed tower has been cordoned off as a "restricted zone" while reconstruction commences. These past few nights, under the cover of darkness, when it is easier to move about High House undetected, I have made my way in its direction, trying to figure out what happened. The token guards that patrol the perimeter switch rotations quite often. It seems no one expects insubordination this deep in the heart of High House, bastion of order for Montane.

Right after the sun dips beneath the horizon, the bell for dinner rings, and I assume my position, hiding in the shadows. Several minutes later, three guards exit the gate into the castle proper. Counting slowly to thirty, I anticipate a group of Bards heading into their wing from the men's barracks. The next group of two guards should round the corner right . . .

Now.

Tucking my head down, I slip behind them and head in the opposite direction, up the steps to the collapsed tower. This is the closest I've managed to get. I overheard the guards chatting a couple of nights ago about how inside the wing is unguarded. But I can't help wondering why. Has nothing been done to stabilize the structure? Surely Cathal has engineers and workers galore at his disposal. It only reinforces my theory that there's something else going on.

The damage looks even worse up close. The broken marble and limestone cast long, jagged shadows down the mountainside. They remind me of something I saw in a dream once, a long time ago. The wind picks up, the darkness beckoning me closer. As if issuing an invitation . . . or a challenge.

"Damn Bards ought to patrol their own mess," a voice breaks through the silence.

I stifle a gasp and quickly slide around the side of a large block of debris. I was too slow calculating the first group's rounds.

"Don't talk like that. You don't know who can hear you," a second guard responds as the patrol draws level with my hiding spot. "I don't know about you, but I need this job."

"Yes, yes. We all know about your sick brat back home." I can practically hear the first guard roll his eyes at his companion.

"I'm sorry, am I *boring* you?" the second guard asks. Their footsteps come to a halt right on the other side of my hiding spot.

"Just be glad he doesn't have the Blot," the first guard responds. "And yes. It's as boring as it was the first fifty times I had to hear about it."

"Could be worse. You could be stuck down in the caverns on back-door duty with Sergeant Kimble."

The first guard grumbles. "I hate that guy."

"I know. You hate everyone."

I peek out at them while they are absorbed in their discussion. My only exit is cut off as they stand in my way.

The mention of a back door in the caverns was quite interesting though.

"Back door has fewer shifts. I could be off-duty by midnight and only have to deal with a couple of hours of Kimble's abominable singing." The first guard is a short, squat man whose gruff voice somehow fits his physique. He's facing away from me, while his tall and lanky younger companion has a good chance of seeing me if I try to move.

I inwardly thank them for giving me such useful information, a small smile touching my lips as they finally walk away and I'm able to safely turn the corner back to the training grounds.

Later tonight, when the shift changes, I'll find this secondary entrance and finally see what's being hidden in the rubble.

Evening has fallen, and the Bards' Wing is mostly empty. The bulk of the Bards are in the refectory enjoying dinner.

Everyone except Ravod, it seems. My heart somersaults when I see him standing near the door. His eyes are narrowed and his arms are crossed over his chest in his usual stance. He taps two fingers absently against his bicep.

"Shae," he says, looking startled as I draw closer. Quietly, he adds, "We need to talk."

I open and close my mouth a few times. Was he *worried* for me? Why didn't he come check on me, then? Inwardly I shudder, remembering his face appearing in the window in the sanitarium. I must have imagined it. I was in a sanitarium, after all.

"Is something the matter?" I ask.

Ravod shifts his hands to his hips, clearly vexed by my deflection. His eyes dart swiftly up and down the hall. I've never seen him so agitated.

"Ravod!" A familiar harsh call cuts him off before he can speak, followed by the sound of purposeful striding feet.

Kennan sweeps toward us, her haunting glare locked on Ravod as she ignores me entirely.

Ravod's eyes meet mine for a fraction of a second before he turns to Kennan. In an instant, his tension and paranoia melt away into a disarming smile.

"Something I can do for you, Kennan?" he asks.

"Don't play dumb with me." Kennan scowls. Unlike me, Ravod seems unperturbed. He regards her with his usual cool indifference as she continues. "I'm not covering for you again. If Cathal had placed *me* in charge of the investigation in the first place, we would already have a suspect. Instead, you can't even be bothered to attend Cathal's debriefing, and *I* get blamed for your incompetence."

"But I thought he already knew who the culprit was?" I interject before I can think better of it.

Kennan rounds on me, eyes spitting fire. "Nobody cares what *you* think."

"There's no need for that," Ravod says, placing his arm between Kennan and me. He shoots me a warning glance before turning to the other Bard. "I understand your frustration, Kennan. I was preoccupied with a lead and will explain everything to Cathal. You have my word."

Kennan clearly isn't finished with him. Her mouth thins to a tight line as she steps closer to Ravod. She's slightly shorter, but her stance is somehow far more threatening.

"You only got your fancy gig because of *my* misfortune," she seethes. "I'm twice the Bard you are. Don't forget it."

"That was not so long ago, as I recall," Ravod replies. "You were cleared to return to duty. I suggest you do so."

Kennan is poised to retort, but her eyes flick to me and she steps back, unwilling to air her grievances in my presence. With a final glare, she disappears into the dining hall.

Ravod sighs, turning back to me. "I must report to Cathal or risk further suspicion." He lowers his voice. "I'll find you tomorrow."

Confused, I nod, and he places a hand on my shoulder. He's about to say something else when he sees my breath catch at his touch. Ravod hastily removes his hand and exits the Bards' Wing swiftly and soundlessly, leaving my shoulder tingling with warmth where he touched me.

I have to shake my head to clear it. My thoughts turn immediately to what Kennan said. What was her misfortune that caused her to be passed up for Ravod's position? I narrow my eyes at the door to the dining hall, as if it will somehow allow me to see into Kennan's mind.

You're cleared for discharge . . . A voice echoes in my not-so-distant memory.

You were cleared to return to duty . . . Ravod's voice replaces it.

Was Kennan taken to the sanitarium?

"What do *you* want?"

I didn't expect Kennan to give me a warm welcome when I plopped myself down across from her, but I had hoped the surprise might delay some of her hatred.

"I only want to talk," I say, forcing my fear down. I can't let her get the better of me.

"I have nothing to say to you."

"Then listen." I'm impressed by how level my voice sounds, considering how terrifying I find Kennan. "If you give me a chance, you'll find we have a lot more in common than you think."

Kennan makes a noise of disgust. "I have more in common with the scum beneath my boots."

286 — DYLAN FARROW

"I know what you did, Kennan," I say, point-blank.

She turns and stares at me. Fear flickers across her eyes and is gone, replaced by hardness.

"The Counter-Tellings," I say. "Cathal told me everything. You tried to sabotage me. Why?"

Kennan scoffs and turns away. "You got what you wanted, didn't you? Cathal's attention? So what does it matter?"

"Why do you hate me?" The question blurts out of me. I can't understand the depth of her anger toward me.

"Do you know what I hate?" Kennan slams her hands on the table, causing her teacup to rattle its saucer. "I hate seeing real potential *languish*."

Does she mean hers or mine? "This is all about power for you?"

"Of course." She says it like it's the most obvious thing in the world. "Real power is subtle. Something you know nothing about."

Bitterness flares behind my eyes, swiftly warping my fear into anger. "Subtle? Don't make me laugh. You've been anything but subtle with me. We could have been friends, you know."

"I know enough," Kennan replies readily. "You think Cathal didn't do the same with me when I was the new girl? You think he won't toss *you* aside as soon as the next one shows up?"

"If Cathal favors me so much," I say, keeping my

tone slow and deliberate, "why did he send me to the *sanitarium*?"

A few nearby Bards shift uncomfortably in their seats upon hearing the word. Kennan goes silent, her eyes widening for a split second.

"You know what I'm talking about, Kennan." I keep my eyes leveled on hers across the table. "That was the misfortune that caused you to lose Ravod's position. If I had to guess, I'd say the others thought you were too unstable to handle it."

Kennan opens her mouth to reply before snapping it shut. Her eyes narrow dangerously, her palms pressing so tightly against the surface of the table that her fingers are trembling.

"Whatever you tried, it backfired." I watch her carefully, as if she is a snake about to strike.

"Yes. There are limits to our gift," Kennan says quietly. "For now. But beyond those limits exists possibility. Knowledge. Solutions . . . Power. For those reasons alone, the limits are worth testing. There's no risk that isn't worth taking."

"You're talking about something specific."

Kennan nods. Her whole body is afire with energy I've never seen from her before. "The Telling alone is not enough. Not when there's so much more out there," she says. "Enough not only to wash these lands clean of the plague, but make it so it never existed. I reached for *that,* and perhaps I failed once, but I won't again."

Without elaborating, Kennan rises from her seat, abandoning her tea and half-eaten meal. As a servant hurriedly clears it away, I stare at the space she vacated, lost in thought.

It's not only about the accumulation of power for her, she wants to *apply* that power. She wants to erase the Blot. Cathal spoke of a conspiracy against him by one of the Bards. And if Cathal took Kennan under his wing like he did with me, perhaps he similarly shared with her a secret to finding such power.

It starts to sink in—the truth. It all comes back to the *Book of Days*.

I wait until High House is silent before venturing into the caverns. As I traverse the winding, labyrinthine corridors, the conversation with Kennan turns in my head.

Does she know of the *Book of Days*?

Has she tried to find it?

The natural next thought follows: Was it she who caused the collapse of the tower? Could she have been looking for the *Book* when it happened?

A feeling consumes me, like the heat of a distant flame—I'm getting closer. I can feel the truth flickering against my skin, but I cannot see it yet.

I pass the outlet that leads to the waterfall, the farthest I've ever gone, and find myself in uncharted territory.

I fumble in my pocket, pulling out a tiny spool of dark thread that mimics the color of the ground. I quickly tie one end to a low rock ledge and unwind a good bit before walking forward. If I keep the thread slack, no one will ever see it.

Hopefully, I won't lose my way.

Multiple pairs of heavy footsteps pierce the silence.

My body goes rigid in fear. I strain to listen.

Footsteps and . . . singing?

Singing very, very badly. I cringe when the distant voice cracks on a high note. Something tells me I've found Sergeant Kimble.

I make sure the thread is still slack and slide into the shadows, peering around the corner at the source of the noise.

Two guards stand in front of a black, wrought-iron gate, protecting the large cavern opening. A portly guard, whom I assume is Sergeant Kimble, is belting out his song, agonizingly off-key. His companion stands nearby, rubbing his temples under his helmet and grimacing.

I count the seconds under my breath. If the guards outside were correct, their shift should change in a matter of minutes.

Finally, Sergeant Kimble reaches the end of his song and appraises his comrade. A look of expectation fills his face. His partner slowly removes his hands from his temples, as if surprised by the silence.

"Is that how you appreciate the musical talent of your ranking officer, Abernathy?" Sergeant Kimble nudges his companion.

"It's . . . very good, sir," the other guard offers meekly. The praise seems to placate Kimble. "But I believe we are done for tonight."

"Pity, the acoustics down here are truly unparalleled."

"Indeed." The other guard leads the sergeant away from the gate.

When their footsteps disappear in the distance, I quickly walk over and press down on the latch, but the gate doesn't budge.

"Of *course* it's locked," I mutter to myself. I grip the iron bars and shake them in frustration.

Footsteps. The next shift is on its way.

I take a deep breath and try to tether myself to my surroundings, like I did in the wasteland with Ravod. But my concentration fails as the thundering of my heart gets the better of me. The guards are approaching.

"Unlock," I mutter quickly as my hands shake, the warm feeling quickly fading. My spool of thread slips from my pocket and clatters to the ground. My voice falters. The Telling fails.

"Did you hear that?" a voice asks in the distance.

If I don't move now, this will all be for nothing. I shiver at the thought of being thrown back into the sanitarium. Or worse. What would be the punishment for a Bard dipping her nose too many times where it doesn't belong?

"Unlock!" Nothing.

I take a few paces away from the gate, clenching my fists and releasing.

It's okay to take some time to breathe. Ravod's voice is gentle and calming against the onslaught of panic.

My foot catches on the thread, and I wind it

up in my hands, clutching it so tightly, my knuckles flash white. I close my eyes and clench my jaw, gripping the latch. I focus on the sting that reminds me of Kennan, the bite of her gloves against my cheek.

I pull the thread tighter and tighter, imagining the lock is in my hands instead, the metal so bent out of shape that it cannot hold on any longer.

"Unlock." The thread snaps into my skin. I clutch my fingers, looking at the thin line of red that seeps through.

A clank of metal makes my eyes shoot up. The lock is completely mangled, like it was stretched apart. There's a click behind the latch and the handle swings down. I rush through the gate, closing it silently behind me.

From the darkness on the other side, I see the lock revert to normal as the Telling fades. By the time the guards arrive, it's as though I was never even there.

The wreckage of the collapsed tower makes my breath catch in my throat. My every step threatens to weaken the damaged structure.

Once I'm safely out of the guards' line of sight, I manage to light one of the torches near the entrance, casting the area in a meager glow. Chunks of debris litter the floor, most of the ceiling is caved in, and a fine layer of dust has settled over everything that is left.

Still, seeing this for myself does nothing to quell my suspicions. Something is hiding here. It *has* to be.

I start gingerly combing through the rubble, trying to spot anything that looks out of the ordinary. Mostly, all I see are personal items. Keepsakes.

Certainly nothing remotely like the *Book of Days*. Perhaps that was a long shot to begin with.

My mind wanders as I continue my search through the sea of rubble. *The Telling alone is not enough. Not when there's so much more out there.* Kennan's words stir unease in my chest. *Enough not only to wash these lands clean of the plague, but make it so it never existed. I reached for that, and perhaps I failed once, but I won't again.*

I think back to Mads and Fiona and Ma and my home in Aster. To the backbreaking work we inflicted upon one another to meet the Bards' demands, to prove ourselves worthy.

We were the blight on this great nation. Or so we were reminded at every opportunity.

I lean haphazardly against a cracked wall. It is not only Aster that is suffering. It is *all* of Montane.

Is that why Cathal wants the *Book of Days*? To fix what has been destroyed?

It is the fabric upon which all of reality is shaped . . . Cathal's voice echoes in my head.

I turn over half a chair to clear my path, thoughts churning. If all of reality is written on those pages, could it be changed? Could someone write something into reality that wasn't there before?

Or write someone back in?

Ma's face flashes in my mind, and sudden, unbidden tears sting the corners of my eyes.

"Stop it, Shae," I whisper. "One thing at a time. Focus."

Cathal only wants to keep it out of the wrong hands. Like Kennan's. A part of me wants Cathal to show up and set my mind at ease, like he always does.

But seconds pass in the dark ruins, and I'm still alone.

I've reached the other side of the ruined tower, and my search has turned up nothing. Reflexively I run my hands over my cheeks, like I used to do as a child when I tried to wipe away my freckles. My shoulders slump as a bitter taste fills my mouth.

There's nothing here.

Dejectedly, I pick my way back through the room. Having already cleared a path, the return trip is shorter. It's a small mercy.

Sidestepping a fallen beam, light catches my eye. My head tilts as I study it.

That door wasn't there before, was it? I rub my eyes, convinced I'm seeing things. But I would have noticed a door like this. It's simple and wooden, almost like the front door to my house back in Aster . . . Nothing like the ornate, gilded passages I've become accustomed to at High House.

And I *definitely* would have noticed the pale blue light issuing from beneath it.

I step closer, running my hand over the surface of the wood. It's solid. And it's still there moments later, so it's not a Telling. It's something else entirely.

I try the doorknob, and it turns easily in my hand. Before I can heed my better judgment, I step through the open door.

The roar of the waterfall greets me.

This can't be right. How am I in the cavern with the waterfall? It's as impossible as the sunlight spilling through the churning water.

But here it is. Right in front of me.

I whirl around, reaching for the door, but my fingers only touch rough-hewn stone, blocking my path. The door has completely vanished.

I am so tired of feeling like I'm going mad. I close my eyes, pinching the bridge of my nose.

But what if my mind isn't playing tricks on me? What if this is the hidden pathway to the *Book of Days* after all?

I regard the waterfall suspiciously before taking half a step closer.

There are limits to our gift . . . but beyond those limits exists possibility. Knowledge. Solutions . . . Power. I hear Kennan's voice as if she were standing beside me, but when I look around, I am as alone in the cavern as I was before.

Perhaps Kennan isn't the one speaking to me.

I center myself and keep my thoughts from tumbling over one another like the waterfall before me. Whatever power is at work here, it's different than anything I've come across before.

But maybe it's just similar enough. I remember the first time I was here—with Kennan. The way she sipped her tea as she sabotaged me with her Counter-Telling. I narrow my eyes and take a step forward. Without any distractions, I channel my focus toward the current. Using my fingers as my guide, I murmur very softly, "*Part.*"

A thrill of warmth rushes through me as the water obeys the Telling, splitting in the center like a curtain. But instead of the cliffside, it reveals the rest of the passage.

I try to keep from gaping as I move toward it. The cavern ends in a series of steps, leading to a replica of the shooting range. A loaded crossbow, a mirror, and a target are set up in a line, as if expecting me.

My training. Could this be the test's true purpose? To find someone who could navigate this passage?

Was Cathal planning this? Is this what he was preparing me for? Kennan must have tried to sabotage me so she could get here first.

I heft the crossbow into my arms, straining only slightly under the weight. I'm stronger than when I first arrived at High House. I feel a small surge of confidence I was sorely lacking the first time I attempted this challenge.

I take a deep breath and concentrate on the mirror.

"*Vanish*," I murmur softly as I squeeze the trigger. The bolt flies free and I stumble backward two steps, but keep my gaze locked on my reflection. It flickers out of reality for an instant. Just long enough for the bolt to pass through.

When the mirror reappears, I hear the satisfying sound of the target behind it being hit.

I step to the far side of the shooting range to inspect my handiwork. The bolt sticks out of the topmost edge of the target. A hair's breadth higher and I would have missed.

Another door, identical to the one in the ruins, has appeared behind the target.

Feeling more assured, I push the door open. My stomach clenches when I'm assaulted by an all-too-familiar smell.

Death. I would know its scent anywhere now.

High House is gone. I'm standing in my home, back in Aster. At my feet is my mother's body, broken and bloody. There is no light except the glow of the golden dagger in her chest.

Ma.

I shake my head in horror, taking one step back, and another. This can't be right.

"This was never part of my training!" I shout, as if denying what I see will make it go away.

No one answers.

Every muscle in my body is trembling. Ma is dead. It is impossible for her to be here.

But every time I blink, there she is, her glassy eyes trained on something above her. I can't face it. I can't face her.

I bolt for the door, but it's gone.

I race along the sides of the room, searching for a way out, but all the windows have vanished. No matter which way I turn, the room reorients itself so that I'm facing the body in the center, just as I was in my memory.

"*Stop!*" I issue all my rage, frustration, fear, and desperation into a Telling.

Nothing happens.

"*Door!*"

No response.

"*Anything!*" I pound on the walls. My head is spinning. I can't breathe. All I see are visions of me running, falling down in soft dirt, a landslide covering it all up.

Little dots drift in the corner of my vision. I'm going to pass out.

I have to regain control. It's an impossible task, the smell and the sight and the silence slamming into me at every opportunity. I choke on my own breath, my face drenched with tears.

"This isn't real," I say. "It's only an illusion."

My training required Tellings to overcome the obstacles I was presented with. This place must operate on the same principle.

I have to keep myself from falling prey to my own weakness.

I need to try something else.

Swallowing the lump in my throat, I force myself closer to the body, to Ma, until I'm right in front of her. I slowly lower to my knees.

I place my hands on the hilt of the dagger and pull it free. My hands are shaking as I toss it aside.

When I look back at Ma's face, her eyes are open. She's alive. I gasp.

No. It's still only an illusion.

She looks at me expectantly. My jaw quivers. I long to touch her, to wrap myself in her embrace. There's a burning in her eyes, and I know what she wants, but I'm not sure I can bring myself to say it.

Her hand is in mine. Cold, but firm. I whimper, clutching it tight, pressing her knuckles to my forehead as tears slip through my eyes.

A small, encouraging smile touches the corner of her mouth, and she nods once to me.

Say it, her eyes say to me. *It's okay.*

Never looking away from her, I channel my energy into a Telling.

"*Rest,*" I whisper. I kiss her head once and lay her gently back down, smoothing her hair so it rests nicely beneath her. "I love you, Ma." I squeeze her hand as her eyes flutter closed. I hold her as my eyes burn, daring not to blink. I drink in every second of her until she falls limp in my arms, her final embrace her way of saying, *Goodbye, Shae,* as she slips into the ether.

When I look up, the front door has reappeared.

The house is as I remember it. I get up and look around one last time. My hand pauses on the doorknob.

Beyond is the *Book of Days*. I know it. I *feel* it.

I take a deep breath and open the door.

I am back inside the bowels of High House, in the darkness of the caverns. As I close the door to my childhood home and watch it disappear into a wall, I realize everything that came before was half real, half illusion. The work of some ancient Telling placed over the labyrinth.

I'm getting closer.

I ascend a tight, winding staircase of stone, lit by flickering torches. Shadows dance on the gray walls, distorting monstrously around every corner.

The staircase is never-ending, and I find myself wondering what is controlling High House. Is it the *Book*? Or the castle itself? There is a very strange power at work here.

My legs ache when I reach the top. An arching doorway lies before me.

Could this be it? Is the *Book* here?

I reach for the door, but it's locked. I peer around the landing. There is nothing but stillness. This seems too simple. A Telling would easily open the door. Far too easy.

Could this be another test? I tense at the thought. *Whatever it is, I can handle it.* I'm not sure if I believe it or am simply trying to reassure myself.

The door creaks loudly on its hinges, and I jump when it smacks the wall on the other side.

The space is thick with darkness. It takes me a few blinks to adjust to the absence of light save for the lone streak of moonlight seeping in through the vaulted window. Flecks of dust scatter and fall.

I risked my life sneaking into the caverns, went through all those tests, suffered through my mother's death all over again . . . for a *storage room*?

I'm in one of High House's myriad towers. There are a few tables, strewn with papers and rusted objects I cannot place. Heaviness roots me to the spot when my gaze reaches the shelves lining the walls; they are stacked with equally strange artifacts. A fine layer of dust covers almost everything. It reminds me of Constable Dunne's office.

A slick layer of sweat beads along my hairline and neck.

Get out, my mind urges desperately.

I whirl back to the door. It's still there. I hesitate a few inches from the doorknob.

The door doesn't disappear.

It's *letting* me leave. Not a test, then.

Hot anger simmers within me. I am so very tired. Tears fill my eyes. I thought I was doing everything right for once.

"What do you want from me?" I cry out in rage, kicking the metal table closest to me. Pain flares through my toes and into my ankle. The table shakes, rattling its contents. Dust rises into the air. It clouds up into the beam of light filtering through the window before settling. I cough and pull at the collar of my damp shirt. I'm unusually warm.

There's a strange smell in the air. I cough again, trying to identify it. It's heavy. Smoky. I know this scent from somewhere.

I narrow my eyes at the table, running a finger over the dust and inspecting it more closely.

Ash.

The burning village in the wasteland flashes before me. *It's not real.* I squint through the dark and really look at the room. Gritting my teeth, I focus on the floor, forcing the memory back. The flickers of truth push through the illusion.

I run to grab a torch from the top of the staircase. The flame breathes new life into the illuminated space, bringing clarity.

Every corner of the room is charred and blackened. Remains of wooden furnishings are scattered. Ugly scorch marks—both old and new—mar the makeshift metal furniture. As I move closer, the light catches and reflects off the strange items I saw before.

There must have been some sort of fire; perhaps these were rescued from it.

I step closer to the nearest shelf, where a number of stone tablets sit in a line, etched with letters and stylized creatures. There's also an odd machine, its clockwork insides ripped out, and a globe encircled by rings set with delicate crystals.

There is a commonality to all the items: the engravings bear resemblance to one another, and something about them triggers a warning bell inside me. My pulse flutters, and my sleeve brushes against a small stack of papers, which do not seem to be coated in ash like everything else in the room. I pick them up uneasily. They must have been placed here recently.

The ink markings on the pages look hurried, as if someone was short on time. Cathal told me not to practice reading without him. His warning cuts through the fear of the writing that causes my hands to shake. Like the book he gave me, the paper feels impossibly heavy.

If there's a clue here, though, I have to find it. Determination, and several deep breaths, eventually smothers my fear.

My skill at reading is still clumsy, and the unfamiliar scrawl on the pages is difficult to decipher. I squint, sounding out the words with my mouth as I go.

Test . . . one: The . . . something unreadable *. . . is prac . . . tic . . . ally . . . in . . . des . . . truc . . . tible . . .*

Who wrote this? I focus on the pointy, hurried handwriting itself for a long moment, trying to find something familiar and failing. I've seen Niall's handwriting from my misadventures in the men's barracks, and this is not it. Even Ravod's letters on the window in the sanitarium were rounder and loopier.

That just leaves every other Bard or courtier or servant in High House . . . Or even Cathal. I rifle through the papers, looking for . . . something.

Test five . . . six . . . seven . . . all the way through twelve. Whoever this was, they went to great lengths to destroy the contents of this room. Some of their methods were astonishingly creative. I keep skimming the contents, hoping to find something useful.

Cathal can't know what I've done here . . .

So it's not him.

I think Ravod suspects . . .

Not him either.

If only Nahra were still here . . .

I don't know who that is.

I wipe sweat from my brow as I lower the papers. Something tiny—a sharp reflection of light within a box—catches my gaze. I cross toward it.

On the table, there's a wooden box with bronze hinges and a glimmering clasp. I pop it open. Hidden inside, I find a menagerie of tiny stone animals—a raven, a wolf. They're lovely, and lovingly carved, no bigger than a child's toys.

I freeze. The material and craftsmanship are painfully familiar. I recognize the shimmering veins on the surface of the material.

My breath catches when, as if from a dream, I see a little stone ox. Like Kieran's.

No. This isn't just like Kieran's little ox statue, it is the very same. I'm sure of it. The stone feels warm in my hand, as if it recognizes me too.

Suddenly, I understand.

This entire room is filled with Gondalese idols. Someone was trying to burn these forbidden items.

Ma tried to burn Kieran's ox once too. It didn't work then either.

My mind is racing. Ma's murderer took this from my home, which means they knew we had something to hide. But they have also been in this room. My breath grows ragged. I'm getting ever closer to the truth, and suddenly I fear what it will bring.

The light flickers, pulling my attention away from the swirling questions in my mind. I clench the ox in my fist and turn quickly to the door.

A cloaked figure moves, like a shadow rising in the darkness. A hood obscures their face. In one hand, they are holding an unlit torch, and in the other, a canister of oil.

Could it be Ma's murderer? I shrink back, clenching my fingers tightly over Kieran's ox until the inside of my palm screams in pain.

"Who are you?" My voice cracks as I stumble backward, knocking over items and papers. They clatter to the ground.

The figure ignores me and mutters under their breath. Their torch bursts to life. Before I understand what's happening, they have poured oil onto the floor, and a sickly toxic smell invades the room.

I try to run, but a blast of wind throws me into a shelf, toppling its contents across the floor.

Whoever this Bard is, they are powerful. Too powerful.

I groan and crumple to the floor. Clutching my stomach in pain, I see the Bard standing over me. With one swift movement, they snatch the ox from my hand and level a kick to my gut.

A shock wave of pain courses through me, and I double over. The Bard drops the torch. It feeds into the oil and blazes with fury. The bright orange flames lick the edges of the metal shelves and desks. It won't be long before the small space is engulfed.

I choke on the fumes, reliving the burning inn and the smirking bandits who set it aflame. The smoke is thick in my lungs, dense and dark, coiling like a snake around my throat.

The Bard turns. My hands grab for the nearest item in my reach—the wooden box the animal figurines had been kept in. It's burning.

I throw it as hard as I can at the retreating figure. It hits them hard on their left hand, slashing through their glove. The Bard yelps in pain, vanishing into the stairway.

My head is swimming as the fire creeps closer to where I lie on the floor. I'm trapped. The flames lick the sole of my boot as the smoke constricts my throat further, choking me into unconsciousness.

"Shae! Wake up. Can you hear me? Shae!"

A deep voice breaks through the darkness of my

mind. My eyes flutter open. A blaze of cold air burns them and they squeeze shut again. A wave of fire follows it through my throat. I cough violently and scramble away from the voice.

"Get away from me!" I shriek. "Don't touch me!"

All I can see and feel is the room burning. The Bard coming back to finish me off. The heat. Kieran's ox . . . Gone.

"Easy, easy." A gentle hand on my shoulder lowers me back down. "You're safe. You inhaled some smoke."

Ravod's blurry face is hovering over me, his brows tightly knit. We're outside on one of the rooftops of High House.

"You saved my life?" My voice grinds out uncomfortably, like sand has lodged in my chest. "How did I get here?"

Ravod hands me a metal canteen. "Slow down. Drink this first."

"What is it?"

"It's water," he says. "And I don't want to hear from you again until it's gone."

I obey without further encouragement, and we lapse into a comfortable silence. I alternate between sipping the water and coughing under Ravod's watchful gaze.

My eyes adjust slowly as our location finally comes into focus. We are at the back of High House, overlooking the mountains and an elegant peristyle garden below. Overhead, the stars are beginning to give way to the grayish light of dawn.

It reflects off Ravod's skin, making him look like he's made of moonlight. Except for the dark smudge of soot on his cheek. The edges of his clothes are singed.

I finish the water and hand the canteen back to him.

"How did you find me?" I ask. He nods, pulling a second canteen off his belt and handing it to me. "Thank you," I say.

"Drink."

I take a thoughtful sip of water, but lower the canteen as my questions finally rush to the surface.

Ravod shifts uncomfortably. "I was on my way to the dormitory, but when I opened the door, somehow it opened to a stairway in the ruined tower." He pauses, worried. "I was about to turn back when I heard your voice. There's an old rumor, a legend really, that the castle will lead certain people where they need to go." A frown tugs at his mouth. "Looks like I was just in time. Any longer and you might have been permanently injured. Or worse." His voice cracks on his last word.

I'm silent for a long time.

"Let me see your hand," I finally say. "The left one."

"Why?"

"Please, I have to see it." I need to know it wasn't him who set the fire.

Slowly, Ravod displays a gloved hand in front of

me. There are so many questions in his eyes, but I can't bear to look at him.

Ravod does not question me, displaying his hand on both sides. His glove is undamaged. "Take off your glove." He does. His hand is unblemished. I look between it and his mouth quickly. He is not using a Telling.

He's not the Bard who attacked me in the tower.

At that realization, whatever was holding me together gives out, and I feel like I'm tumbling into an abyss.

"I was so close," I whisper.

"What happened in there?" Ravod asks.

I sniff, which turns into another cough, and I take a few more sips of water before answering.

"There was another Bard, but I didn't see a face. They set fire to the room. I couldn't fight back. I only managed to chuck a piece of burning wood at them. Obviously it didn't help much."

His body tenses. "Whoever they are, I'll find them. This is a violation of everything we stand for."

"This is much bigger than a rogue Bard." I gaze at him levelly.

"There were some disturbing things in the tower," Ravod says. "I would hate to think you're mixed up in that."

"If you think that's true, why save me?" I ask. "I was there looking for answers, nothing more or less."

Ravod's lips narrow into a line, and he turns away, looking thoughtfully at the mountains.

"I believe you," he says slowly. His voice is quiet, as if he has been holding back from saying those words for a while. "I didn't want to for a long time. But once you pointed out the cracks, I couldn't ignore how deep they really were," he says. "And I knew they were there all along, I just didn't want to see them."

"Ravod, none of this is your fault." I rest a hand gently on his forearm. He flinches, and I think he's going to pull away, but he relaxes fractionally.

"A contraband-riddled tower collapses, a Bard tries to kill you, Cathal put you in the sanitarium . . ." he whispers, and saying the words aloud seems to finally allow him to understand what they mean. His face contorts with disgust. "Shae, Montane is *dying*. There has to be a reason why."

Ravod is right. The world is a mess. But maybe it isn't too late to change that.

"We need to find the *Book of Days*," I say. "It can fix everything."

Ravod gives me a sad look. "The *Book of Days* is a myth, Shae. A bedtime story. If one of the other Bards told you it's real, they were messing with you."

"*Cathal* told me about it," I reply. "He wants it and thinks I can find it for him."

"Is that why he taught you to read?" Ravod asks. He immediately notices my eyes darting away defensively and continues, "I came to check on you in the sanitarium. I wasn't allowed in, obviously, but I saw Cathal in there with you. It's how I knew you'd understand my warning."

I recall Ravod, and his warning, in the darkened cell window of the sanitarium. That was real. One less potential bout of madness to worry about. I nod in answer to his question, and Ravod goes quiet. The silence is uncomfortably heavy between us.

"Why does Cathal want the *Book of Days*?" he finally asks.

"I . . ." My heart thuds with a dark, sickening jolt. "Cathal never explained why. He just said it would help me discover the truth about my mother's murder." I am unafraid of the word as I say it.

Ravod fidgets, but says nothing. His dark eyes search for something on the horizon.

"Can I ask you a question?" His voice is low.

"Anything."

He doesn't ask immediately, and I begin to wonder if he is reconsidering asking at all. When he does, he keeps his gaze locked on whatever he is looking at in the distance. I have to strain to hear him.

"Let's say you find out the truth about your mother. What then?"

I've been so preoccupied with finding out the truth, I haven't thought of what happens after.

"I guess I'll know when I find out."

"And what if you don't like the answers you discover?"

"Could it be worse than not knowing at all?" I counter.

He considers this. A breeze passes by, shifting a lock of black hair across his forehead. With effort, I resist the need to smooth it from his brow.

"I never found out what happened to my parents," he confesses. "My father was not a kind man. At his worst, my mother would take his temper upon herself so I wouldn't get hurt. It was like that for years. One night, when I was about six years old, it reached the worst I'd ever seen. I was in the corner, trying not to listen, but I drew their shapes in the dust on the floor and crossed them out. When I looked up, they were gone. I never saw them again." His face is emotionless, but there's a deep sadness in his eyes when he finally looks at me. "My first Telling."

His parents. He lost them too.

My heart breaks for him as I absorb what he said. I see traces of the terrified little boy in the face of the young man before me. Everything clicks into place. Why he's so guarded, so controlled. Why he doesn't use his Telling.

"That's—" I stop, not knowing what to say. "You shouldn't have had to go through that."

Ravod tears his gaze away from me.

"I'm not saying this for pity. I want you to understand that I respect you," he says. "I know that's not what you want to hear from me. But it's true."

I draw my hands away from his. Coldness settles over me as disappointment curls around me like a shield. The same disappointment that pierces me every time Ravod shuts down on me, closing off any hint of emotion. I manage a smile, remembering with a mixed pang of awkwardness and heartache how I confessed my feelings to him . . . and his rejection. But even if my affection is one-sided, I am still grateful that he chose to confide in me.

"Shae," he says my name slowly. "It takes a lot of courage to speak up for what you want. I'm . . ." He trails off, taking a deep breath. "I'm not that person yet."

"Maybe I'll wind up being a good influence on you." I smile brightly.

"A bad one, more likely."

I shove his arm, the laughter in my chest stirring up my cough. He sobers somewhat, gesturing toward my half-drunk canteen of water, which I resume drinking from thankfully.

"Ravod?" I ask after I finish.

"Yes?"

"You said High House leads people where they need to go." I try to gather my thoughts as they come. "Maybe it led us both to the tower for a reason."

"It's possible, I suppose." Ravod's expression is a wild mix of emotion I can't read. "This place, I've come to realize, is not what it seems." He pauses. "It's far more dangerous."

Back in my quarters, my thoughts are like shards of broken glass scattered on the floor.

I shiver involuntarily as I sit in bed. Even with my blankets wrapped over me, and my legs drawn up to my chin, I can't seem to get warm. Ravod told me to rest and lay low until he can figure out which Bard was with me in the tower.

But I can't rest. I did enough of that in the sanitarium.

My hand wanders to my bedside table, to the silver comb Fiona gave me. Picking it up, I imagine she's holding my hand. I picture her and Mads in my mind's eye, smiling reassuringly at me, giving me strength as only my dearest friends can.

I carefully fix the comb in my hair. It feels good to have a piece of home with me in a place like this.

My bravery falters when my thoughts drift to the Bard who attacked me. They killed Ma; they tried to kill me. If I sit here idle, it will only be a matter of time before they realize I survived and they try again. Next time, I might not be so lucky. Ravod might not be there, just beyond the door, to save me.

The *Book of Days* is somewhere in this castle, and

more than ever, if I want to stand a chance against any of this, I need to find it.

But how? The thought keeps circling back to me.

Chewing my lip, I think back to Ravod's words.

There's an old rumor, a legend really, that the castle will lead certain people where they need to go . . .

Maybe there's a way for it to lead me to where I *want* to go.

I toss my blankets aside. A simple Telling is not enough to overcome the intricacy of the ancient powers at work here. If I want to exert my will over the castle's, I need to lend my Telling permanency.

My eyes fall on my needles and thread, discarded in the corner.

I embroidered Tellings in Aster, without even meaning to. I can embroider them here with intention. I bring my supplies to my bed, threading the needle and pulling my sheet free. If I can't find the door, maybe I can bring the door to me.

I take a deep breath, centering myself before plunging the needle into the sheet, focusing all my thoughts and energy on the Telling.

My fingers grow warm, then hot, as I weave a door into the fabric. The air crackles with energy. The silhouette of a door begins to form in the wall across from me; it is trapped in the hazy place between thought and reality.

There's a tug, a resistance to my sewing as the

castle counters me. I felt something similar the first times I tried using my gift, when Kennan used her Counter-Tellings. I didn't know what was happening then. This time I know to block it out, however difficult, and persevere.

My needle grows red hot under the strain of my Telling and the struggle of being countered. My fingers burn, and it takes everything in me not to give up. I grit my teeth against the pain. I *will not* stop.

A high-pitched ringing reaches a sudden, piercing apex in my ears. With a final searing sensation in my fingers, the needle snaps into tiny pieces. Blood drips from my fingers. When I look up, the door I tried to summon is gone.

"No!" I cry out.

I cradle my hands as the room sways. I breathe in and out, trying to catch my breath. I hadn't realized how much energy I exerted with failed Tellings. With no needle and no door, I'm another step behind.

I have to try something else. There must be *something* lying around that I can use to bring the door back, and there's no time to waste.

Pulling on my boots, I venture into the hall.

I'm so wrapped up in my thoughts that I almost don't see the light issuing from my neighbor's door. I halt in my tracks.

Maybe I can ask one of the other female Bards to loan me a needle? If someone is awake at this hour, it's worth a try.

I compose myself as best I can and knock.

There's a pause, long and quiet, before I hear footsteps. The doorknob turns and a familiar face appears. There's a hint of surprise that she masks immediately with a scowl.

"What do *you* want?"

Of course this is Kennan's room. My usual good luck wouldn't have it otherwise.

"I'm sorry to interrupt you this late, but I—" Alarms shoot through me. Her left hand. A burn mark is visible beneath the poultice she applied to treat it.

My blood runs cold. She rushes to shut the door, but I wedge my foot in between the door and the frame in time to see beyond her, to the familiar stone ox lying on her bed.

"You." I can barely breathe. I force the door open with strength I didn't even know I possessed, fueled by raw shock and overwhelming fury. Kennan's eyes widen. She steps back.

"So." Kennan sneers, her face cracking into a malicious smile. "You finally figured it out?"

I say nothing, advancing on her and curling my fist. When I draw close enough, I punch her in the face as hard as I can. My fist comes away bloodied, and I wince.

Kennan falls into the wall, clutching her nose.

"Why did you kill my mother?" My voice is low and deadly. It sounds like someone else talking. It's taking all my willpower not to keep hitting her until she never gets up.

Blood trails down Kennan's nose and drips into her mouth, coating her teeth as she bares a snarl at me.

"She said it was *real*," she growls.

Kennan is fast to her feet, leveling a kick to the middle of my chest. There's a sickening *crunch*. I see spots as I fall. Not even my anger can keep me from crumpling to the floor.

Kennan bolts.

Between the smoke inhalation and being winded by her kick, it takes all my power simply to keep breathing.

I watch helplessly from the floor as my mother's murderer disappears down the hall and out of my reach.

It was Kennan.

For several minutes I lie dazed on the floor. The spot next to me is spattered with Kennan's blood, and the sight churns the anger already writhing within me. It's not enough. She deserves to bleed as much as Ma did, and even that might be too good for her.

Clutching my ribs, I struggle to my feet and steady myself on the edge of the bed. I clench my jaw, breathing through the pain, and search her room. Recent revelations notwithstanding, I have to find a needle before I'm discovered. Kennan may have already summoned guards to double back on my location. Who knows what lies she is willing to give to save herself.

My hands sweep frantically over the meager contents of each space I search. Kennan's quarters are immaculately tidy. Fortunately, I find a small sewing kit in the drawer of the bedside table. I shove it into my pocket and head for the door.

My mind tries to reconcile Kennan the murderer with Kennan the ruthless trainer. The woman I tried so hard to find camaraderie with, to trust. It's hard to picture Kennan, even at her most austere, as a killer. It's difficult for me to attach the title to someone

I know, no matter how deeply I dislike them. Murderers were scary figures from cautionary tales. They seemed almost as imaginary as Gondal.

Gondal! My eyes snap back to the desk. I grab Kieran's ox, clutching it for dear life.

I hobble back to my room, locking the door behind me.

I rip out the thread from my previous attempt, ready to make a fresh start. I concentrate my thoughts on the *Book of Days*, pushing everything else from my mind.

The needle flies through the fabric. The Telling starts, smoother and more immediate.

I watch the wall out of the corner of my eye as the door begins to manifest. I focus on the end result—willing the door into existence, deftly stitching around the resistance I meet.

The needle grows red hot, but I'm faster this time. I complete the final stitch. The needle snaps, burning my fingers. I frantically look at the door as it flickers in and out of view.

Until, finally, it affixes itself in reality.

"That's more like it," I whisper to no one in particular as I get up from the bed, gripping the little stone ox in my pocket. For luck.

I open the door.

The hallway I'm in is dark, cut through the stone of the mountain like the lower caverns. The same luminescent stones line the walls. I step cautiously as I move deeper in. I keep my guard up. The castle makes it impossible to know reality from illusion.

I see a faint, rectangular light ahead, the corners of a door. It pushes open easily and plunges me into light.

I'm in the refectory—or at least, a room that looks *exactly* like it. I see the rows of long tables, all empty. There is an eerie undercurrent as my steps echo a beat after I take them. Everything is as it should be, except . . .

Veils of light enfold the room, wrapping around and contorting everything in it. They shift and flicker around one another. I have to close my eyes and open them again to fully understand it. There are different versions of the space, different versions of *reality*. Limitless possibilities. It's like standing in a room made of mirrors.

When I look at my hands, the shroud shimmers over my own skin. It's not an illusion, not exactly. I'm in the same refectory, but on a different layer, one accessible only through the altered reality of my Telling.

All around me, there are faint streaks of movement. Dreamlike silhouettes of people move within the various layers of reality. If I try to look at them directly, they disappear, but I can follow them on the periphery of where I gaze.

This labyrinth isn't a separate space within the castle; it's in an entirely separate realm of existence.

As if two truths—or even limitless truths—are capable of existing at the same time. That is why no one could find it. It is everywhere and nowhere at the same time. We are in it, and it is hiding from us, at every turn. No one thought to look right under their noses. I didn't.

Hidden in plain sight. I wonder, has the *Book of Days* been hiding all these years in this separate realm?

"Three more disturbances have taken place . . ." I hear an unfamiliar voice, cutting in and out before fading. I glance around the room, searching for the source.

"Our manpower and resources are stretched too thin . . ." Another voice. It reaches me from across the room, across dimensions until it disappears.

A third voice. "We receive less and less from every tithe we collect . . ."

Roughly a dozen older Bards, including Niall, are clustered around a map of Montane at the end of the room. They rapidly flicker in and out of sight. When I step closer, the images condense somewhat. The figures are still ethereal, but more firmly anchored in front of me.

"At this rate of attrition, we won't be able to maintain our numbers for much longer," one Bard says, crossing his arms. "We're squeezing blood from a stone."

"We can't afford to lose face or pull back. The chaos will only spread," Niall counters, drawing a few nods from his peers. "We control them. Collect extra from the towns that haven't been hit yet by famine. They just need the proper motivation."

"And when the famine ravages everywhere else? Then what shall we do? How do you propose we motivate them?" The first Bard struggles to control his voice.

"The way we always do," Niall replies readily. "Our agents in the villages will plant rumors, and control and monitor the flow of information. Keep the people suitably frightened."

"You're risking widespread panic," another points out. "The people are *already* frightened."

"Then they'll be all the more eager to double their tithes in exchange for our favor, won't they?"

I make tight fists, letting the bite of nail pressed into skin ground me. Not too long ago, I was one of the people they're talking so casually about manipulating, controlling, and extorting.

As quickly as the vision appeared, it dissipates. Disgusted, I turn away.

The door I used to enter the room has, predictably, vanished. But instead of trapping me, several others take its place.

It really is a labyrinth, I think as I watch the doors alter, shift places, and realign. There is no pattern, only random movements. I'm not sure how to pick the door that leads to the *Book of Days*.

Unless it doesn't matter.

"There's an old rumor, a legend really, that the castle will lead certain people where they need to go . . ."

"All right, High House." I brace myself and approach the nearest door. "Do your worst."

I regret those words almost immediately as I stumble along the uneven floor. There is minimal light here. Only a thickness to the air that makes me feel as if I'm walking underwater. I'm in the ghostly bowels of the castle. A place lit by braziers that cast shifting shadows across the stone walls and thick, metal doors.

The sanitarium.

It is more frightening than I remember. I use the phantom figures that glimmer in this plane to guide me. Their movement is punctuated by bloodcurdling screams, always shifting and fading through the spaces where existences collide.

The end of the cells spills out into a larger, circular room. It's sterile and the lights are blindingly bright against the whitewashed walls. The sound of screaming is loudest here.

There are peculiar holes on the floor, and I jump back when my foot sloshes against a dark red liquid draining into them. Perhaps most unsettling are the apparatuses set up in the center. Each one is different, and obviously meant to contain a person, but it's nearly impossible to say what the purpose of such disturbing machines might be. When I look up again, people's silhouettes flash and contort inside the room. They lie on beds, their hands and feet bound by metal shackles. Their gaping mouths open, their shrieks echoing a second too late.

Would this have been my fate if I had not been discharged? A shiver penetrates deep in my bones. Bile rises in my throat, but I swallow it down.

Ghostly figures manifest at the center of the room, hovering over a bed. Their faces are covered by masks.

"Another death? Unfortunate. Prep the next one," a tall man says to a young woman. "Cathal wants a complete report by sunrise. Did you get a reading from the last test?"

My heart twists in horror. Cathal is in charge of this?

"The data is inconclusive, sir," she responds. "There's still no evidence to suggest that a Bard can be 'cured' of the gift. Or that it can be bestowed artificially."

The man shrugs. "If it can be done, it would boost efficiency. That's what Cathal is interested in. If it can't, then we'll know conclusively and can pursue other avenues."

"At least there's no shortage of test subjects." I can nearly hear the grimace on the young woman's voice from behind her white mask.

"They're Bards. They've given their lives for High House," he says reverently. "They are doing their duty as we are doing ours. Reset the devices and bring out the next one."

My breath comes out shakily, grating against my

throat, still raw from the smoke, as the figures dissipate into another realm.

I feel a lurching sensation as I turn, as if the castle is contorting impossibly around me, the same way a dream would. This time, I'm in Cathal's solarium.

It's dark, with only the faint light of one torch and the gossamer fabric of the phantom realm I'm in to illuminate the room. The leaves of the exotic plants and the angles of the statues and furniture make everything seem unnatural and elongated.

The door opens quietly, and I turn toward the sound, expecting to see Cathal. My brow knits when instead I'm faced with Kennan.

My rage flares. If only I wasn't trapped on a spectral plane and could punch her again for what she did to my mother. And a third time just for myself and everything she put me through.

I seethe, watching as she tiptoes around the furniture, casting wary glances around her.

The door opens again, louder this time. I remain still for a moment, until I remember I can't be seen. Kennan slips behind one of the chaise longues, nimble as a cat.

"Come out of there, Kennan, it's just me." Niall strolls into the room. "I see you're up to your old tricks."

Kennan comes out of hiding and faces her fellow Bard. My gut twists as I watch them. Maybe they were accomplices all along.

"Stay out of my way," Kennan says. "It was Cathal

who weakened the structure under the tower that night. I *will* prove it."

"Don't you dare go pinning that tragedy on Lord Cathal." Niall glares at her dangerously. "Even if you had a shred of proof, no one will believe a woman with a known history of . . ."

"I know what I saw!" Kennan snaps, interrupting him.

Niall scoffs. "Do you? Do you really?"

"I . . ." For the first time, I see Kennan falter. Then my surroundings fade to darkness again.

High House was supposed to be a bastion of truth and order. That's what we were always told. Could this be a trick of the labyrinth? I don't want to believe that Cathal is capable of such atrocities. I don't want to believe that anything masked in a mantle of righteousness could be so evil.

How many Bards has Cathal sent to find the *Book of Days*? How many Bards have met this fate?

Am I next?

I step back, looking frantically for a door. An escape. Several appear, like before. I rush to the nearest one and barrel through it quickly.

Am I doomed to madness?

Succumbing to insanity again feels like a mercy. Anything is better than the truth.

I run.

I find more rooms. More corridors. More darkness. Everywhere I turn are the specters of High House. Door after door after door . . .

My heart is hammering in my chest. I stop, finding myself in the hallway of the female Bards' dormitory. Right back where I started.

The doors don't go anywhere except in circles. This is how the others were trapped. How I might be trapped if I don't think of something.

I trusted the doors before. Trusted High House. I let it lead me.

But perhaps I should be taking charge.

I close my eyes, concentrate, but I can barely catch my breath, can't think straight. I'm dizzy with frustration, with exhaustion, with *fear*.

I press myself flat against the stone wall and sink to the floor. I want to cry but nothing comes. I don't know how to do this. I don't know what's real anymore.

Panic rushes through me, that this is all a nightmare and I'm still standing in the doorway of my home in Aster, screaming in horror over Ma's death. That I am hurtling downward in a chasm of uncertainty and I will never, ever stop falling.

This must be what madness feels like. It is worse than death.

Cathal said the labyrinth nearly killed him. I understand now what he meant. Death, or permanent entrapment in this endless nightmare, is starting to seem like a real and distinctly terrifying possibility.

My body aches under the weight of everything that's happened to me. I can't stop shaking—not even when I hear a soft sound reaching me as if from across a great distance.

I squint. Imogen stands at the end of the hall, framed in shadow. Her curls loose around her face. From so far away, she looks tiny, and I'm reminded how young she is—not much older than I was when I lost Kieran.

How did she know? Why does she always appear whenever I feel alone, whenever I need her?

My name is Imogen, she'd said. Like my favorite ewe from back home.

It hits me like a thousand boulders.

She isn't real either. She's a Telling. Nothing more than an illusion. She *is* me. My younger self. A figment of my desperation.

"No," I murmur, trying to hold my voice steady. "You aren't real." My voice scrapes against my throat. "I'm alone."

She steps closer cautiously.

Her face is half hidden in the dim light. She reaches toward me. Her hand touches my shoulder, and I shudder. Her touch *feels* real. I'm so confused, so scared, so overwhelmed, I don't know what to think.

She kneels before me. This close, she doesn't look exactly like me. Her eyes are darker. She has only a small beauty mark under her eye instead of a multitude of freckles. Her hair is wilder.

I blink. I seem to be between dimensions now; half in reality, half in the labyrinth.

"Shae," she says softly. "You're *not* alone."

"That can't be . . ." I say, not wanting to trust her, not ready to trust anything. "You're only a Telling. A figment of my imagination."

She quirks her head. "Well, *that's* unexpected," she blurts out. It's so direct, I almost laugh.

Instead, I swallow. "How are you here? Why are you always appearing right when I need you?"

Imogen sighs and looks away. When she looks back at me, I see the hint of a smile in her eyes. "He told me to watch out for you. To make sure you were okay."

"He?" Is she talking about Cathal? Ravod?

"All I can say is, I know how strong you are, Shae. I've seen it with my own eyes." Gently, she reaches out and brushes my hair from where it's fallen into my face. "You should really give yourself more credit."

Before I can respond, she flickers out of sight, and I'm alone in the labyrinth.

Imogen's words weave through my thoughts. She's right. I've been so worried about making Cathal believe me. Wanting Ravod to believe me. I never tried believing in myself.

I recall everything that happened—everything I witnessed. I repeat the story of Ma's death inside my head, and I look at it unflinchingly—the way the constable lied and changed his story, how he patronized me and made me fear others blaming me. The look on Fiona's face, even as she handed me my bag—her fear that what I was saying was true.

Mads too. He told me to stop fighting, to stop looking for answers. It wasn't because he thought I was crazy. He was afraid of what I'd find.

It's not enough to send myself back. I must know. I think of the others who have been sent here to wander aimlessly until they lost their minds. Scrambling to stand, I press my palms against the walls. I close my eyes and channel my breath.

"Truth."

The fabric of reality responds with a series of weak pulses, warping through the heat in my fingers. Something below the surface seems surprised by the word, as if it was never asked for such a thing.

But I'm not asking, I'm Telling.

I plant my feet more firmly on the ground, bracing against the current that binds me on the spectral plane, pushing against all my senses and locking myself in place. I take a deep breath, allowing the current to wash over me.

I anchor my Telling in reality as Ravod taught me, summoning the memory of my mother's murder, the event that set me on the path to find answers. It gives me clarity. My anger at the injustice of her death pulls the threads of my intent together. I weave in all the pain and hardship I've endured along the way, creating a bulwark against the waves pushing against me.

"I won't be moved." My Telling is a scream against the rising tide. *"I want the truth."*

The current swells to what feels like a breaking point . . . and abruptly stops. A passage manifests in the wall in front of me, crumbling the stone. It's not another spectral door. There is no shimmer of illusion around it, no flickering. This one is real.

A shudder courses through the air. An electric current. A crack running through the fabric of the labyrinth. I close my eyes.

When I open them, I'm standing in the same place, but no longer in the in-between plane of existence.

Before me is the door to the *Book of Days*. At last.

27

I expected a bit more fanfare for the room where the entire record of reality is kept. Instead, I'm in a small stone room, set below an oculus that streams moonlight onto a simple podium at the top of a short flight of stairs.

Motes of white dust float through the light, disturbed for the first time in what must be ages. Three statues of robed men, each holding a book, stand vigil on the perimeter. They are cut from the same greenish stone as the rest of the room. One statue is holding up the domed ceiling. The simplicity is startling.

Something about this room feels final. Like High House has finally let down its barriers.

My legs shake with every step I take up toward the podium. I swallow the trepidation in my throat.

I reach the top and look down at the podium.

The *Book of Days* . . .

. . . is not there?

The podium is empty.

I stare blankly at the podium. A couple of torn pages lay scattered on it. I lean forward, steadying myself on the podium, but wanting to scream.

Someone else got here first. How could that be?

I touch the papers, turning them over. I blink when I see my name written in a rushed hand . . .

Shae,
Forgive me. It was necessary.
—R.

The leaden disappointment in my chest shifts uncomfortably. I am too exhausted to even realize what it means for a moment.

Ravod found the labyrinth first. He solved it. He stole the *Book of Days.*

My finger moves back and forth over his words as I read them over and over.

Forgive him? It was *necessary*? Is this a joke?

The second ripped page has symbols on it that are almost too faded to see . . . until it moves.

I pick it up, studying it a little closer in the bright shaft of moonlight.

The lines are shifting over the page like water, forming symbols I don't recognize. The longer I look at it, the stranger it seems. The images drift from side to side like they are swimming in a pond. Slowly they form a glyph that takes the shape of an ox. Letters appear beside it.

Gondal.

Is this fragment of paper from the *Book of Days*?

Footsteps sound behind me.

I shove the note and book fragment into my breast pocket and whirl around.

"Hello, Shae."

Cathal.

He steps into the light. Half a dozen armed guards and another four Bards crowd in around him.

"Cathal." I'm not sure how to begin to explain. Or if I should.

"You have been an immense help. I will take it from here," he says, marching up the steps toward me. A wolfish grin of anticipation overcomes his face. He strides to the podium, pushing me aside.

He looks at the empty surface and back to me. Confusion etches across his face.

"The *Book* is gone," I say.

He grabs me roughly by the collar. "*Where is it?*" he hisses. His face is rigid, with no trace of any of the amity he has shown me before.

I can only stand in shock at his iron grip. This can't be Cathal. He is my ally. My mentor. Cathal was the first person at High House, in the whole *world,* who believed me when no one else would. It seems utterly impossible that this man glaring down at me is the same person who encouraged me, had faith in me, helped me . . .

Used me.

My insides plummet and writhe sickeningly inside me.

This is the real Cathal. The man who leaves Montane to suffer while he dines lavishly in his castle, throwing balls for dignitaries to mask the truth. Who sends his Bards to instill fear and desperation in his subjects while bleeding them of their resources. And when the Bards break free of his control, he imprisons and conducts tests on them in the sanitarium.

This is the man who sends countless Bards to die in search of the *Book of Days.* Including me.

We were never allies. I was another cog in his machine. Another tool for him to use and discard.

I was a fool.

My anger blazes inside me, red hot. Perhaps I made a mistake by trusting him, but his mistake is underestimating me.

I'm still alive, and I can fight to make things right. I hold his gaze. Something deep inside makes me brave.

"Somewhere that you can't kill innocent people for it," I lie. Then I spit in his face.

Cathal recoils, jerking his arm to throw me roughly down the steps. I land on my hip, wincing. He takes a handkerchief from his coat and wipes his face, stepping down after me, his cool demeanor restored.

"I have many means of encouragement at my disposal to persuade the truth from you," he says. "I will use force if necessary."

Cathal's guards descend on me, grabbing me tightly by my upper arms and hauling me to my feet.

"I'll tell you *nothing*," I snarl.

He regards me with distant eyes, all warmth and familiarity gone. I feel like knives have buried themselves all over my body, piercing deeper into me than any wound. Seeing him like this, a cold, calculating despot, is even more painful when it's being leveled against me.

I *trusted* him.

"Wait, my lord." A Bard runs quickly to the edge of the podium. Lodged in its corner is a ripped piece of cloth, torn from the hem of a Bard's uniform, singed slightly at the edges and smeared with ash.

I still against the guards, hoping they don't know enough to connect it to Ravod.

"*Hmm.*" The Bard gives the scrap to Cathal. He clenches it in his fist. "Search the grounds. Now." A few Bards leave immediately as Cathal rounds on me. "I will give you time to reconsider," he warns, "but not much. I am not one to tolerate such a betrayal of my trust, Shae."

"You're the one who betrayed me!" I fight against the guards. "You said I was like a daughter to you!" I choke on the words as the weight of his actions knifes me again. "You made me believe . . ." I try to search for some sign of empathy in his face, some recognition of what he's done. He stares back at me coldly. "Was everything you told me a lie?"

He pretends to consider, his mouth arched in a vicious smile.

"Cathal is my real name," he says finally.

I thrash my weight against the fists restraining me, screaming half from hurt and half from fury.

"The more I tell you, the more you believe, the more it becomes true." Cathal shrugs. "And deep down, that is what you wanted, is it not?"

"You're a monster." My words grind out through my teeth.

Cathal merely rolls his eyes. "Careful, Shae. You do not have much time to waste with struggling."

"What do you mean?"

His response is a curt nod toward my hands.

My heart stops when I look down. The tips of my fingers have turned a dark, sickly blue, and all-too-familiar veins have begun to thread beneath my skin.

The Blot.

The aching heaviness of a fever registers first. Then the sensation of being pulled onto a hard, flat surface.

I struggle to keep consciousness as I'm dropped somewhere.

Am I back in the sanitarium? I try to lash out, but only manage to writhe languidly against the firm grip of the hands pinning me down.

Firm, but surprisingly gentle.

"Careful, there's no need to hurt her," one of the guards says.

The voice is as familiar to me as my own. Even in the midst of my rising fever, I can place it. It feels like forever since I've heard it, but it's unmistakable.

I struggle to open my eyes. My head falls to the side, and I see a flash of silvery blond hair. Longer than I remember. Broad shoulders and muscular arms . . .

Another trick. I can't trust anything I see in this castle.

The last thing I hear is the sound of an iron door clanging shut. It sends an ache through every muscle in my body. A coughing fit painfully pulls me under into a dark blue abyss.

"Well, *this* certainly isn't how I thought things would turn out." The voice is the first sound I've heard in ages.

I turn toward it. The back of my head feels like it's grinding against the stone underneath it.

I wait until the throbbing in my skull stops before I open my eyes. I have a strange surge of relief when I find out that I'm only in a regular prison instead of the sanitarium. My cell is about half the size of the bedroom in the dormitory and constructed from dark stone. The only aperture is a barred iron door.

Beyond, there is the silhouette of a woman. Her hands grip the door. One bears a burn mark.

"Kennan?" Air passes over the dark veins in my throat when I speak. I don't sound anything like myself. "What are you doing here?"

I feel foolish even asking. I know why she's here. She's come to gloat. Or finish me off.

"You were supposed to be there," Kennan says, without preamble, "at the house. With your mother. You were the one we were supposed to kill."

"Come to finish what you started?" I wheeze. The effort of speaking is enough to cause another coughing fit.

Kennan shakes her head. "That's not what I intended."

"I'm tired of riddles." I pant in shallow breaths.

"Fine," Kennan says, taking a piece of paper from her pocket and unfolding it. "Tell me what this means to you."

I glare at her, but she doesn't move. With effort, I struggle to sit. Every bone in my body feels like it's being set on fire as I push myself off the stone bed and shamble to the door of my cell.

Kennan does not flinch as I take the paper between my blue thumb and forefinger. I tilt it toward the light issuing from the hall, the only illumination I'm afforded.

It's one of Niall's maps, a detailed rendering of my house and the surrounding valley. Only, there is a landslide drawn where there once was pasture.

"Niall caused the landslide?" I frown. "Why? To cover up that you killed my mother?"

Kennan fixes me with a level stare, her pale eyes deliberating. Her mouth twists briefly before she answers.

"I . . ." She pauses. "I *think* I killed your mother."

She's lucky she is on the other side of an iron door and I have no energy to perform a Telling. It's taking all my strength to remain upright.

"What, you're not *sure*?" I ask through clenched teeth. "Seems like the sort of thing someone ought to remember."

"My thought exactly," Kennan says, her voice quiet. "I've been trying to find out the truth. I wanted to fix it. I thought the answers would be in the *Book of Days*. I . . ." She looks away. "It doesn't matter. But you deserved to know."

"You're a piece of work, Kennan," I seethe at her. "You certainly seemed contrite when you performed all those Counter-Tellings and tortured me during training."

"You—" She stops abruptly, before whatever insult she had lined up can slip free. She takes a breath and starts again. "If you failed, you would have been safe. I did it to protect you, to keep you hidden."

The truth of her words clicks into place. "Hidden from Cathal," I whisper.

"Who else?" Kennan rolls her eyes. "He did the same thing to me, you know. Played on all my vulnerabilities, pretended he was my only friend. It was an act. He wants the *Book of Days* and doesn't care who he destroys in the process. I barely escaped the labyrinth with my life."

My whole body is shaking. "Even if that's true, why would I ever trust you after what you did to my ma?"

"Will you shut up for five seconds? I'm *trying* to make this right," Kennan snaps. Her tone is no different than usual, but the look in her eyes has changed from frustration to regret.

I steady myself, tightening my hand around a bar. "Then make it right. Say what you came here to say." I sigh. At this rate, the plague will claim me before I make any headway with Kennan.

She takes a deep breath. "The tithe was only part of the reason we were sent to Aster that day," Kennan says. "Cathal told me this task would absolve me of my failure to get the *Book of Days*. We were tracking a rogue Bard, one that has eluded us since long before I came to High House. Our sentries in the wasteland uncovered information that led us to believe she was hiding in Aster."

"She?"

Kennan cocks her head. "Did you not know your mother was a Bard?"

I freeze. The question hangs in the air like a storm cloud about to erupt. Ma? A *Bard*?

"Niall and I were tasked with apprehending her. She was to be brought in alive. She resisted," Kennan continues. "The last thing I remember is reaching for your mother, but a Telling hurled me at the wall. I don't know whose it was. When I came back to myself, Niall was pulling me from the house, promising not to share with anyone what I'd done."

"And you believed him?"

"I don't know," she says. A moment passes between us in silence. "All I know is that I've had nightmares every night since. I've seen terrible things." Anguish creases her face, a pain I've come to know well since arriving at High House. The madness that seeps in and the fear that there is nothing you can do to control it. "You seem to know what I mean," she adds.

"The madness," I say, nodding.

Kennan pauses, her eyes locking meaningfully on mine. "Except I don't think that's true."

"Why would . . ." I trail into silence under Kennan's gaze. It's a terrifying thought, but she might be right.

I think back to what Cathal said. *The more I tell you, the more you believe, the more it becomes true.* The madness, and the idea that women were somehow more susceptible to it, was just another lie to control us.

"Do you really think it's impossible, after everything you've seen?"

I take a deep breath, ordering the shuffle of thoughts racing in my head. "So . . . you wanted to find the *Book of Days,* why, exactly?"

"I thought I could make things go back to the way they were. Undo what happened," Kennan admits. "Erase my mistakes."

"You said my ma spoke to you," I say. "You told me, 'she said it was real'?"

Kennan shudders, but nods imperceptibly. "Gondal."

I gape, unable to speak.

"She said she helped people find it. That they lived free of High House there." She hesitates. "You didn't know?"

I shake my head in disbelief. The thought that Ma *spoke,* and to Kennan of all people, has to be some kind of cruel trick. But when I think back to my time with Ma, and her silence after Kieran's death, I wonder if I ever really knew my mother at all.

"Why say this now?"

"I don't have to like you to know it's the right thing to do."

I fall back, unable to hold myself up any longer. The quiet is painful as it stretches.

"And I'm tired of hiding. This guilt . . ." Kennan grimaces. "It's made it hard to recognize myself. The longer I hold on to it, the more I lose. Maybe I didn't kill your mother—"

"You didn't save her either."

Kennan's eyes flick upward to mine. For the first time, I see the enormity of the pain she's been carrying. She hid it well.

"I won't ask for forgiveness that's not in your power to give," she says. "But I would like to atone for my action—or inaction—if you will allow me."

I hold her gaze. Her pale eyes stare back, unblinking. Perhaps I will never understand Kennan's morality, but I don't doubt her sincerity.

"And how do you plan to do that?"

"I'm going to get you out of here," Kennan replies. Before I can respond, she turns on her heel and disappears from view. As soon as she's gone, two guards emerge and silently take up positions at either side of the door.

I draw a ragged, heavy breath. I hate to admit it, even to myself, but all this time, I've been waiting for Ravod to show up, for him to inform me that he wasn't the person who stole the *Book,* that it all wasn't a setup. I wish I understood. Why and where did he take it?

I look down at my shaking hands, dark with plague. Pushing up my sleeves, I see the veins have spread past my elbows. They burn beneath my skin, on my legs, my back, up the curve of my jaw. It might not matter whether I escape or not.

My fate is firmly sealed.

It's hard to know how much time passes in a tiny, windowless cell. Hours can pass in a delirium-fueled heartbeat, or take an eternity when gasping for air between bouts of coughing.

In the brief moments when my mind is clear, I'm haunted by Kennan's revelation. Ma was a Bard. She hid her past from me my whole life. My heart breaks not being able to ask her why.

I can see the curvature of Ravod's form behind my closed eyes. His words are etched into the deepest recesses of my mind.

What if you don't like the answers you discover? his voice echoes.

I pull out the fragment of the *Book of Days*—mercifully, I was never searched—and turn it toward the light. The guards don't like looking at me. Every time I cough, they flinch. They fear that I could infect them too.

The ink shimmers, moving fluidly over the paper, creating symbols and icons I can't interpret. I watch them shift for several minutes, wondering what kind of language this is.

I pull Kieran's ox from my breast pocket, comparing

it to the ox that formed on the page. They are nearly identical.

As though the paper senses the ox in my other hand, its lines dissolve in a pattern toward it. Mountains, rocks . . . a path.

No. A *map*.

It charts a course across Montane. My eyes watch, tracing houses, caves, passages. Images flicker beside each one, listing unfamiliar letters, save for a single symbol of a crescent moon beneath each landmark.

Slowly lines compose a small house surrounded by sheep in a mountain valley. My home. Letters form beside it. The same symbol.

Before I can wish for the image of my house to stay a little longer, it fades. Several dozen more places follow, all leading east. At last I see a house tucked into some trees in a distant, barren forest beyond the wasteland. A symbol. And a strange, yet comfortable feeling resonating deep within. Letters begin to form beside each glyph.

Safe.

The lines shift one last time, dissolving into one final word . . .

Gondal.

I gasp, which turns into a hacking cough that wracks my whole body, squeezing my lungs tight inside my chest.

I sit up. My blue fingers are shaking violently as I clutch the fragment of paper.

My mother was a rogue Bard. She ran a safe house for refugees fleeing to Gondal. Fleeing from High House. Fleeing the lies, the death, and the tyranny. She *died* for it.

I snap out of the revelation when the door of my cell whines open. I quickly stash the paper in my pocket as a tall figure darkens the door. My heart furiously protests the boundaries set forth by my chest, hammering louder than I've ever heard it.

In the dim light I can make out a guard's uniform. My gaze travels upward, locking onto a pair of blue eyes I thought I had imagined.

"Hello, Freckles."

My words are slow to obey me, and even then, I find it difficult to summon them.

"Mads?" The name escapes in a whisper.

He steps closer, a grimace tugging on his lips.

"I guess this is pretty awkward." He stops when he sees me flinch. "I'm not here to hurt you."

"How are you here?" I ask, looking between the sigil on his chest and his face several times. "*Why* are you here?"

Mads sighs, maintaining the distance between us. Even in the dim light I can see the familiar warmth in his eyes, behind the conflict.

"My family fell on hard times awhile back. My father asked High House for reprieve, but it came at a cost—my secrecy in aiding the Bards," Mads admits, his voice soft. "It was always my job to report the goings-on in Aster to High House."

There is a yawning distance between us. So much has changed since the time when I thought we were two mere ordinary people.

"Why didn't you say anything?"

"I almost did, more times than you'll ever know."

"But you didn't."

Mads catches his lower lip between his teeth. "I *couldn't*. Only my family could know." His voice lowers. "I suppose I just thought one day you would be . . ."

His words taper off into a heavy silence. We both know how the sentence was supposed to end.

"How much did you know?" I ask finally. "About my ma? About me?"

"I swear, I knew nothing," Mads says. I always thought he was a terrible liar, but now I'm not so sure. After everything I've been through, my trust is at a premium. "Even when they refused to give their blessing for my proposal, they wouldn't explain further."

"They refused?" I frown.

Mads's face is embarrassed as he rubs the back of his neck. "That was something I was *actually* planning to never share with you." He pauses. "All my life I was told I was doing the right thing. I thought I was building a life I could be proud of. I know it's a feeble excuse."

"We all thought we were doing the right thing," I mutter. Didn't I hide my truth from Mads all along too?

"That doesn't make it okay." Mads shakes his head. "I should have been there for you. I should have listened to you. I should have *helped* you. Instead . . ." He lets out an uneasy breath. "I don't know. Maybe I couldn't have changed anything. But I didn't even try, and I'm going to regret it the rest of my life."

"What changed your mind?" I ask, peering up at him, tears beginning to slip from my eyes.

"I thought you had run off to the wasteland," Mads says. "It wasn't until Imogen told me what happened that I realized you were here."

I blink. "Imogen?" I ask. "How do you know Imogen?"

"We've been friends for a while, ever since I started in High House's employ," Mads replies. "When I found out you were here, I asked her to keep an eye on you."

I remember what Imogen said, back during my ordeal in the labyrinth. *He told me to watch out for you. To make sure you were okay.*

It was Mads.

"She was the one who put me in touch with your friend," Mads continues. "She's been a huge help."

"My friend?"

"Your trainer. The tall girl? With the amber eyes? I think her name was Kendra?"

"Kennan." I decide not to linger on the specifics of my relationship with her.

"She told me everything. Some of it was . . . difficult to hear." Mads winces. "But you started something just by refusing to believe the lies. Kennan saw it. And now so do I."

I frown. "See what, exactly?"

"Everyone in Montane is watched closely. You know that," Mads says. "Turns out, people like me who do the watching wind up destroying people like you, who dare to ask questions. I don't ever want to be a part of anything that could hurt you."

Slowly, as if approaching a wounded wild animal, Mads kneels in front of me and takes my hands without hesitation. He doesn't even look at the dark blue veins, his eyes locked on my face. The tenderness in his expression and the touch of his large, callused fingers are achingly familiar. I've missed him so much.

"So, Freckles . . ." He lowers his voice to a whisper. "Ready for a prison break?"

I have to admit, in all the scenarios I considered, not once did I expect Kennan and Mads to team up to break me out of High House.

I can't help grinning, and a memorable smile touches the corners of Mads's lips. The last time I saw it in earnest was when we were kids, sneaking into his mother's kitchen to steal some freshly baked cookies. Kieran fell ill the next day, and for a long while, I foolishly thought my cookie thievery was the reason why.

The bittersweet memory fades as Mads gives my hands a gentle squeeze and stands, holding a finger up to signal me to wait. Not that I have much choice. I don't think I can walk without assistance. The veins in my legs sear into me with every movement.

Mads moves to the door, winking slyly at me over his shoulder. The guards don't pay him any mind until he balls his hand into a fist and knocks the nearest one out with a single, rapid punch. The second guard barely has time to react before Mads spins around, kicking him in the gut. The impact sends him stumbling back and his head connects with the wall. Mads flinches at the sound it makes, but his attention quickly diverts back to me.

My jaw drops. "Who *are* you?"

"I've gotten into a scuffle or two in my time here." Mads grimaces. "Was it impressive?"

"Not if we get caught," I say. He chuckles and helps me to my feet.

"We'd better hurry, then," Mads says.

I shuffle beside him, biting my lip to try to ward off the pain radiating through my body. The dark veins seem to stretch the more I exert myself, constricting my every movement.

"Mads, I'm going to be honest . . ." I wince as each step becomes more painful than the last, and we haven't even reached the exit to the cell block. "I don't know how long I can last."

"It's only a bit farther," Mads replies. "Don't give up on me, Freckles."

The faith in his voice gives me enough of a boost to keep going. The prison level consists of a hall of iron-barred cells identical to mine, constructed from rough stone and lit by flickering torches. It is quiet and deserted, unlike the sanitarium. The implications of that make me queasy.

At the end of the hall, Mads produces a ring of keys from his belt and fits one into the door.

"So . . . all those hunting trips?" I ask.

"I was here." Mads nods tightly. "I never meant to lie to you."

My mind goes back to the night of the ball, when I followed Imogen. I'd dismissed my recognition of him, no longer trusting my own mind. But it *was* Mads. He was here, trying to watch out for me despite everything.

"It's all right, Mads," I say, with a gentle squeeze on his forearm.

He's not entirely reassured, but doesn't argue as the lock clicks and the door swings open.

"I'm definitely not going to be welcome back here after this." His mouth twists.

"You and me both."

Mads shifts my arm on his shoulder and helps me forward.

"I know the way out of the castle, but it's going to be tough getting past everyone unnoticed."

The door has deposited us into a lavish hallway, a little quieter than the main castle. The windows are high up so we must be on one of the lower levels, right above the caverns.

Mads pulls me into a shadowy alcove, behind a statue, right as a coughing fit strikes me. I barely manage to stifle it as a patrol of guards passes us. It feels like hours go by before they disappear around a corner.

"On my mark," Mads mouths. "Now."

The end of the hallway leads to a large marble staircase spiraling up into the castle. The walls are hung with banners emblazoned with the High House sigil and the golden thread catches the light from intricate circular windows that ascend with the steps. Even the thought of climbing them feels like a death sentence.

We duck beneath the stairs, hunched over each other as deep into the shadows as possible. The patrol from before has doubled back, but their unhurried pace suggests that my disappearance has not yet been discovered. I struggle to contain my coughs until their footsteps fade up the stairs.

Mads rubs my back when another violent one escapes me. I can feel the veins lacing deeper into my body, burning and strangling every part of me from the inside.

This is what happened to Kieran. The thought rises

unbidden. *He never let on how painful it really was. He was so brave, and I never truly understood until this very moment.*

The coughing quiets, replaced by a shiver from the fever. Mads's strong arms come around me and I collapse against him.

"Mads, if I don't make it out of here—"

"Don't." His voice is gentle, but tinged with fear. He tightens his hold on me. "You're going to be fine, Freckles."

"You're not afraid of getting sick?" I ask.

"My pa always says no one arrives safely at their grave," Mads replies. "I'll take my chances."

I smile into his chest, listening to the steady beat of his heart. "Thanks, Mads."

"It's the least I can do," he says. "If I were a Bard, I'd use a Telling to heal you."

"That's not . . ."

That's not entirely how it works. A spoken Telling has no permanence, not like the symbols in the *Book of Days* or in my sewing. Or writing, I'd wager.

My mind takes me back to the repository when Cathal pushed me aside. His rough grip on my collar. The cold emptiness in his eyes when he sneered at me. The moment his mask of kindness was discarded. The image appears unbidden in my mind, but clear as crystal.

I do my best to banish the hurt from my heart. The broken trust. The lie that he cared about me.

The look on his face when he was no longer pretending I mattered; the darkness in his voice as he threw me in a cell. This is worse than the pain of the Blot. This is a pain I will never be rid of, not fully at least, not for a long time.

If I live that long.

It wouldn't surprise me if he had given me the Blot.

"Mads . . ." I whisper. My eyes widen. The truth was there the whole time.

I push back from him, raising my hands. They are even darker than before. Moving my fingers sends shock waves up my arms. I let out a low moan of pain.

"What's wrong? What is it?" Mads looks near panicking.

"Touching the pages of ink didn't give me the Blot. *Cathal* wrote it into me." I shiver, only partly from the fever, remembering the notebook Cathal would write in as he sat by my bedside in the sanitarium. "I *saw* him do it."

Mads's eyes flick between my hands and my face. I can see him warring with disbelief—and I don't blame him. If Cathal has the power to give someone the Blot, who else has he done it to?

I look back at my hands. Cathal's Telling is strong and locked into reality with ink. But it's still only a Telling . . . and I'm a Bard.

"Heal."

My Telling is spoken in a whisper, but carries every ounce of focus and strength I can muster.

"Heal," I repeat fiercely.

Slowly, the veins begin to withdraw, the pain subsiding to a dull throb. I'm not cured. I'll need to continue countering Cathal's written Telling, perhaps forever. And I don't even know how long my Counter-Tellings will last. But I'll live, which is more than I had ten minutes ago.

Mads is staring at me with wide eyes. I grab his hand, pulling him out from under the stairs.

"Hurry," I say, "we don't have much time."

No one on the upper floors bats an eye at seeing a Bard and guard emerging from the lower level. Even if the Bard is somewhat disheveled and sweating nervously. At my side, Mads looks remarkably composed. But his nose is crinkled. Only I could recognize his way of hiding his worry.

"Should we make a run for it?" he whispers.

"Too obvious," I say. "We need to slip out unnoticed, and we're running out of time."

"Shae, we don't have a choice."

The panic has spread to my throat, but mercifully, the courtyard at the entrance to High House appears deserted. Mads grips my hand tightly at my side as we rush to the gate.

"Going somewhere?" a familiar, steady voice asks, stopping us in our tracks.

My breath hitches when Niall steps casually in

front of us, blocking the path to the gate. Mads starts to step in front of me, but I hold him back.

"Let me pass," I say. "I promise, I'll leave High House and never return."

Niall raises an eyebrow. "I don't think so."

With a nearly imperceptible Telling, he's suddenly standing right in front of me, his gloved hand closing around my neck.

"I thought you looked familiar," he says. "The rogue Bard in Aster. You're the missing daughter."

"Don't touch her!" Mads growls, making to push Niall away.

"Away." Niall waves his hand dismissively. His Telling pushes Mads several feet back, knocking him to the ground. It gives Niall enough time to pull a blade from his boot and hold it to my neck. He shoots Mads a warning look as he scrambles up. Mads's mouth is pressed to a thin line, his hands held up defensively.

"Kennan didn't kill my mother, did she?" I ask quietly.

He lets out a harsh laugh. "Kennan didn't have the courage to do her duty. She couldn't handle the responsibility of our position." Niall sneers. "Why do you think she was sent to the sanitarium? She got cold feet. She was ready to join your mother's failed cause." He pauses with a dangerous smile. "I don't share those reservations. I am a Bard of High House, and I will lay down my life for Cathal."

The fury I had directed at Kennan returns a hundredfold, my entire body wanting to attack.

The blade inches closer to my throat.

Before I can think better of it, I jerk my knee up to his stomach as hard as I can. Niall doubles over and stumbles. It gives Mads enough of a window to grab his arm and wrench the knife from his grasp.

As they grapple, I step back, anxiously looking for a weapon. The only things in my pockets are the *Book of Days* fragment and Kieran's ox.

I hold the page in front of me, frustrated at being incapable of helping. A drop of blood falls from my neck with a soft splat on the page, followed by another. Two more. Niall must have cut me with the knife, and I didn't notice. The drops of blood make a thin line where it drips. It almost looks like the beginnings of a stick figure.

Ravod's horrible tale comes back to me, of what happened to his parents. What his Telling was truly capable of.

I dip my bare finger into the blood, focusing on Niall's face. My rage. Shaking, I complete the figure.

And, with two swift motions, I cross it out.

A cold gust of mountain wind sweeps through the courtyard. I look up over the edge of the page.

Mads is midswing, but his punch doesn't land. Niall is gone.

Mads glances at me, confused.

A wave of sickness threatens to knock me over. "I'll explain later," I rasp, horror gathering in my throat. I've done something terrible. I might have to do more before this is all said and done.

But there's no time to overthink it. I grab Mads's wrist as we race ahead toward the gate, Telling it open. Mads pushes one waiting guard into another, causing enough confusion for us to pass through. Another quick Telling turns the metal gate red hot behind us as it slams shut, keeping our pursuers back and sealing their way forward.

Mads and I flee haphazardly down the mountain. I can hear the shouting of guards in the distance as we finally make it to freedom.

EPILOGUE

Sunset casts the wasteland in an orange glow as High House recedes into the distance behind us. I don't realize I'm out of breath until Mads slows down and I come to a stop beside him.

The memory of what I did to Niall flashes back to me with a swell of nausea, and I stumble almost imperceptibly. But I did what I had to do. He killed Ma with just as little regard for her life.

I won't become him. That will only happen when I stop caring. A part of me knows I'll be struggling with this for a long time. Maybe the rest of my life.

I turn to Mads, anchoring my hand on his arm. "Are you okay?" I ask.

"We . . . we did it," he gasps between breaths. He is leaning on his knees, panting. "We really did it. I don't think I've run like that since . . ."

"Since the great cookie caper?" I finish his sentence. The memory of stolen cookies and childish laughter warms me.

"You remember that too, huh?" A smile lights up his face. "I suppose with experience like that, it's no surprise we managed to pull this off."

I can't help smiling back, despite the knowledge

we can't stop for long. "I'm sure your ma will be happy to have you back at home, after all this."

Mads's grin falters. "Yeah, you're probably right." But a look gives him away. "She would be." Mads admits with a crooked smile, "And she'll be about as happy with me about this as she was after we stole the cookies she spent six months saving rations for."

"Does this mean . . ." I pause. "You're not going back to Aster, are you?"

Mads takes a deep breath, drawing himself upright. He gazes off into the distance somewhere behind me.

"No," he answers with a smile. "No, we're not."

I frown at him. "We?"

"Shae!" a voice calls in the distance, and I'm certain I'm hearing things. When I turn, I see what Mads has been staring at. My heart leaps with joy.

"Fiona?"

Kennan approaches on horseback. Surprisingly, Fiona is seated behind her, arms wound tight around Kennan's waist. When Kennan draws closer, Fiona looks unsteady as she dismounts. It takes a second for her to find her footing before sprinting toward me. The force of Fiona's hug nearly topples us both.

"You're really here." I cling to her, afraid she might not be real. When I pull back, I realize I am crying.

"Shae, I'm so sorry. I was terrible to you. I—"

"Don't be," I cut her off. I fiercely hug her again, knowing my heart had forgiven her long before this moment. "I'm so happy to see you."

"I've missed you so much," Fiona says. Happy tears are in her eyes. "When you left, I was certain I'd never see you again and . . . Wait." She stops, emotion filling her voice. "Let me start over. When you left, I . . ."

"Fiona." I smile. "Did you rehearse this?"

"Exhaustively," Kennan interjects, pinching the bridge of her nose. "I can probably recite it for her at this point."

"Never mind the speech, then," Fiona says. "All I want to say is that losing you broke my heart. Everyone in town said you were dead. I . . ." She takes a deep breath. "I won't lie, I struggled with what you said. But you've always been truthful. I wished over and over that I could go back and listen to you instead of driving you away. I told myself I'd do anything to have you back. When Mads approached me with the truth, that you were *alive* but in trouble . . . I knew what I had to do. Even if it meant leaving my family. But, Shae, you're my family too. So, I'm here to help."

"Fiona." My heart feels like it's about to burst, even as my joy goes to war with my worry. I pull her silver comb free from my rescue-matted hair and gently tuck it into her golden locks.

"You kept the comb." Fiona gasps.

"Of course I did. It reminded me of what's really important." I take her hands in mine, sobering somewhat. "But, Fiona, things are going to get tough from here. There's a lot you don't know. You might not want to know it."

"It's sweet of you to worry, but my mind is made up. I've had a long time to get to this point," Fiona says. "And your friend explained everything to me."

"We're not friends," Kennan and I say in unison.

"What's important is we know the truth," Fiona says. "Or, enough of it, at least. We're going to set this right."

"Our priority is finding the *Book of Days*," Kennan says. "That's not going to be easy."

"It won't be," I agree. "But I know who has it. And I think I know where we are going to find him." I pull out the pages torn from the *Book* that Ravod left behind. Even now, his disappearance stings. I hope he's okay, wherever he is.

Gondal. The place beyond. The safe haven, somewhere past the horizon. The place I imagined Kieran had gone to when he died. A place that is not a superstition, illusion, or myth.

That's where we're headed.

To a place that is real.

ACKNOWLEDGMENTS

So many wonderful people helped make *Hush* a reality. First and foremost, Lexa Hillyer and Deeba Zargarpur, for all the extraordinary time and talent they poured into this story from beginning to end. I owe more gratitude than I can possibly express to Vicki Lame, the best editor a gal could ask for, and to Editorial Director Sara Goodman, as well as my publisher, Eileen Rothschild. Thank you for seeing the value in such a story and for all the amazing work you have done in bringing that story beyond the borders of Montane and into our world.

I am so fortunate to have such a wonderful team at my back from Wednesday Books. Christa Désir for her meticulous copy edits, Production Editor Melanie Sanders and Production Manager Lena Shekhter, as well as Managing Editor Elizabeth Catalano: a heartfelt thanks. For getting this book into the hands of its readers, my thanks to Brant Janeway and Alexis Neuville for marketing and Mary Moates for publicity; also Tracey Guest, Meghan Harrington, and Jessica Preeg. Anna Gorovoy brought these pages to life visually, and Rhys Davies beautifully rendered the official map of Montane. Olga Grlic designed the magnificent jacket of this book.

A huge thank-you to the creative talents of Kim Ludlam for copy and concepting and Lisa Shimabukuro for designing the most amazing ARCs.

I am unendingly grateful to my agent, the incomparable Emma Parry, Lynn Nesbit, and Janklow & Nesbit for all they do, not least of all helping me achieve my lifelong goal of being an author. And a huge thank-you to Kamilla Benko, Alexa Wejko, and Wendi Gu, who could not see this project through to the end but without whom this book simply would not exist.

A little under a decade ago, I told my husband I wanted to quit a desk job I wasn't finding fulfillment with, to try my hand at writing full-time. He encouraged me to follow that dream without hesitation, and continued to encourage and support me every step of the way. I would not be the writer I am today without this man. Thank you, my love.

I also would like to thank my family, especially my mother for always standing by me and believing me when I chose to speak my own truth. Sue, for passing on your gift for writing and so much more. My brother Ronan, for being my rock and my best friend whose fearlessness and creativity always pushed me to be fearless and creative. My sister Quincy, for dutifully listening to me read my very first story aloud from start to finish and helping me realize I wanted to be a writer. All my gazillion siblings: Matthew, Sascha, Lark, Fletcher, Daisy, Tam, Thaddeus, Isaiah, Minh, Heather, Chris, Matt, and Ali, I love you. Also, a special shout-out to their respective spouses and children, my amazing siblings-in-law, and my equally amazing nieces and nephews. I owe a huge thanks to my godmother, Casey Pascal, for a lifetime of encouragement. And to my in-laws, David and Frances, both for the aforementioned husband as well as for their love and support over the years.

Special thanks to my friends, especially Priscilla Gilman, my soul sister, I cannot thank you enough for everything you've done for me. Katherine and Emma Pascal, Jacqui Teruya, Emily Friedhoff, whose friendship kept me going—I am eternally grateful for you.

A NOTE FROM THE AUTHOR

When I was growing up, the world of books was a refuge for me as my family was assaulted by a powerful individual dedicated to ruining our lives and our credibility. Using the overwhelming power of a verbal campaign that was supported only by obfuscating legal documentation, an entire generation was led to believe in a false narrative.

Today, this type of situation has become very visible to the public at last. And yet, we still live in a world fragmented by the easy, almost addictive spread of news, both real and false, a world that breeds skepticism toward victims and gives a platform—and power—to those who spread lies, hate, and fear.

Sometimes it requires incredible bravery, and risk, on the part of an individual to stand up and expose the truth, to persevere in a sea of doubt. This is a story about the importance of holding fast to one's own voice and sense of justice in a climate where it's easy—normal, even—to be gaslit and deceived, not just by a single predator or even a loved one, but by entire institutions, even the ones we have entrusted to keep us safe.

Hush is about that bravery and that risk. It's about

the need for something concrete to hold on to in a time of illusions, distortion, and loss. It is a story about the power of words and truth.

As writers, it's our job to weave the stories of our imagination into being, much like the Bards of Montane. But our stories are not only the reflections of the author's hopes, fears, and obstacles—to many they are a reminder of their own. My hope is that this story is one that will continue to make more space for others' truths to come to light.

Thank you—for reading, for believing, for persisting.

Sincerely,
Dylan Farrow